W9-DEG-187

Back in the mid-eighties, I wrote *Texas Anthem*. It was the first of a family saga set against the western frontier from the end of the Mexican-American War to the turn of the century. *Texas Born* soon followed and carries us forward several years from the events chronicled in *Texas Anthem*. Big John Anthem has become a successful and respected rancher and carved his own empire out of the Big Country of West Texas. He has sired two sons and a daughter, all of them mavericks, and a real challenge for their parents as we discover in this and subsequent adventures.

The Anthem family is a robust collection of men and women shaped by the land, a strong and independent breed, often flawed and perhaps too headstrong, but the kind of folks who will stand for justice, live life to the fullest, and cast a tall shadow. I am pleased that St. Martin's Press is re-printing all five novels in the series.

I reckon this is where I'm expected to tell you how I lived a life of towering adventure, saddle-broke a hundred wild mustangs, pitched a tent in Tibet, hunted Cape buffalo, served with distinction, rode with the wind, tramped the wild places and the crooked highways . . . oh, heck with it. That's not me.

I was the kid who sat in the front row of the balcony of the movie theater and spent every Saturday afternoon with the likes of John Wayne, Burt Lancaster, Kirk Douglas, Lee Marvin, Charlton Heston, Gregory Peck, and the list goes on; a kid who thrilled to the sight of charging Comanches, saloon brawls, and shoot-outs in dusty streets, not to mention sword fights, heroic last stands, dueling pirate ships, and chariot races. And when I wasn't at the theater, I was reading the same, yondering by way of the written word, finding the lost and lonely places, and dreaming I would one day be the tale-teller, spinning legends on the wheel of my imagination.

Sure, I've done some things, been some places. But so have you. All that matters now, my friend, is the story we share. I have tried to craft these books with a sense of legend as well as history; finding just the right blend of thrills, drama, romance, and a dash of wit. Whether or not I have succeeded is in your hands.

KERRY NEWCOMB
MARCH, 2001

ST. MARTIN'S PAPERBACKS TITLES
BY KERRY NEWCOMB

The Red Ripper
Texas Anthem
Texas Born

TEXAS BORN

KERRY NEWCOMB

(PREVIOUSLY PUBLISHED UNDER THE
PSEUDONYM JAMES RENO)

St. Martin's Paperbacks

PUBLISHER'S NOTE

This novel is a work of fiction. Names, characters, places, and incidents either are the product of the author's imagination or are used fictitiously, and any resemblance to actual persons, living or dead, events, or locales is entirely coincidental.

TEXAS BORN

Copyright © 1986 by James Reno.
"Just a Note From the Author" copyright © 2001 by Kerry Newcomb.

ISBN: 0-312-97717-4

Printed in the United States of America

Signet edition / November 1986
St. Martin's Paperbacks edition / March 2001

St. Martin's Paperbacks are published by St. Martin's Press, 175 Fifth Avenue, New York, NY 10010.

10 9 8 7 6 5 4 3 2 1

For Patty and Amy and P.J.
with love

My thanks as always to Aaron Priest, who does it better than anyone.

My thanks to the kind, patient, and creative talents at NAL, and special gratitude for the efforts of my editor, Maureen Baron.

And last but not least this pilgrim's humble thank-you to Buck and Tim and Killer . . . "So Long, Rough Riders!"

But ye shall die like men,
and fall like one of the princes.

—Psalm 82:7
KING JAMES BIBLE

TEXAS BORN

PROLOGUE

1863

The cry of the coyote was carried on the wind. Fair were the golden hills, the pale-green meadows luxuriant with chino grass and sage and crimson flowers bright as prairie fire. All this beauty spread out below the pine-crowded battlements of Mescalero Lookout, a mountain and sprawling ridge rising out of the arid west Texas landscape. In the distance, between the gateway of the pines, loomed Blue Top, another peak, and beyond it, though hidden from sight, Luminaria Canyon and home.

Cole Tyler Anthem knelt in the emerald shadows high up on the wooded slope and turned his attention to the creek spilling down from the boulder-strewn crevice in the side of the mountain. There, like some great open wound, Mescalero Lookout suffered its gash and bled its clear cold waters from its granite heart.

This was Texas.

This was John Anthem's land, and Cole was his son. Even at thirteen, Cole was cut in his father's image, showing size and strength in his sturdy limbs, and fierce resolve in his sun-browned features. Cole's long, straight hair was flaxen like his mother's, but there ended Rose

Anthem's influence. Cole's temper and dreams were fueled by ambitions that marked him his father's son.

Cole rolled over on his back and searched in his pocket for a scrap of newspaper. The *Uvalde Star*. It was a water-stained wrinkled piece of paper, almost three weeks old. Emblazoned on the page, VICKSBURG SURRENDERS. *Grant enters the city. Eleven thousand troops paroled.* Farther down the page, below the detailed account of Vicksburg's fall and an impassioned plea for all good Southern men to rally to the aid of a divided Confederacy, was a notice that a new Texas battalion was being formed in San Antonio and the deadline to join was August 20.

Cole read the enlistment notice for the fifth time that day. There was still time to reach the river city, still time to get into this war before it ended. And there might never be another chance to test oneself in battle, to reach for a share of glory.

A twig cracked and boots scuffed on the surface of the boulder Cole was propped against. Cole stiffened and felt a twinge of apprehension—after all, the mountain wasn't called Mescalero Lookout for nothing. His fingers closed around the Springfield percussion rifle cradled in his lap, then relaxed as his brother Billy squirmed beneath Cole's makeshift blind. Billy settled himself next to his brother in the pocket Cole had cleared for himself among the rocky debris left over from a winter landslide.

Though they were twins, Billy was smaller than Cole, his skin fairer, and his gentle, sensitive features more closely resembled his mother's. His hair was blond and thickly curled, his eyes were a warm brown, not harsh blue like Cole's. At fiestas and fandangos the older girls and ladies always seemed to make a fuss over Billy Anthem, attracted to his good looks and by his innate politeness. His well-mannered behavior was usually in direct contrast to that of his brother.

"You think I was an Apache?" Billy grinned.

"The noisiest one in all creation," Cole replied, and lifted a finger to his lips. "I haven't sat up here three full days just so you could spook away every critter that comes to the creek to drink."

The two brothers had made camp on the other side of the mountain, out of sight and scent of the creek and any animal that might be frightened off. Cole was hoping for a chance at a whitetail. At thirteen, Cole had yet to make a kill and had only recently grown enough to be able to handle his father's Springfield rifle. Billy liked to tag along but left the hunting to his brother. He enjoyed the solitude and tranquility of these desert mountains too much to ruin the peace with rifle fire.

Billy slid down and sat alongside his brother, noticing the wrinkled page of newsprint. "Pa told you to forget such notions as joining up."

"As far as he knows, I have. And don't you be telling him different when he gets back." John Anthem was on a cattle drive to Shreveport.

"You needn't worry about me, but you better not let Rachel know about it, 'cause she'll run and tell Mama first thing." As Billy took the paper to read, Cole nodded in accord with his twin brother's opinion of their younger sister.

Billy whistled softly. "Just what do you expect to do even if you could join up?" he asked, unable to fathom his brother's desire for fame and glory. Though he had a more practical nature, Billy respected Cole's wishes and dreams.

"Seems to me they need couriers and such. I can ride

like the wind. Ain't no one quicker. And I'd do my share of fighting if called on," Cole said.

"Best you forget it. As I recollect, it was right after we heard about the siege of Fort Sumter, Pa came to dwell on the matter. He said war is a man's work, a man's triumph, and a man's folly. You may be older than me by a few minutes, Cole Anthem, but you aren't a man yet by a long shot."

"I will be before long," Cole whispered, resolve in his voice as he peered over the lip of the boulder in front of him.

Billy started to speak, but Cole suddenly waved him to silence and reached for the Springfield. His hand closed around the heavy walnut stock and lifted the weapon into position. He slid the barrel between the branches of the lightning-shattered pine tree that screened him from the creek below.

Shifting his position, Billy spied a whitetail buck standing about three feet tall at the shoulders and better than six feet long from head to erect white tail. The animal gingerly approached the creek, paused and craned its head to either side, became statue-still, took a hesitant step, and froze again. Billy marveled at the way the animal had materialized out of the forest, taking form and movement out of the emerald gloom, finding substance in the private stillness of the slide-scarred slope.

In that moment, he remembered a story his father had told him of the time in his own youth when he had made his first kill. John Anthem had marked *his* passage into manhood with the blood of a white-tailed deer. The blooding was a sacred ritual to almost every frontier-bred youth. Billy began to understand his brother's determination and persistence in this hunt.

The buck raised its head, four-point antlers jutting

skyward. Twenty-five, maybe thirty yards away. Cole would have wished for an easier shot. He held his fire, willing the animal closer and grateful for every step the animal took. He centered the sights on a patch of reddish fur above the left shoulder.

A blue jay startled Cole as it attempted to land on the branches of the dead wood and realized at the last second that there were humans behind the boulder and rotting wood. The bird voiced its outrage and fear in a raucous cry that ranged higher and higher in pitch as it spiraled upward from the blind.

The buck recognized the blue jay's pealed alarm and halted in its tracks just at the edge of the narrow creek. Cole squeezed the trigger of the rifle. The buck seemed to be looking directly at him, as if in some strange way in communion with the boy, linked to him, bonded— killed to killer. The deer could have bolted and yet it remained, poised and vulnerable, like a sacrifice.

Billy jumped as the rifle roared and recoiled against Cole's shoulder. Black smoke rose to sting the eyes and blind both boys. It slowly dissipated. Then Cole jumped to his feet, roaring in triumph, and bounded out of the scheduled niche. Billy saw the buck, lying prone across the creek, paw the water in a futile gesture, shudder, and die.

"I took him," Cole shouted. "Did you see that?" He stumbled, regained his balance, and bolted the remaining few yards down to the animal's side.

Squirrels darted up tree trunks out of harm's way. A doe leapt from cover and scampered off out of range. Cole yelled and raised the rifle before remembering he had already spent its single charge—powder and shot were back in the blind. He lowered the rifle and used the stock for support as he lost his footing for the third time in his excitement. He stumbled and skinned both knees as he slid to the dead animal's side.

The white-tailed deer acted as a natural dam. The springwater built up on one side, then crested the reddish coat and spread out to continue its flow down the wooded, boulder-strewn incline. Cole noticed an undulating ribbon of crimson marking where the creek flowed over the animal's mortal wound, a puckered, nasty-looking hole.

Cole sagged back on his haunches and reached out with trembling hand. He worked his fingers into the wound and brought them out dripping with blood, crimson to the knuckles. He began at his forehead and wiped down, marking himself with the blood of the beast. He shuddered. And sensed a longing in himself for the goodness of life, felt an inner drive to run free and catch the wind.

Billy approached, taking his time to traverse the treacherous incline, but Cole did not notice him at first. The hunter was lost in the enactment of ritual. He leaned forward and drank from the creek as it flowed over the draining wound and tasted life's fluids, washed from the flesh of his kill. Billy held a few paces back and waited in respectful silence, in truth, moved by the savage display.

So, in the late summer of 1863, Cole Anthem was blooded. He became a man—at least in his own eyes— and felt free to pursue a man's work, a man's triumph . . . and folly.

PART ONE

★

1

1874

Big John Anthem had laid claim to his land in the wild west Texas mountain country back in 1850. He had fought Indians and Mexican raiders, petty thieves and jealous cattlemen, to keep his claim.

He called his kingdom Luminaria and took a wife who bore him two sons and two daughters. And in all this golden, lonely, lovely range his word was law; his judgment, justice.

In the fall of 1874, eleven years after the blooding of his son, Cole, John Anthem rode out of a thicket of scrub oak and mesquite and down into a washed-out arroyo where two raggedly dressed hide-hunters were busily skinning a fresh-killed steer whose hide wore the Slash A brand, John Anthem's mark.

Slash A was the only brand worn on cattle that grazed over four hundred thousand acres of range. If there were any cattle to be killed, John Anthem or one of his men would do the killing and there would be a good reason: for food or to cull a sick steer from the herd.

Anthem had no use for hide-hunters. And his thoughts were of retribution as he walked his sorrel gelding past a high-sided wagon half full of skins. Flies were thick as grit in a sandstorm around the campsite where carcasses rotted in the sun. Anthem studied the two men in the morning light and sensed the tension rise in their gullets. A third hide-hunter emerged on horse-back from behind a cover of mesquite and monks-hood.

The skinner on horseback—a young man, no more than eighteen years old—sat astride a brown mare and cradled a Spancer carbine in the crook of his arm. The youth's features were hidden beneath the brim of his battered hat.

Anthem shifted his attention to the men by the campfire. One was a hard case nearing forty, sporting a scraggly beard and deep-set eyes. His lips peeled back to reveal a row of crooked teeth. Stringy blond hair hung to his shoulders. His partner looked a few years younger, a lifetime hungrier. There didn't seem enough meat on the man to cover his bony frame. He was tall and bearded, wearing a rancid-smelling woolen coat despite the warm autumn air. All three of the hide-hunters wore homespun shirts and buckskin britches.

The older of the threesome glanced at his companion and took a step forward, angling himself so that the revolver holstered on his right was hidden from view. The bearded man started to move to get himself in a better position.

"That's far enough, Stringbean," John Anthem said, walking his range horse up the arroyo and reining the sorrel to a halt about thirty feet from the hide-hunters' campfire. The bearded man halted in his tracks as Anthem's cold blue eyes bore into him, for Anthem's tight-lipped, weather-scarred face showed the mercy of a cornered cougar.

John Anthem was a big man, six feet tall and at forty-four years, a touch thick in the waist, but slabs of work-hardened muscle crowded the shoulders and sleeves of his faded red shirt. He held the reins of his mount in his left hand, his right already resting on the grip of his Colt Dragoon. The percussion pistol had been converted and bored out to handle a big .45-caliber cartridge. The gun was heavy and hard to handle, and packed a wallop as mean as the man who wore it.

"Reckon you be Big John Anthem hisself," the older of the three remarked. He seemed to be the leader of the disputable-looking trio. "Well, folks call me—"

"I know who you are," Anthem growled, in obvious bad temper. "You're the three sons of bitches who have been butchering my cattle and leaving them to rot. I'd rather Apaches steal 'em. At least they do it to fill their bellies. But you three scum . . . The hell with your names, I don't intend to erect any markers over you. I'll leave you where you fall, like you've done my stock for the past month."

There was silence then, for the three men needed to weigh their chances or find the courage, to grow wings perhaps and fly like all hell away from Anthem's land. It was morning—late, though—and the sun was crawling toward noon.

The smell of blood was in the air. If there had been a breeze, the fragrance of chino grass and sage and the faint scent of pines would have favored the arroyo, for mountains loomed behind the campsite. But there was no breeze and the stench of blood clung to the clearing like a gloomy portent of trouble to come.

"You talk mighty bold." The stringy hair hide-hunter grinned.

"I've talked enough," Anthem replied with an air of casualness that belied his actions. He yanked the Colt

Dragoon from its holster as the two hide-hunters afoot
reached for their own weapons. The Dragoon spat flame
and followed with a deafening boom. The leader of the
three flew backward into the flames of his own campfire.

The hungry-looking man in the coat levelled a
Confederate-issue cap-and-ball and loosed a wild shot
that blew away a clump of trumpet flowers and sent a
hummingbird winging to safety.

Anthem fired once more and the bearded man
screamed, clutched at his chest, and dropped to his
knees. He seemed to shrink into his coat as he doubled
over and died.

The young rider broke for cover, dropping his rifle
and lashing his horse unmercifully. He gained the cover
of the trees as Anthem brought his Dragoon to bear.

John Anthem held his fire, cursed, and dug his heels
into the sorrel, and the range-bred gelding broke toward
the camp. The leader of the thieves rolled out of the fire
and sat upright, smoke rising from the back of his shirt
and the charred wisps of his matted hair. His eyes widened as he looked at the crimson stain spreading over
his shirt. He raised a Navy Colt at Anthem on his charging sorrel. It took an eternity to cock the damn gun, and
an eternity was too long. The hide-hunter shrieked and
tried to cover his face, but fell back as Anthem rode him
down, leaving the hide-hunter's trampled corpse in the
settling dust, the dead man's blood mingling with that
of the freshly skinned steers.

In the glare of the sun-washed walls of the arroyo, upon
the hard packed earth, treacherous with the residue of
flash flood and the wind's erosion, Lendel Bass rode for
his life. He raked his rusted spurs along the mare's flanks
and chanced a glance over his shoulder just in time to

see John Anthem on his sorrel burst from the thicket and leap a cache of deadwood left by a now-vanished flood. Young Lendel Bass felt his heart shoot into his throat and he turned his attention to the trail ahead. But there, too, he found the winding escape route blocked.

Where the walls fell away and the arroyo widened into an open meadow, another horseman waited astride a hammerhead Appaloosa. The rider was a slight man in his mid-thirties. His hair was long and raven-black. He wore a sombrero, a nut-colored short coat, and flared pants. His blousy shirt was open to the waist, revealing the smooth coffee-colored expanse of his chest. A gun belt circled his narrow hips and a bandolier hung from his right shoulder, its loops crammed with shells for the sawed-off scatter gun he gripped in his left fist.

Lendel knew that horeman by description, and if his spirits sagged at the sight of John Anthem, they plummeted now. The vaquero could only be Joaquín Almendáriz, called Chapo for the wild horses of the barrancas.

Like his father before him, Chapo Almendáriz was segundo of Luminaria. It was rumored he had once been a cutthroat and bandit who had roamed the Sierra del Hueso to the south. Whatever his past, Almendáriz was no man to ride the wrong side of, but what choice was there.

Lendel Bass whipped his horse and rode straight on toward the Appaloosa as it pawed the air.

Chapo fired the shotgun into the ground a few feet ahead of the oncoming hide-hunter. Both barrels spat fire and black smoke as double-O buck-shot blasted a small crater in the path of the brown mare.

The animal leapt sideways and neighed in terror as gravel stung its legs like a swarm of wasps, and Lendel Bass lost hold of the reins. He felt his feet slip out of the stirrups, and a second later he was airborne. The young man slammed into the side of the arroyo and slid down the wall as his legs buckled. For a moment, he lost consciousness. But the sharp rocks digging into the small of his back brought him around. He fumbled at a sheath at his waist, dragged free of his skinning knife, and forced himself to stand. He stumbled and staggered toward the segundo on his Appaloosa.

Chapo's hand dropped over in a cross draw and a long-barreled Colt appeared in his right fist, its seven-and-a-half-inch barrel centered directly on Bass. Chapo shook his head as if silently scolding the young man for his foolishness.

Bass noticed that the segundo had dropped the reins and yet the Appaloosa obeyed the vaquero's shifting weight and the pressure of his knees. The animal advanced a few paces and stopped. As Chapo thumbed the hammer of the Colt, Lendel Bass lowered his head and dropped his knife. He heard the sound of an approaching horse and looked up at the creased, leathery face of John Anthem.

The man on the sorrel holstered his Dragoon, and Bass took comfort in the gesture. It was his first time at rustling and stealing hides, and he hoped the two men would understand that he was a good boy at heart. He even owned a bible tucked away in the saddlebag on his brown nag. He mustered up a sheepish grin.

"Pilgrim, your two friends are dead," Anthem said.

"Seems to me, sir," Bass said, doffing his hat and looking from Anthem to the segundo and back to Anthem, "Uh . . . seems you've saved me from bad company."

Anthem raised his eyes to study the projection of volcanic rock upthrust out of the flood-scarred wall behind

Bass. It looked to be about twenty feet up the arroyo and was the proper angle to support a man away from the gravel-strewn wall. John Anthem looked over at Chapo, whose expression was one of slow realization and disapproval.

The man on the sorrel removed his own weathered stetson and wiped his forearm across his forehead and close-cropped pale-red hair that the sun had almost bleached the color out of.

"I don't know how I can ever thank you, Mr. Anthem. I had one foot on the path to perdition, but you sure have helped me pluck it off and set it square on the road to righteousness," Lendel Bass exclaimed with all the fervor of a camp preacher leading his wayward flock to a river baptism.

Anthem untied his lariat, tossed it upward over the projecting rock, and caught the loop where it dangled.

"Mr. Anthem . . . uh . . . sir, what do you intend for me?"

"Son, I aim to hang you."

Bass paled and almost collapsed right then and there. Again he appealed to the rancher's sense of mercy. "Sir, this act demeans you."

"Like you demeaned my herd by about forty-three steers, according to my segundo's count," John Anthem snarled. He dropped the loop over the hide-hunter's neck and jerked it tight.

"*Compadre*, no," Chapo blurted out. He nudged the Appaloosa forward to try to block the sorrel, but Anthem veered his mount to the side. With the end of the lariat wrapped around the saddle horn, Anthem backed the sturdy mare away from the wall of the arroyo, jerking Lendel off his feet and into the air. As the rough hemp bit deep into his flesh and choked off his wind, Bass reached up and grabbed for the length of rope overhead to take the strain off his neck.

"Damn. What a piss-poor hangman I'd make," Anthem grumbled as he tied the rope off around the base of an ocotillo growing out of the slope.

Chapo looked around at the hide-hunter, who slowly and painfully was working his way hand over hand up the length of the rope to the rock projection. He would have a nasty flesh burn, but he would live.

"I had to spend so much time hunting you and your 'bad company' that it's likely I'll miss my son's wedding," John Anthem called up to the dangling figure. "Be glad my wife isn't here; *she'd* have tied your hands. And the next time I catch you on my land, I'll remember to tie your hands myself." Anthem shook his head in disgust. He glared at Chapo, who grinned and slowly exhaled.

"You had me fooled that time, Big John."

"Yeah," Anthem replied. He glanced up and saw that Bass had reached the projection and was struggling to loosen the noose around his neck. "You can keep the rope, sonny. Better think long and hard before you ever drop it over something that isn't yours."

"I think he's been read to from the book," Chapo said. "He'll remember."

"What day is it anyway?" John Anthem asked.

"Near as I can reckon, September twentieth."

Anthem winced. His son Billy was due to be married on the twenty-first. Rose had been making preparations for nigh on to a month and had extracted a promise from John that nothing would interfere with his being present for the vow-taking and fiesta. "And here I sit a good two days' ride from my own front door."

Smacking his lips and running a hand over his stubbled jaw, Anthem raised his eyes to Lendel Bass, who had finally freed himself from the lynch rope and was clinging gratefully to the slope. Compared to the tempest that awaited John Anthem back at the ranch, the hide-hunter got off light.

2

Rose McCain Anthem, still as lovely as her namesake flower, stood on the balcony of the hacienda. Her hair was a sunlit cascade of yellow-gold tresses that flowed down over her shoulders. Her features were fair and browned; crows' feet wrinkled around her eyes when she smiled, which she often did. She was a tall woman and big-boned, a forthright and honest beauty, a woman of strength and femininity.

As she studied the winding road that followed Luminaria Creek, her brown eyes seemed to take in the entire canyon, then lifted to check the grassy ridges rising five hundred feet to east and west from the floor of the darkened canyon. Night shadows spread outward to engulf the floor of the canyon, though the sunset lingered on the crest of the ridges. The canyon opened to the south about half a mile away where the waters of the creek emptied out onto the plains.

Rose leaned upon the balcony railing just outside her bedroom. Her arm curled around a timber post supporting the latticework roof overhead. The balcony ran the length of the two-storied hacienda and not only offered a dramatic view of the canyon but also provided battlements in case of attack. The adobe walls wore the scars of battle, pockmarked from musket ball and arrowhead.

A low wall ringed the hacienda and accompanying bunkhouse and stables. Rose sighed and lowered her gaze to the courtyard below, which was festooned with paper lanterns, luminarias that sparked as bright as sunlight on the creek below in the canyon.

The hacienda crowned a broad swell of land in the center of the canyon just east of a wide creek. Upon this knoll John and Rose had built their house and defended their land against Apache, Commanche, and a host of desperadoes who had tried to take it from them. The twins, Billy and Cole, had been born during a Commanche raid. With only the help of old Poke Tyler, Rose had brought her twin boys into the world with the smell of gunsmoke stinging her nostrils and gunfire and war whoops ringing in her ears. Her first act, after she tucked her babies close to her side, was to load a brace of Walker Colts for her husband to fight with. That was twenty-four years ago, though it sometimes seemed only yesterday.

Rose walked to the east end of the balcony and looked out on the grave plot with its black iron fence that framed a square of ground. Half a dozen white markers rose out of the tall yellow grass, but two especially were dearest to her heart. Rebecca Faith Anthem, born December 8, 1864, died December 27, 1864. She had shared a single Christmas, poor little one, poor frail and premature babe. The other marker was for Cole Tyler Anthem, born 1852, and died . . . when, where? He had run off to war, lured by the call of adventure and the promise of glory. And never returned. At first Rose had clung to the possibility that he might be alive as stragglers from the armies of the Confederacy drifted west toward the goldfields, or south to fight in the revolution rocking Mexico, where embattled Maximilian and his French troops struggled to contain a rising tide of rebels led by Benito Juárez.

John had erected the marker five years after the South's surrender. He had driven it down into the rocky soil and laid his doubts to rest. His son was dead. Rose Anthem never thought of the grave as empty. After all, part of her heart was buried there.

Rose walked back to the middle of the balcony and watched the Mexican women clearing away the great oaken tables that yesterday had been filled with stoneware platters and pots and racks of fire-glazed cups. The wedding banquet waited in the summer kitchen out behind the hacienda. And there it would stay, thanks to her husband's absence. Rose sighed and thought of the incorrigible man she had married, remembering his assurances that he would be back for his son's wedding service. The opportunity to catch the skinners plaguing Luminaria was just too ripe to miss.

"Any sign of him?" Billy Anthem said, stepping through the doorway.

Rose turned toward her son. Billy stood as tall as his mother. He was slimly built. His clean-shaven features and delicately boned countenance hid a volatile temperament. His eyes were gentle and brown as the earth, like his mother's eyes, but lacking the golden highlights that added to her beauty.

John Anthem had never been able to accept the fact that Billy harbored ambitions other than running the Slash A. Billy preferred his books, especially his journal. He took pleasure in observation and solitude and moments of introspection. He preferred writing to roping, dreaming to doing. Billy had another quality that Rose found endearing even as it gave her concern. He was hopelessly romantic. Too often he allowed his heart to rule, to sweep him into situations that called for one to proceed slowly, to see clearly and not rush headlong into something . . . like marriage.

Rose held out her hand to her son. "He will be along," she said.

"It's too late now, Mother," Billy bitterly replied.

"Nonsense. Your father's only a day late. Laura is still here. She and her father can just spend the night with us again. The bank in Uvalde can get along without Griffin Prescott for a little while longer."

"Mr. Prescott left with Reverend Schraner this morning, while you and Rachel were gone for your swim. The reverend waited all day yesterday as a favor to me. Mr. Prescott was furious and accompanied him. I can't blame Reverend Schraner. He's the only doctor between here and Uvalde, and Martha Wallers over on Blue Creek is due anytime."

Billy Anthem hooked his thumbs in his belt and began to pace. He paused at the corner of the porch and frowned down at the tables as the women continued to clear the remnants of a wedding that never was.

The wives of the vaqueros who lived in adobe houses back up the canyon had spent the day returning the courtyard to normalcy. The courtyard was a peaceful place crisscrossed with rock walks and stone-bordered beds of wild roses and trumpet flowers. Madrone trees grew there too; their twisted branches of peeled bark and pinkish wood were strangely soft to the touch, much like the skin of a peach.

"Laura wants us to go on to Uvalde and be married there. It might take weeks to bring Schraner back out to the ranch," Billy said, already suspecting his mother's reply.

Rose stiffened. She smoothed the wrinkles from the deep-blue velvet bodice of her dress. "We can ask your father." Billy started to protest. She cut him off. "I know it is hard. But you are the only son he has. And being at your wedding is important to him."

"Just not as important as this ranch," Billy grumbled.

"He loves you, Billy," Rose said, crossing to him.

A breeze set the olla gently swaying in the shade of the porch. A clay dipper on its knotted cord clattered gently against the side of the egg-shaped stoneware container of water hung in a net of braided hemp.

"But he loves this ranch more," Billy said. "He always has and always will."

"Luminaria is his life. It's mine, too," Rose gently answered. "The land is as much a part of us as the blood in our veins, as our own flesh. Little Faith sleeps in its embrace."

"I just wanted him to think of me, of what I wanted for a change," Billy said, scowling.

"Everything he does is for you; Luminaria will be yours someday," Rose said in a vain attempt to make him understand. "Yours and Rachel's."

"Only because Cole isn't here. Poor Father. Cole ran off and got himself killed and left John Anthem with the worst of the lot, me." Billy looked over at his mother and saw how his words had hurt her. He walked over as she lowered her head, her golden hair spilling forward, and put his arms around her shoulders. Words of apology were in his heart, imprisoned there by his own wounded pride, the hurt and frustration his father had caused him.

Cole is dead and I will never cut his image. The shadow I chase is my own for better or worse. Thoughts hammered in his mind. The wounded expression in his mother's eyes hurt. Her pain was his, but it didn't change things. He felt a stranger to his father. The words "I'm sorry" remained unspoken.

The alarm bell on the crest of the east ridge shattered the mounting tension between Rose and her son. Both of them spun around as the brass bell pealed forth and echoed down the long hills sounding its alarm: rider approaching. It had to be John and Chapo, Rose thought, her knuckles whitening as she braced herself against the adobe wall and leaned over the balcony. A young red-headed girl rode a brown mare through the ranch hands lounging in front of the bunkhouse. They scattered out of her way. She sat easy in the saddle and her willowy frame moved in graceful oneness with the mare.

And right behind her, walking, hurried an old man in buckskins. Rose watched as Rachel left old Uncle Poke-berry Tyler staggering in the dust. Poke Tyler wiped the grit out of his eyes, patted the dirt from his beard, glanced toward the bell on the ridge, and headed for the nearest horse. He climbed into the saddle, waved his hat to the woman on the balcony, and slapped it down across the rump of his mustang.

Rose waved back and watched as Poke rode down through the lengthening shadows of night that stole ominously up the walls of the canyon toward home and hearth.

The travois slid up the side of a wheel rut and settled with a tooth-jarring thump that sent a spasm of pain cutting like a knife all the length of John Anthem's broken leg. He grimaced and craned his head around to glare at the sorrel gelding pulling him homeward. The walls of Luminaria Canyon appeared to open as if to receive him.

"Go ahead. Hit another," he called out, his speech slurred. "And find a chuckhole for yourself." The gelding shook its head and whinnied. John lifted a whiskey bottle to his lips and took another pull. "Ahh . . . just enough."

Riding ahead of the travois, Joaquín Almendáriz turned in the saddle and looked back at Anthem, who began to sing about the moon shining bright on pretty redwing.

"With howling like that, maybe I better put you out of your misery," said the segundo. "I'd do the same for any horse."

Anthem leaned up on his elbows and fixed his segundo in a withering stare. He started to offer a retort, but the distant pealing of the alarm bell in the canyon cut him off.

"We've been spotted by the lookout," John said. He shouted for the sorrel to stop and grabbed a handful of tail and the gelding obeyed. Anthem rolled off the side of the travois. He yelped in pain but managed to shift his weight onto his sound right leg. Bracing himself against the mare, he fumbled for and found the oak branch he was using as a makeshift crutch. Two shorter branches and several strips of rawhide had provided a leg splint.

John Anthem shuddered as a wave of nausea washed over him and the world tilted crazily before his eyes. Chapo seemed, for a minute, to be riding up a steep slope toward him. But John willed the world to straighten itself, and the landscape complied.

"Big John, what are you doing?" Chapo asked, worried.

Anthem brought out a knife and, with a single flick of his wrist, sawed through the rawhide straps holding the travois to the gelding. He reached up and flipped the rig over on its side. The gelding trotted forward a few paces and Chapo leaned over to catch the reins.

"I don't aim to be carried into Luminaria. Least-ways not alive," Anthem insisted loudly. He finished the whiskey and tossed the bottle aside. His leg didn't hurt so much now.

"You may not have to worry about living much longer," Chapo retorted.

John Anthem ignored him and hobbled around to the right of the sorrel. He rested a hand on the pommel of the saddle, took a deep breath, and told himself this wouldn't hurt.

He lied.

But John made it up into the saddle without biting through his lower lip. When his vision cleared, the world quit spinning, and the lava burning a course through his injured limb turned to mere blood once again, he nodded to Chapo and muttered "Let's go" in a humble tone. At the sound of distant gunfire he glanced up to see his daughter, Rachel, and Poke Tyler emerge from the mouth of Luminaria Canyon. Rachel, in her exuberance, fired several signal shots from her carbine to welcome her father home. John hated any sort of fuss, and yet the sight of his flame-haired daughter racing toward him at breakneck speed filled him with proud affection. She was a spitfire right enough, better with a horse than most trailwise drovers, and at nineteen in the full bloom of her beauty.

"She'll break her fool neck running the horse like that . . . over broken ground," John said. He hiccupped and belched. God, how much had he drunk, he tried to re-call—one bottle or two?

"She's more saddlewise than her father," Chapo said.

John Anthem repositioned himself, and a flash of pain knifed through him like a white-hot blade, stifling any protest. It was difficult to offer a defense with his leg in a splint. He waited for his daughter to approach.

She reined in, slowed her horse to a trot. And Poke Tyler followed suit behind. Dust billowed around them, obscuring all four riders for a few seconds.

" 'Bout time you showed. Hope you're packin' scalps to make it worth losin' yours," Poke said. He was bald and leather-looking, with a stubble of silver for a beard and a line of broken yellowed teeth revealed in his smile. He was scarcely as tall as Rachel, but despite his size and age of nearly sixty years, John knew Old Poke could hold his own with any man.

Rachel was slim and graceful, full of poise one mo-ment, tomboyish and skittish as a bronc the next. She brushed a strand of red hair out of her eyes and looked at her father with eyes as piercing blue as his own.

"Papa, you told me I could go with you this time. But you went and snuck off and didn't even wake me," Ra-chel blurted out. "You left me to have to dress up and everything."

"We weren't riding line, girl," John replied thickly. "Chasing hiders is no job for a young woman . . . oh . . ." He winced.

Poke noticed the travois John had thrown aside. He looked at Chapo and followed his gaze to John's broken leg, seeing it the same time as Rachel did.

"Oh, my God, you're hurt," Rachel exclaimed, her anger draining at the sight of his injury.

"That's a fact," John said, and started forward, keeping his sorrel to a steady walk.

"Broke?" Pokeberry Tyler asked.

"Fractured below the knee," John said.

"Still won't save you from Rose," Poke replied.

"He was hoping it would," Chapo said.

Poke shook his head. "Nah, it'll just put him at her mercy." He shook his head. "Bad luck, Big John."

"Better luck 'an 'em hiders we caught," Anthem slurred. He grabbed the saddle horn to steady himself.

Rachel, riding along side him now, wore an expression of grave concern that made John feel old.

"Is Billy married?" John asked.

"No," Rachel said. "Mama wouldn't let him without you there. Now the preacher's left and Laura's father too. And everybody's mad as blue blazes at you."

John winced. He shook his head and groaned softly. Only this time, it wasn't because of his leg.

Welcome home.

Rose and Billy, waiting on the porch of the hacienda, watched John Anthem ride up through the gateway and into the courtyard.

John grunted with relief as he walked his sorrel up to the hitching post and angled himself to show off his broken leg. He hoped it would buy him a few moments' respite. He noticed, in a sweeping glance, that the courtyard had been stripped of any decorations. One of his vaqueros approached to help him down from his horse. He waved the man aside and held out his hand to Billy, who waited in the shadows of the porch. Billy Anthem pointedly turned around and headed inside the house. John stiffened, but did not call after his son.

"Good hunting?" Rose asked, defusing the tension as

she stepped out of the shade and into the fading sunlight. She motioned for the vaquero to help her husband down.

"We won't lose any more cattle to those hide-hunters," John announced in a loud voice.

"He read 'em from the book," Joaquín Almendáriz said, leaning over from his Appaloosa to take the reins of the sorrel from the vaquero.

"Papa's hurt," Rachel exclaimed as she leapt down from her horse.

"I can see, daughter," Rose said. As long as John Anthem could ride into Luminaria, she wasn't worried. "He doesn't look to be suffering overmuch."

"He plumb broke his leg trying to make it back on time," Poke added, hoping to win some sympathy for his friend.

"Chapo makes a fine trail nurse," John said as he braced himself against the pain and leaned into his crutch. He nodded to the vaquero who had assisted him, dismissing the man.

"Doc Schraner left this morning," Rose said. "He waited as long as he could. Laura's father left with him."

"I heard. And the wedding?" John asked, looking around at the deserted yard, trying to focus. An empty belly and all that whiskey did not mix.

"There was no wedding, Mr. Anthem," said Laura Prescott, walking up to him. She was a dark-haired girl with pale white skin. Like fine porcelain, her beauty was fragile and fair, her features prim. She was used to demanding respect for the simple reason that she was a Prescott, one of Uvalde's fine families. "Maybe no one else will say it, but I will . . ." she began, hands on hips and drawing herself up.

"Fine," John said. He patted her on the shoulder and lurched past. "But not now." He continued up onto the porch and headed into the house without looking back.

The lower half of the hacienda was divided into a broad, open living room and a separate dining room with a long rectangular table. The table was covered with pies left over from the fiesta that never happened.

The kitchen could be entered from the dining room and a study/library stood on the other side of the living room. The study, John Anthem's retreat, occupied a rear corner of the house. It was his place of privacy, its walls lined with the books that had provided much of his children's education. A stairway straight ahead and dividing the living room from the dining area led upstairs to a carpeted hall and four bedrooms.

Billy Anthem was standing in front of the living-room fireplace; its massive hearth and empty, soot-streaked interior loomed over him like the mouth of a cave. One hand was thrust into the pocket of his frock coat as he leaned on the mantel. A shot glass full of rye whiskey was in easy reach, inches from his fingertips. He turned toward the front doorway as John Anthem limped into the room, with Rose and Rachel following, and a much-distraught Laura Prescott closing the door behind them.

John maneuvered his way past the carved furniture that dominated the living room. Great high-backed chairs and heavy couches built to last were covered with brushed leather. The couches were cushioned with pillows Rose and Rachel had stitched, stuffed with down, and embroidered with tiny satin flowers of blue and wine red and delicate pearl white. The room smelled of sage and whiskey, the aroma of peach and wild-strawberry pies drifting in from the dining room.

"Well," John said, facing his son. He tried to focus on the young man. "I'm late, but I'm here."

"You're drunk."

"Yes . . . yes . . . I am most assuredly, uh, drunk." He turned to the women and bowed. He swept his hat down and across in a gracious gesture that almost toppled him onto the rug. He managed to avoid disaster by bracing himself on his cane.

"Come to bed," Rose said, catching him by the arm. She steered him toward the stairway.

"Rachel," John said, looking over his shoulder, "bring me some coffee upstairs. And maybe one of those pies, if there is one of yours among them."

"I made the strawberry," Rachel replied, beaming.

"My favorite," John said, and he looked at Laura. "That is if Miss Prescott doesn't mind me robbing a little from the celebration table."

"Mind? Hardly. After all, it is your house, Mr. Anthem. And I have no doubt but that you will do just exactly as you please," Laura said, and picking up the hem of her skirt, she hurried across the room to hook her arm in Billy's. "But there is one thing you won't have your way in . . . this marriage. Billy and I will be wed no matter what you do."

Rose had to suppress her satisfaction. It did Big John good for the women in the house to stand up to him. At least Laura was showing some backbone. Maybe there was hope for the union, after all. She hurried her husband up the stairs before he could offer a retort, leaving the bride-to-be to her minor victory.

The covers on the brass bed were turned down and inviting, and John headed straight for the cool, comfortable-looking sheets. A breeze ruffled the curtains and the parted drapes provided a view of Luminaria Canyon, its gray walls of stone a shadowy corridor now opening up onto a golden plain in the distance. The blue sky darkened and a scattering of stars dotted the deepening heavens.

"Hey, lady," John said, a wicked twinkle in his eye, "why don't you lay across this big brass bed?" He reached out and encircled his wife's waist, lost his balance, and almost fainted as pain erupted up his right leg.

Rose managed to support him until he reached the bed. The springs creaked beneath their combined weight.

"Well, here we are John Anthem," Rose said. "Now, what do you intend for me?" She spoke to their reflections in the mirror on the walnut vanity across the room from the bed. "Of course you had better hurry before your daughter shows up with the pie."

"Oooohhhhh," the man beside her groaned, and lay back on the bed.

Rose stood and walked around to his feet and pulled his boot off. He only wore one. Chapo had cut the other away from his injured leg.

"Thanks," John said with a sigh of satisfaction.

"I have taken your boots off before. I think it was part of my marriage vows."

"No. I mean for not yelling at me. My head is going to feel four sizes bigger in the morning." His hand slid over as he reached for her.

"I'm hoping you'll feel bad enough on your own," Rose said, keeping her distance. "At least when you've sobered up."

Rachel knocked once on the door and entered without waiting for an invitation. She balanced a tray containing a whole strawberry pie and a blue-enameled coffeepot and two thick mugs. She carried the tray to the bed and set it down on the maplewood bedside table.

"I brought you some coffee, Papa."

"Good girl."

Rachel sat on the edge of the bed and leaned over to kiss him. She smelled of wild flowers and fresh-cut hay, and John wondered how he could have had any part in making a girl so lovely as this.

"I guess I must be the only one in this house who isn't angry as a mud dauber in a drought over you being late for the wedding," Rachel said. "Billy and Laura were in the living room, talking soft like they were afraid someone might come a-spying on them. Then Billy left. He looked real hurt. That makes me sad. Not Laura, though. I don't care if she's angry or giddy as a colt."

"Shhh, child," Rose admonished. "Laura is going to be a part of this family someday. Billy loves her and I think we ought to respect his judgment."

"Sure," said Rachel, brushing a scarlet ringlet back from her forehead. "And pray for the best." She stood and hurried back to the door. "I'm gonna go find Chapo. I want to hear how Papa shot up those hide-hunters. Poke says it ain't proper business for a lady."

"He's right," John's voice came drifting up from the pillows.

"It's proper business for me. I'm an Anthem, unless I'm wearing a cross brand that no one has told me about."

"Rachel," the girl's mother blurted out in a scolding tone, but Rachel disappeared out into the hall and shut the door behind her, effectively cutting off Rose's attempt to correct her.

"Did you hear her?" Rose asked, turning to her husband and shaking her head in exasperation.

"Yeah." John laughed gently and closed his eyes. "She's Anthem, all right." He yawned. "Through and through." He worked the kink out of his shoulder blade and settled deeper into the mattress. "Rose . . ."

"Yes." She sat on the bed and put her hand on his leg. If his leg hadn't been broken . . . Her thoughts dwelled on a most unladylike notion that put any of her daughter's to shame. She felt a delightful warmth rise up from her loins and course the length of her body.

"I never intended to hurt Billy," John said, his voice fading. "But this other thing had to be done. Those hide-hunters figured every Slash A rider would be gathered here for the wedding and didn't even try to conceal their smoke. Chapo and I caught them with the skinning knives in their hands." He reached for her hand and pulled her closer to him. "You understand why it had to be done."

"I understand you, John Anthem. But if it makes Billy feel better, I'm going to be furious as heck with you for the next couple of days," Rose softly replied.

"I love that boy. Dammit, why has he got to go marry some bluestocking won't live anywhere but in the city?"

"She's very beautiful, and he's in love."

"I need him . . . here . . ." The words were fainter now, spoken as he slowly exhaled and drifted into sleep.

Rose continued to sit by him, holding his work-roughened hand.

If hard years had worn away John's youthful handsomeness, they'd left something better; an enduring core of manliness. Though he was often too blunt for his own good, Rose would have him no other way.

Yes, a big man, a good man. And hers.

She reached over to take the tray and covered the pie with a cloth napkin. As she stole quietly from his bedside, she paused once to inspect the splints on his battered leg. The break did not seem too severe. She prayed it was only a fracture. If he was able to hobble up the stairs, then that was probably a favorable sign. The injury ought to heal despite the lack of proper doctoring.

Rose glanced out the window at the crimson streaked sky. Sounds of ranch life drifted up from below: horses passing by: clanging iron as Prometheus, the black cook, summoned the ranch hands to supper; dogs barking; the cry of an owl; *mamacitas* calling their children by name.

"All's right with the world," she softly said as a gentle breeze pushed the curtains inward. "John's home."

She fooled herself into thinking the peace would last.

3

Chapo emptied a bucket of oats into the trough and muttered softly in Spanish as the Appaloosa nudged his arm aside and began to feed, ignoring the mound of hay Chapo had heaved over the stall railing to supplement the bait of oats. He considered giving the animal a rubdown but decided to let it wait until morning even if it meant enduring another of Poke's lectures on the care of horses.

The stable was a large one, eight stalls to a side. Carriages were kept in the broad center aisle as well as a pair of buckboards used to fetch necessities from Uvalde: canned goods and side meat, dried fruit, lamp oil, cartridges and black powder, salt, sugar, and plenty of sacks of Arbuckle's coffee.

Chapo liked the smell of a barn, the mingled scents of weathered wood, of grain and leather, horses, and dry hay. Nothing better than a solidly built barn, he thought, unless it was a good saloon.

Saloons.

The Thrown Shoe Emporium and Imbibery in Uvalde . . . now there was a saloon worthy of the name. He enjoyed its partylike atmosphere.

Chapo remembered another party in town—one definitely not in a saloon. It was the first time he had set eyes on pretty Miss Laura Prescott. A spring dance, and she was the finest lady there, something special. She had danced with him and let him walk her out beneath the moon and favored him with a kiss from her sweet lips. He was Joaquín Almendáriz, the dark and lethal segundo of Luminaria, almost a son to John Anthem.

Yet not a son. Not like Billy, who caught Laura's fancy a few weeks after the dance. Suddenly Chapo was no longer welcome at the Prescotts as a social caller. Laura remained civil to him—she was too much a lady not to be—but her flirtations ceased. She became cool and proper and no longer conspired to meet him for an evening walk or to share a cool drink on the front porch of her father's house.

Billy had a lot to offer a girl like Laura—position, prestige, and he was much younger than Chapo, too. And he'd never been an outlaw, riding the lost canyons of the barrancas, south of the border. Chapo didn't blame Laura. No doubt she made the right choice. But it didn't make the hurt any less.

His attention distracted by his troubled thoughts, Chapo turned from the stall and stepped right into Billy Anthem's roundhouse punch. The blow knocked Chapo back against the stall gate. The segundo sat down on the hard-packed floor and shook his head free of the spinning lights while a sound like a flash flood roared in his ears. The noise gradually diminished as Chapo caught his breath and his sight returned. He stared up at the slight figure of Billy Anthem standing over him. Big John's son had his coat off and the sleeves of his dress shirt were rolled up over the elbows. Chapo spat blood

from his bruised lips. The whole left side of his jaw
ached.

"I knew you could push a pen; I didn't think you
could hit like that," Chapo said. He braced himself
against the gate and stood.

"It was your idea to hunt down those hide-hunters,"
Billy said, his pale cheeks flushed with anger. "On my
wedding day. You knew Pa would have to go along."
Billy tore loose the string tie around his throat. "You
wanted to ruin things just because Laura chose me over
you."

Chapo frowned, his eyes narrowed. He wiped his
mouth on his sleeve. "You're wrong, Billy. I'm gonna
forget what you said." He reached up and gingerly
touched his swollen lower lip. "And I'll forget this."

Billy dived into him, battering his fists against
Chapo's hardened midsection. He tried a right cross to
the jaw, but Chapo blocked it and shoved the younger
man back.

"You just improved my memory," Chapo snarled, and
pumped a left jab that doubled Billy over and sent him
to his knees. Chapo could have finished him then, but
he backed away and withheld further punishment. "Let
it be, *compadre*. I don't want to hurt you."

Billy pushed himself to his hands and knees. Still staring at the dirt and struggling for breath, he waited for a
blow that never fell.

"All . . . your doing . . . couldn't have her . . . you . . .
jealous of us," he gasped. Billy lunged forward, butting
Chapo in the stomach, then straightened, and the top of
his head clipped Chapo's jaw. The segundo staggered
and shoved away from his younger assailant. Billy followed in, jabbing with left and right and keeping Chapo
off balance. A hard left rocked the segundo, the hard

right that followed ought to have put him down.

Chapo took the blows, shook them off, and leapt like a panther. The move was completely unexpected. Chapo's full weight crashed into Billy's upper torso and bore the young man over on his back, the segundo astride his chest.

Billy grunted as the air was swept out of his lungs. Chapo rolled free and sprang to a crouch while Billy gasped anew and curled on his side in a fetal position as he struggled for breath. Clay and straw matted his hair, his fine clothes were smeared with dirt, the shirt torn at the right shoulder.

"Had enough?" Chapo growled. He was angry now. Billy Anthem had pushed him too far, and when Chapo Almendáriz got pushed, he got mean.

"Yes he has," Rachel said, stepping around a carriage and between the two combatants. She knelt by her brother, put a hand on his arm.

"Go away," Billy said in a raspy voice.

"When I didn't see you downstairs with Laura, I was afraid you'd be here," Rachel said with almost parental tenderness. She fixed Chapo in a glare of blue fire.

"He started it." Chapo shrugged, bandanna in hand and dabbing at his lip. "Billy came looking for a fight."

"He didn't have to find it, Joaquín," Rachel snapped. She always referred to him by his Christian name in her anger. He was like another brother to her. He had filled the hollow in her heart left by Cole's departure and death.

"Oh, hell," Chapo said. He swung around in disgust and headed out the way he had come, his battered sombrero dangling between his shoulder blades. He donned his sombrero, drew tight the leather strings beneath his chin. Then he touched the broad brim in a gallant fare-

well and walked through the open doors toward the
bunkhouse.

Rachel looked down at her fallen brother. She was
angry that he had fought with Chapo, who was so special
to them both.

"Supper will be ready within the hour. Better come
on to the house and clean up."

"I'm all right," Billy said, breath returning at last.
"Where is he?"

"Gone," Rachel replied. "Lucky for you." She helped
her brother to stand. He doubled over and rubbed his
ribs, grabbed his short-brimmed hat off the earthen floor.
"There'll be another day," Billy complained.

"Not if you want to grow old and die in bed," Rachel
said.

Billy ignored her and dusted himself off. It wouldn't
do for Laura to see him like this, a common brawler. He
walked down the aisle, steadying himself against the carriage and buckboard as he followed Chapo's head out
of the barn.

"Big John would have handled this better," Rachel
called out.

"I'm not Father," Billy shot back.

"I know," Rachel said in a soft voice. "And now, so
does Chapo."

They dined on calabacitas, a seasoned dish of Mexican
green squash and corn, rice cooked with peppers and
tomatoes, and strips of steak layered high upon a stoneware platter brought sizzling from the fire. Rose sat at
one end of the long oak table; the place opposite her, at
the other end, was empty. John Anthem was asleep upstairs. But his high-backed thronelike chair was not the
only empty place at the table. Rose glanced over at the

chair to her left and wondered about Chapo's absence. It wasn't like him to miss an evening meal. Though he preferred to live alone in a cabin back in the canyon, he always took his meals at the family table.

To her right sat Billy, looking the worse for wear. Laura shifted uncomfortably beside him. Across from the bride-to-be, young Rachel ate with healthy appreciation of her own cooking. She paused between mouthfuls to allow everyone their chance to compliment the cook, but no one cared to seize the opportunity. Billy ate sparingly, concentrating on vegetables and rice. His stomach hurt too much for beef. Laura nervously tore at a square of corn bread, littering her plate with the crumbs.

"Maybe I ought to wake Papa," Rachel suggested.

"No. He needs the rest," Rose said.

"Even Big John is human," Billy said. His mother frowned at him. Billy shrugged. "Well, he is. Just folks around here lose sight of it."

"His son most of all, it would appear," Rose reminded.

Billy took no heed of her remark. He dabbed at the food on his plate. Through the window, the faint music from a softly strummed guitar lingered on the air. And there was laughter, the sound of merriment from the houses of the vaqueros in marked contrast to the tense gathering around the dining-room table in the hacienda.

"Hear them," Billy said. "Anthemistas . . . I call them. They worship Father."

"They are grateful, for homes and work. They are loyal to John and he is loyal to them," Rose said. "I will have no more of such talk. Do you understand? Enough!"

Laura eased back behind her beau. She had never

heard Rose Anthem raise her voice, had never seen her really lose her temper. And she did not want to. But Billy was not to be cowed. Especially in front of his intended bride.

"You are quite correct, Mother. The table is no place for what I have to say." Billy slid his chair back and stood, tossing his cloth napkin aside. "If you'll excuse me . . . what I have to say should be said to my father."

"He's resting," Rose said.

"I'll wake him," Billy snapped, and walked out of the dining room. There was silence as they heard his footsteps on the stairs.

John's sleep was troubled, and his thoughts drifted to the past, to the years of civil war. He thought again of the letter Cole had left his parents along with a freshly tanned deer hide. Rose had found the letter and kept it for John, who was away on a cattle drive. Two weeks had passed by the time he returned . . .

Dear Father,

By the time you get back from the drive I will have joined up. Maybe some of the beef you brung to Mississippi will wind up in my belly. Don't you and Mama fret, for I can take care of myself. I'll come home with a chest full of medals, you just wait and see. If I tarry much longer the fun will be over. So I am off.

                                        Cole

P.S. I killed the deer.

He was gone. Gone. Gone. John had ridden in vain to San Antonio, hoping to somehow catch up to his son. But the militia had already pulled out, weeks earlier.

That was back in the summer of 1863 . . . eleven years ago. And Cole Tyler Anthem had not been heard of again.

Cole . . .

"Cole," John spoke the name aloud and came fully awake. He sat up as Billy lit an oil lamp on the bedside table.

"Sorry. It's only me," Billy said. "I didn't mean to wake you. I just wanted to let you know Laura and I will be pulling out tomorrow morning."

"What?" John rubbed a hand over his face and tried to make himself more alert. The effect of the alcohol still clouded his thoughts.

"We're going to be married in Uvalde. There's a parson in the town who'll see to it," Billy said.

"What about your ma and me?"

"You can show up late. That ought not to bother you," Billy said.

John Anthem scowled and his brows knotted in a frown. "Boy, when this leg is healed, I aim to whop some respect into you—if not toward me, at least for your ma."

Billy folded his arms over his chest and shook his head. His father seemed to know only one way of facing things: head-on. There was no step-aside in him.

"Mama's welcome to come along if she will," the young man said. "But I reckon she'll want to stay here with you. Either way, Laura and I are leaving at sunup."

"Why? I've built a kingdom here for you! A kingdom! By God, I'll stop you," John said, and swung his legs over the edge of the bed and tightened up in agony as his left leg throbbed anew. "Damn," he muttered through clenched teeth. How could his son be so ungrateful?

"How can you stop me? You can't even get out of bed," Billy said. He stepped back and headed for the door. He opened it, then hesitated in the doorway as if wanting to say more, to make his father understand.

"I'm sorry, Papa," Billy finally said. "I'm sorry Cole died and left you only me to set your hopes on. I've made up my mind to see this through. Laura and I will be married in Uvalde. Mr. Prescott will put us up. He needs someone to help him in the bank and the school is hurting for a headmaster . . ." Billy's voice trailed off. His explanation wasn't cutting through the pain and whiskey-soaked fog shrouding his father's mind.

John Anthem lay back on the bed and stared up at the ceiling, no longer hearing his son. "Goodbye," he said without emotion.

Billy nodded and closed the door.

4

That night it rained, a drowning downpour lasting through the early-morning hours. It beat against the clay-tile roof and battered the shutters. Thunder rumbled like a battery of cannon loosing a volley at the mouth of Luminaria Canyon. The foot-thick walls of the house itself seemed to tremble, yet prevailed against the attacking elements.

Billy woke, sensing a presence in the room. His eyes searched the darkness of his bedroom. He glimpsed movement, heard the rustle of a cotton nightgown and the pad of bare feet across the floor. For one fleeting moment he thought it was Laura. His passion for her burned, unfulfilled because she had declared her intention to remain chaste until their wedding night. So, he realized it couldn't be her, unless . . .

Then, in the glare of lightning he saw it was only his mother. She came to sit on the side of his bed. Her flaxen hair hung loose across her shoulders. Her eyes bore into his, catching him awake.

"Mother?" he stammered.

"I checked Rachel's room to be certain Laura was still abed and not here. I didn't want to interrupt anything between you two," Rose said. "And don't look so shocked. Your father and I were young once. Still are, for that matter."

Thunder roared and a glare lit the room, flickered like candlelight, and died.

Rose pulled her dressing gown around her and shivered. "Nights like this always leave me chilled. Even in the middle of summer. By October, any day might find a blue norther on the skyline."

Billy continued to peer at her from over the edge of his sheet. His mother was as perplexing as she was beautiful. He never knew what to expect from her, nor what course of action she might choose to take. Perhaps that was why Father loved her so much.

Billy loved her, too. Loved her especially because she accepted him for what he was.

"I couldn't sleep. I lay awake, thinking of tomorrow, knowing you would leave." Rose reached out and took his hand. "There has to be a reason, something more than your father being late for the wedding. Your hurt was much deeper."

Billy sighed and, rubbing a hand over his youthful features, sat up in bed. In the flickering glare of the storm that briefly illuminated the room, his wiry torso shone silver and supple as he folded his hands behind his head.

"I want to cast my own shadow. Not Cole's," Billy finally said. "I loved him too, Mother. But not enough to be him. I can't be him, no matter how much Father wants me to be." The young man glanced at the shutters and listened to the storm that raged without. Laura would be frightened. She hated thunder. "Laura loves me for what I am. She helped me to accept the fact that ranching isn't in my blood. I doubt it ever will be. Now, if only I could get Father to accept it."

"John can be a most stubborn man," Rose said. She stood and walked to the window, facing south down the valley. She opened the shutter and stared out at the rain patterns swirling over the surface of the windowpanes.

"I don't want to hurt you, Mother. But Laura and I will be married in Uvalde."

Rose looked around at her son. She knew him better than he knew himself. Being a clerk or a schoolmaster was not for him. Nor was ranching. She had watched him grow and sensed in him a wanderlust and dissatisfaction he had yet to recognize. He was love-blind, and only time would help him to see.

And yet, who was she to judge Laura? After all, love had taught Rose Anthem a thing or two about living. They were lessons etched in memory.

"You do what you have to do, Billy Anthem. And don't worry, I'll talk some sense into your father. Give me a few days. Not only will John Anthem be at the wedding, but he'll kiss the bride." Rose closed the shutter, and in the flash of lightning and the crack of thunder Billy noticed that his mother never flinched. If anyone could handle Big John, it was Rose McCain Anthem, he decided as he listened to her footsteps move toward the door. A latch clicked open and she was framed in the doorway for a couple of seconds. Then she was gone.

Billy eased down into the bed. He listened to the storm and resisted the urge to wake Laura and entice her to his room. He wanted to hold Laura, to feel her grow warm in his arms. Billy hungered for her with a sudden desperation even he did not understand.

Chapo Almendáriz hungered, too. But he doused the fire gnawing at his entrails with another jolt of whiskey and stared out at the rain. He eased his chair back against the wall and watched the rain pour in an unquenched torrent off the porch roof fronting his cabin.

Poke Tyler stepped out on the porch and rubbed the small of his back and groaned aloud. His voice was drowned out by the thunder. Chapo glanced aside and passed him the bottle.

"Damn cards never let me win," Tyler grumbled, and looked over his shoulder at the deck of cards arranged upon the table in neatly ordered rows, a short stack of cards left amid the uncompleted game of solitaire.

"Blame not the cards but the player, old one," Chapo said with a grin.

"Seems I recollect your pa saying them same words to me once," Poke said between pulls on the bottle. He gasped and set the bottle down beside the chair.

"I was just thinking of him myself," Chapo replied. His father, Memo Almendáriz, had thrown in with John Anthem, forsaking the bandits' life. He had wanted something better for his son. He had died in the service of John Anthem, and Anthem had raised Chapo like a son.

"He was a man to ride the trail with," Poke said, hooking his thumbs in his vest pockets. His faded gray shirt was blotched with rain, and his boots were scuffed and caked with mud. He looked off across the valley at the hacienda looming cold and lifeless in the glare of the storm. Were they all asleep? Troubled sleep, no doubt, he said to himself. He yawned and tilted his head back, making no move to conceal his weariness. He thought of his nice dry room out beyond the kitchen.

"You'll have to use the footbridge down in the woods, but you *can* make it home," Chapo said, his darkly handsome features growing sharp and studious as he appraised Tyler's condition.

"Maybe I'll stick around until you bring out the good stuff," Poke said, nudging the half-full bottle of "who hit John" with the toe of his boot.

"That is the good stuff."

"God in heaven," Poke proclaimed with obvious distaste. "Maybe we both ought to turn in. I'll bunk on your floor."

"Go ahead," Chapo replied. He tilted forward in the chair and picked up the bottle. "But this rotgut is the only nursemaid I need." He turned toward Poke, who was looking at the bruises on the segundo's face, a legacy of the fight in the barn. "Tell Big John I'm fine," Chapo added.

"He don't know I'm here, and you're drunk," Poke said, his calloused leathery fingers combing his silvery-white beard.

"Drunk?" Chapo shouted back. He tossed the bottle into the air, rose from the chair, his hand a blur at his side as he palmed his revolver. The six-gun belched flame and the bottle exploded against a backdrop of sheet lightning. "What have I got to get drunk about? Everything is fine." Chapo momentarily lost his balance and then steadied himself against a post. Smoke curled from the barrel of his gun. "Just fine, you old bastard."

Poke nodded. The storm gave him courage. "We been together a long time, younker. I seen you grown from a boy to a man as good as your pa," Tyler answered. "So you rant and rave all you want. Pop a few more bottles with the toy you carry on your hip. Play it hard, boy, for all the world to see. But to Pokeberry Tyler you can say the truth. She don't love you, Joaquín Almendáriz. And that's somethin' you better understand. 'Cause you and Billy are like brothers. It would break John Anthem's heart to see you two lock horns."

Lightning shimmered and lit the muddy hillside, and the bottle shattered in the rain. Chapo lowered his gaze to the gun in his hand.

"Chapo?" Pokeberry said.

Thunder rumbled down the hills. Raindrops spattered and drummed a brisk tattoo upon the roof. It filled the puddles. Tiny geysers of muddy brown water exploded in their midst.

"Segundo?" Poke repeated.

But Chapo Almendáriz had no answers, not even for his own heart's pain.

5

The old trail cook, Prometheus, helped with the last of Laura's hatboxes, lifting them onto the wagon bed. Billy worked them into place there and began to arrange the remainder of the trunks and carpetbags for better balance. The black cook walked around to the bride-to-be and lifted a basket up to her.

"There's a whole chicken fried the way Billy likes it," Prometheus said. "And some of my biscuits and a jar of honey I stole from my bees down by the creek. Put a tin of tea in there too 'cause Billy tells me you likes that to drink of an evening."

"Thank you," Laura said, taking the basket from the black man. "You are very kind to think of us." Laura placed the basket under the bench seat.

Prometheus sort of bowed and doffed his battered felt hat. As he walked back around, he glanced up at the gray sky and inhaled deeply, testing the air. "Smells like rain," the cook pronounced.

"Maybe it will hold off," Billy replied, patting the dust off his frock coat. He looked up at the balcony of the hacienda half-expecting to catch a glimpse of his father watching these final preparations.

"Leaving's a powerful hard thing to do sometimes," said Prometheus, sensing the young man's concern. Sweat streaked the black man's massive forearms. He wore a homespun sleeveless cotton shirt. His features wore the luster of polished ebony.

"So is staying," Billy added. He climbed down from the buckboard and reached out to clasp the cook's proffered hand.

"Take care of yourself," Prometheus said, and glanced in Laura's direction. "You too, ma'am."

Billy watched him walk away, then turned as the front door of the hacienda creaked open. Rose Anthem emerged from the house. She paused on the porch for a moment and stepped into the morning's sullen light. She noticed the threatening clouds but made no comment.

Rose wore a high-necked woolen dress of deep blue that set off the brilliant golden curls that framed her features and spilled down over her shoulders. Tiny lines beneath her eyes betrayed her lack of sleep. Rachel, in her nightdress, stepped around her mother, out into the yard.

"Did you have your coffee," Rose asked her son.

"Yes, ma'am. I made it. I left the pot for the rest of you. Figured it would show Rachel what real coffee tastes like," Billy added with a grin.

"I know more than you ever will about good coffee," Rachel blurted out as she came down off the porch and stood with hands on hips in front of her brother. "I can outride, outshoot, and outcook you any day of the week, Billy Anthem."

"Outargue too." Billy laughed and took her in his arms.

Rachel struggled indignantly at first, then surrendered and wrapped her arms around her brother's neck. "Oh

Billy, don't go. We lost Cole. I don't want to lose you as well," she whispered. She hugged him tight and the tears that welled from her eyes moistened his cheek.

"You come see us, little sister," Billy softly said, his lips brushing her ear. He eased his hold and Rachel broke from his embrace and rushed back up onto the porch and disappeared inside the house.

"I thought I would be in the way," Rose said. "I felt it was better that you handle things on your own. So I stayed upstairs on purpose."

Billy nodded in appreciation. "Nothing to be said now anyway."

"Oh, I can think of something," Rose replied, and stepped over beside Laura, who looked down at her future mother-in-law with a mixture of reserve and suspicion. The two women had not experienced much warmth in their dealings with each other. And yet in these final moments of departure, Rose surprised the younger woman. She reached up to clasp Laura's hand in a gentle grip.

"I hope you will be happy." Rose patted the hand in hers. "Billy loves you. And I believe that you love him as well. So, I will try to be brave about losing my last son, and wish you both much joy." Rose brushed a yellow strand out of the corner of her mouth. The air was fragrant with sage and the aroma of frying bacon and baking bread. She breathed in deeply, savoring the smells of the world that she and John Anthem had made. But it was their world. Laura and Billy had a right to make their own. Rose stepped up on the wheel and kissed Laura on the cheek. "Be happy."

Laura Prescott's guarded expression dissolved and she embraced Billy's mother.

"I can be a cold person at times," Laura managed to

say in a voice suddenly choked with emotion. "I . . . oh, I . . ." She was genuinely moved, caught completely off guard by Rose Anthem's sincerity.

"Go on now," Rose said, climbing down. "You two have that right. I don't know how long Big John will be laid up, but as soon as he's able, we'll be coming in to Uvalde to visit. And I am counting on being able to call you daughter then."

Laura dabbed at her suddenly red-rimmed eyes and made room on the bench seat for Billy, who had paused to give his mother a hug. Gratitude was plainly evident in the strength of his embrace. When he stepped back, Rose smiled and retreated to the porch. Billy lifted his eyes once more to the balcony overhead. He looked back at Rose, who shook her head, reminding him that he was hoping for too much from a man as stubborn as John Anthem.

As Billy climbed up onto the seat and took the reins in hand, the sturdy brown geldings hitched to the singletree started forward. The buckboard rolled away from the house and headed toward the arch in the low wall surrounding the hacienda. Once the wooden gates were open and the buckboard had passed beneath the arch, Billy chanced to lift his gaze to the canyon's western wall. There, he spied a solitary horseman, motionless as a statue on the crest of the rim. He recognized the Appaloosa and knew that lonely figure astride the animal could only be Joaquín Almendáriz. Billy shifted in his seat, flicked the reins, and called to the team of horses to increase their pace. Metal harness jangled, leather popped, the geldings' hooves kicked up clots of mud in the rain-softened earth.

Chapo was not the only person to watch the wagon leave. Back in the hacienda, hidden in the privacy of his room, John Anthem leaned upon his crutch. He kept to the shadows so as not to reveal himself, and watched his son ride away and tried to understand . . . The last of his sons . . . his sons were gone. Cole so wild and hungry for adventure and glory, like most young men. Then there was Billy, the ungrateful, who turned his back on Luminaria and all it offered. The hell with him, John thought, and immediately regretted it. No, not Billy. My son, I love my son. He shifted his stance. Pain blazed a course through his limbs. But John remained by the window until the wagon was lost from sight.

John Anthem heard the door shut quietly behind him and he turned to see Rose standing with her back to the door, lips pursed, brown eyes smoldering. He tried to disarm her with a smile, but she remained unmoved.

"Did you see them leave?" she asked.

"Yes," John said. "I watched him. Now leave me alone. My head hurts and I have a broken leg."

"I'd break the other one if I thought it would shock some sense into you." Rose advanced on him.

"By heaven, I think you would," John said.

"How could you behave like that?" Rose shook her head in disgust. "Your own son."

"How could I? Am I the villain now? Damn it Rose, what about me? And the ranch? Everything I've done was for him." John sat on the edge of the bed and lifted his splintered leg onto the mattress.

"No. Luminaria was *our* dream, John Anthem. We carved it out of the wilderness for ourselves. We made our life here because it gave us joy and purpose." Rose walked past him to the window and threw wide the shutters to let morning air fill the room.

"Have you forgotten Everett Cotter?" she asked.

"I'll never forget Everett," John retorted, leaning back against a pillow.

Everett Cotter, a rancher from San Antonio, was the man who had raised John and Rose, survivors of a massacre, and given them a home. But Cotter had a son, an ambitious young man who at last, unable to live in his father's image, destroyed himself and almost succeeded in killing Rose and John out of sheer jealousy and self-hatred. "Never."

"Well, if you start to, just take a look in the mirror," Rose said.

"That's a hell of a thing to say," the man on the bed complained. "Cotter and I are two mavericks on opposite sides of the range."

"Prove it," Rose said. She faced him, hands on hips, cheeks flushed with emotion.

"How?"

"Come with me to Uvalde, just for a few days, to be with Billy. To let him know that just because you can be a bad-tempered blowhard and one first-class bastard, you still love him. And that when your leg's not broken and you aren't drunk, you can be sweet and dear."

John grimaced at her description. He made such a face that Rose had to laugh. She knew she had won him over.

"All right. We'll make a bed in one of the wagons, and as soon as I'm able, we'll head on into Uvalde," John said. He knew when he was whipped. There simply was no arguing against the woman when she was on the prod.

"Charlie Gibbs is leaving for town in a day or two," Rose said, tapping her chin, then brightening with an idea. "I'll have him drop a letter off. I'm sure Billy will wait if he knows we both want to be there for the wedding."

She bent down and kissed John on the forehead. He made a grab for her rounded derriere, but she skipped out of the way and headed straight for the door to the room.

"I'll have Rachel bring you some breakfast."

"I'm not hungry," Anthem said. "I already ate my fill of crow."

Rose smiled and quietly closed the door.

The sky was the color of powder smoke. Clouds glowered on the horizon and draped Mescalero Lookout in gray. Billy Anthem studied the horizon and wondered if leaving home had been such a good idea. The heavens threatened more turbulent weather. He glanced aside at his bride-to-be. Though he hoped for an uneventful journey to Uvalde, he knew a storm was on its way, and he remembered a cave near the base of Mescalero Lookout. As he turned the geldings off the road to Uvalde, thunder rumbled in the distance.

"Is there a problem?" Laura asked.

"Only that it's fixin' to rain again. If we don't find shelter, we'll wind up soaked before the day is done," Billy said, his eyes on the angry thunderheads rising up from the horizon as if to block their way east. Billy applied the whip and the geldings broke into a brisk trot.

"I'm sorry about what happened . . . I mean, with my father," Billy said.

"He is a very hard man sometimes," Laura said. "But I suppose I can't blame him—after all he is losing you." She sighed and patted Billy's arm. "Life certainly won't be dull having him for a father-in-law." The girl laughed. "A little excitement in my life couldn't hurt."

Billy leaneed over and kissed her, then returned his attention to the horses.

Luminaria lay behind them about a day's ride to the northwest. Another two days ride would bring them to Fort Davis and a chance for comfortable lodgings. The Anthems were in good standing with Maj. Oregor, the garrison's commanding officer. John Anthem had supplied the fort with beef for the past three years. Army patrols were welcome to bivouac in Luminaria Canyon and enjoy Anthem's hospitality. In return, the presence of the U.S. Cavalry kept the Commanches, Apaches, and Arapaho at bay.

Thunder bellowed again and Billy cursed himself for a fool. Laura pretended unconcern as her grip tightened on the seat. The buckboard, true to its name, pitched from side to side over the rough terrain as the chino grass gave way to rocks and shallow gulleys still muddy from previous storms. She dabbed at her neck with a silk kerchief. Perspiration beaded her forehead despite the cool autumn air. Snaking her arm through Billy's, she mustered a brave smile.

"Why, William Michael Anthem, I think you planned that we'd have to ride out a storm in some dreary cave where you'd have me at your mercy," Laura said, struggling to be heard.

"The notion entered my mind," Billy shouted above the clatter of the wagon.

Great heavy raindrops began to fall. Billy winced as an ice-cold drop slapped the back of his neck and rolled down his spine. Laura reached behind the seat for her parasol, thrust through the ropes securing one of her trunks to the wagon bed.

Billy started to apply the whip to the sweat-glistened geldings, but the animals needed no prodding as a lurid fork of lightning skewered the ground behind them and the rain began to increase with stinging intensity. He feared they would never be able to outrace the storm to Mescalero Lookout. But a thick grove of cottonwoods lining the banks of the creekbed offered more protection than the open prairie. Under Billy's guiding hand, the team of geldings veered once more and headed at a gallop toward the dry wash less than a hundred yards ahead.

"Hold on," Billy shouted as the wagon careened from side to side.

Laura clutched his arm and managed a garbled reply that ended in a startled cry as the wagon's iron-rimmed wheels crushed a maguey and pitched violently, almost overturning. A few seconds later the buckboard settled back on all four wheels. But Laura had lost her parasol in the process. The wind had lifted it away and set it spinning over the ground. The parasol vanished down a gulley, its pattern of pink and blue silk flowers making a colorful tumbleweed. Laura had no time to mourn the loss. She was much too busy trying to keep from joining the parasol.

The storm broke and the rain fell in slanting gray torrents that battered the travelers and turned the soft earth to a treacherous muck. Billy ignored the pelting raindrops and fixed his gaze on the line of trees. A hundred yards became seventy-five—then, as he held his team to a gallop, became fifty. A minute more and they would be under a canopy of branches. I'll tether the horses and we can crawl under the wagon, Billy planned. Despite the discomfort, curling up on a ground tarp alongside Laura Prescott was an appealing prospect. And he laughed aloud and glanced aside at Laura, whose dark tresses were already matted to her head, her sunbonnet a forlorn scrap of sodden cloth. She heard him laugh, and looked up at him, surprised and questioning his sanity as the cloud burst assailed them.

"I love you," he shouted. Those were the last words she heard.

Billy thought it was thunder at first, then the sound correctly registered. It was the sharp crack of gunfire. A rippling fusillade from the direction of the cottonwoods. The geldings crumpled beneath the impact of half a dozen slugs. The singletree snapped and drove the wagon upright. Momentum flung the wagon over on its side and sent its occupants tumbling. Billy was airborne before he could react. The sleeve of his coat tore away as Laura, who clung to his arm, was hurled like a rag doll onto the rocks. Billy shouted her name, hit the ground hard, and took a mouthful of mud. He rolled over twice and covered his head in his arms as the buckboard, blotting out everything else, came crashing down. Wood groaned, exploded. Trunks shattered. Metal and leather ripped free. The wreckage missed him by inches and continued on down into a gulley.

Thunder echoed the rifle fire, and though the wind eased, the rain continued to drench the earth. It seemed to be forcing Billy deeper into the mud. It battered his shoulders and tried to bury him. He shoved himself upright and crawled across the reeling distance, as the world continued to spin, as the rain tried to hide his love in its relentless downpour.

"Laura!" he gasped, and the blood from his swollen lip mingled with the mud. "Laura!" And the name tore from his winded lungs as he fought for breath. He crawled past the twisted body of a horse. His muddy hand reached the first of the boulders, and Billy, pulling himself upright, found her.

Laura Prescott was draped over a weather-pocked

limestone boulder. She was bent backward, in an unnatural arch. One arm was propped up by smaller rocks, her stiffening fingers closed around the torn sleeve. Her neck was twisted to the side at a horrible angle. Her lips were parted, in a silent scream that death had cut mercifully short. Water had begun to collect in her mouth.

"AAAhhhh!" Billy staggered back, turning to run from the hideous sight, and stumbled to his knees. He stood again and ran into the storm. He screamed again and doubled over and clutched his stomach. His whole body shook and remained trembling as the young man fought to control himself. When he straightened, Billy caught a glimpse of a man and a woman emerging out of the watery curtain that obscured the landscape around them.

They were dressed much alike, in the short coats and tight trousers of vaqueros. Broad-brimmed sombreros shielded their features. They both looked approximately Billy's age, the woman a few years older. She held a Spencer carbine in the crook of her arm. The man cradled a Winchester. Billy focused on them and his lips pulled back in a snarl that transformed his face into a mask of hate. He did not know these two. But they had killed Laura. And he was going to kill them.

Billy lunged toward the strangers. He had no weapons but his fists, his own rifle was lost among the wreckage. But he didn't care. Fists would be enough. Hate stilled the spinning world. Hate gave his poor bruised battered body strength. But hate wasn't enough. Billy leapt toward the man. As his hands clawed for the Mexican's windpipe, the woman stepped in to her companion's defense. She swung her carbine in a vicious sweep that Billy saw coming but had no time to duck.

The wooden stock crashed against his skull and the

powder-smoke clouds closed in around the young Billy Anthem. They smothered him and his pain.

An image of Laura, dead among the rocks, flitted through his mind. Then nothing at all.

6

Billy opened his eyes and stared at the wall of the cave. For one brief moment Billy thought he and Laura had reached the safety of Mescalero Cave and that the wreck had just been a horrible nightmare from which he had awakened.

But his bound hands were real. His aches and bruises did not ease upon waking. And the serapeclad figures gathered around the campfire were no figments of a troubled mind. One of them noticed Billy was awake, and ambled over to kneel down beside the bound man. Billy looked up into the haughty brown eyes of a strikingly handsome woman. Her skin was dark as her deep-set eyes, brown as clay. Her long black hair was held in a single thick braid that hung down her back. She wore a blousy checkered shirt. Bandoliers criscrossed her ample bosom and mud-spattered trousers clung tightly to her shapely physique. She wore a scarlet bandanna around her forehead, Apache-style, a look of the savage her wicked smile did nothing to soften.

"I am Natividad Varela," she said. She glanced over her shoulder as a slight man Billy's age approached. "This is my brother, Rafael."

Rafael wore a tight-fitting black waistcoat and trousers flared over black boots of Spanish leather. His coat was stitched with silver thread in a floral motif across the chest and back. A concho belt circled his waist, the silver disks shining brightly against black leather. An ivory-handled revolver rode in the holster on his right hip. He was thin-skinned, a patchwork of tiny blue veins coloring his high cheekbones and a pencil-thin black moustache adding age to his boyish face. He touched the brim of his sombrero and walked back to the fire as a hulking figure emerged from the storm and filled the cave mouth. The other man was of solid stature, not tall but wide-shouldered. His bearlike upper torso was balanced on short thick legs. He tossed back his sombrero, let it hang down his back to reveal a shaggy mane of black hair. Discarding his rain-soaked serape, he headed for the fire.

"My other brother," said Natividad. "Hector, come here."

The big man grabbed a cup of coffee and walked over to his sister's side. Though they were the same height, Hector seemed to dwarf the woman because of his enormous girth. A brace of Colt revolvers were tucked in the black sash circling his waist. Two men could have worn his rust-colored waistcoat. Ridges of flesh encircled his neck beneath an unkempt black beard. He swallowed a mouthful of coffee and squatted down beside Billy. His belly strained against the fabric of his shirt.

"Have some coffee? Aurelio brews it bitter," Hector said. He ran a finger inside his lower lip and scooped out a measure of coffee grounds and wiped his finger on his trousers. He tilted the tin cup, and the steaming liquid sloshed out upon Billy's closed lips and dribbled down his chin. "Hey, Aurelio, I don't think this one likes your coffee to much."

The oldest member of the group, a crafty-looking man with silver hair and goatee, looked over his shoulder and shrugged. "I don't like it either," Aurelio said in a gravelly voice. His face was seamed with age, from a lifetime spent among the deserts and mountains south of the border. His eyes were wise and rather red. "You have taste, Señor Anthem."

Hector took the cup away. He was certain the coffee had burned, but the young gringo had refused to flinch.

"You can stand pain, *amigo*," Hector said. "It is good you are strong."

"We will see how strong," Natividad added.

Billy recognized her now, remembered her and Rafael walking toward him through the rain, the faint wisps of powder smoke curling from the barrels of their rifles. Billy remembered poor Laura, her pretty neck broken, the rain in her mouth.

"Aaahhh," Billy screamed, and shot upright. His hands, though bound at the wrists, caught Natividad by the throat. She pulled back and only succeeded in yanking her attacker upright. Billy held on and squeezed with all his fading strength. "I'll kill you," he rasped. Hatred and grief transformed him. Billy, the gentle son, the mannered brother, wanted only to kill, to rip flesh with his talons and tear with his teeth.

Billy saw a huge arm sweep down and break his stranglehold. Natividad stumbled and fell back on her rump. Billy raised his arms to shield himself from Hector's second blow, which strangely didn't fall.

Rafael was standing by the fire, his silver-plated Colt leveled at Billy.

"No," Hector softly ordered. He put his body between

Billy Anthem and the muzzle of Rafael's pistol. "We need him alive." He knotted his hands into fists. Water dripped from his matted hair, his thick brows furrowed in an ugly frown. "Put the gun away, *muchacho*."

"I am no child," Rafael snapped. The revolver wavered in his grasp.

"*Sí*, but sometimes you act like one, eh?" Hector said. He placed his meaty fists on his waist, making of himself an even wider barrier. "Put the gun away." His tone was sterner now, and ripe with meaning; Hector had no intention of repeating himself a third time.

Billy could not see around the big man. He listened, heard the crackling of the campfire and the droning sound of the rain that continued to fall. Droplets beat a steady rhythm at the mouth of the cave, ceaselessly shaping the limestone entrance, drip by drip, carving pools in the rock surface. Billy listened and waited and in the silence heard the slap of metal on leather, a gun being holstered.

Natividad cursed and started toward Billy, her eyes ablaze with anger. But Hector, moving with surprising speed, caught her arm and propelled her back toward the fire, planting a resounding slap on her rump in the process.

"Enough. We have what we came for. Tomorrow we must ride," Hector said in a booming voice.

Billy's mind reeled. None of this made any sense. Who were these people? Why had they attacked him? His mind sought answers, but to no avail. He felt dead. Dead as Laura lying alone in the rain.

Hector Varela turned and squatted by his prisoner. He checked the leather ropes binding the young man's ankles and wrists. Feeling was only now returning to

Billy's arms from the blow that had broken his choke-hold on Natividad Varela.

"Your woman is dead," Hector said. "I wanted there to be no killing. We shot into the air. But the ground was rough and the wagon pitched her out. It would be easier if she were alive. Now one of us will have to stay behind and give our terms to your father."

A kidnapping? Laura Prescott had died for a ransom. And how much would Big John be willing to pay for the son who had deserted him and his dream? The speculation was so macabre, so ironic, that Billy laughed out loud, interrupting his mountainous captor.

Hector stared at Anthem as if Billy were deranged. "A few weeks fighting the rats in my father's *sotano* and I think you will not be so amused, *señor*," Hector said.

The laughter died, leaving only a cold aura of hatred emanating from the young man bound hand and foot.

"Maybe I will regret not letting Rafael put a bullet . . . here." Hector touched a calloused finger to Billy's forehead, tapping him between the eyes.

"Señor Anthem, yes, we know you, your sister, your whole family . . . now, I cannot expect you to cooperate on our journey together, but do not give us trouble or I will let my sister have you. Natividad hates, like my father hates, and she has ways of making you wish you had not been born a man. *¿Me comprende bien?*"

Billy fought to remain impassive as his whole being reeled with confusion and remorse. This wasn't happening. It wasn't happening. He lay back and stared up at the ceiling of the cave. He heard Hector Varela mutter *"Bueno"* and grunt as he stood and returned to the campfire. Billy fixed his gaze upon the stalactites overhead, looming for all the world like dragon's teeth.

We're camped in the mouth of a dragon, Cole. He

and his brother had bedded down here, long ago. Mere boys who regaled each other with ghost stories and scared themselves so bad that neither had slept a wink. A dragon's mouth. Cole liked the image.

Billy had wanted to bring Laura here. It seemed only fitting. A rite of passage from one life to another.

Laura was dead. And their future together had died with her and was lost forever. Billy twisted his face to the wall, dug his cheek into a jagged formation until blood flowed and physical pain replaced his heart's anguish. He resolved to stay alive and to endure . . . for Laura.

And for revenge.

7

John Anthem worked the crutch into his armpit and kept the weight off his right leg. A dry cool breeze lifted the dust out of the corral and sent it billowing across the wheel-rutted drive leading in from the canyon road. He stood near the corral and rested his hand upon the battered wagon his riders had brought home last evening. The buckboard teetered on its makeshift axle at the merest hint of pressure, and he drew his hand away.

Two days ago, Billy and Laura had departed for Uvalde. Eighteen hours ago, Charlie Gibbs, one of the Slash A's ablest hands, had ridden up to the hacienda to report his tragic discovery: the wrecked buckboard and the lifeless body of Laura Prescott. Charlie had brought in the girl's body, wrapped in a blanket and draped across his saddle.

But where was Billy Anthem? John lifted his eyes to the ridges. He had posted lookouts on the rims, and every vaquero was heavily armed. His line riders were ranging the countryside, hoping to discover what had happened to his son. Charlie had reported finding the tracks of a half-dozen horses leading to a cave and that Billy's geldings had been shot dead.

John stared at the wagon, muttered a bitter "Damn," and lowered his gaze to the broken leg that left him so helpless. He wanted to be in the saddle, searching the hills for his son. Was Billy alive or dead? John slapped the wagon with the palm of his hand angrily and started back toward the hacienda. The wagon trembled and settled against the corral fence. What was the use of standing out here? The wagon wouldn't tell him anything.

John crossed the courtyard with slow, labored steps. Pain was far easier for him to endure than his crippled pace. He had never felt so goddamn useless in his whole life.

The yard and bunkhouse were deserted. A few vaqueros remained to take their places behind the roof battlements and up on the rims while the rest of his men scoured the hills for Laura's killers. Perhaps they had used their mischief as a ruse to draw off Luminaria's defenders. If such were the case, they might now be massing in some arroyo, preparing to assault the ranch itself. John Anthem would like nothing better.

He wanted someone to strike out at for what had been done to Laura. Though John had never been close to the girl and blamed her in part for Bily's dissatisfaction, her death had caused him pain.

"Mr. Anthem?" Prometheus, the cook, stood on the porch. He held an enameled coffeepot and cup. "I was just fetching you some coffee. Figured you could use it 'bout now." He filled a cup with the strong black brew and handed it over to Anthem. "Ain't nobody around to cook for, for I figured to give Miss Rose a hand putting things away in the kitchen and root cellar. She told me somethin' she read once, from that Shakespeare fella, he wrote them plays. Anyway, Miss Rose was sayin' how 'the banquet feast becomes the funeral meal,' and it plumb sure made me sad for your troubles."

"Thanks, Prometheus," John said, standing up alongside the black man on the porch. John started to hobble inside when the bell on the east rim began to peal a warning down the valley.

John Anthem changed direction and lost his balance. He tripped on the crutch and fell forward, a flash of pain torturing his broken limb.

Prometheus, sidestepping, wrapped his arms around the bigger man to keep him from a nasty fall.

"Thanks," John muttered, embarrassed at his own clumsiness. "You'd better get a gun," he added.

"Got me a scattergun just inside the front door," the cook replied.

John nodded and walked a few paces out from the porch. He looked up to see Rose and Rachel standing on the balcony. Rose wore a light-gray cotton blouse and darker homespun skirt. Sober clothes for sober times, John thought. He noticed mother and daughter both were armed with Colt revolvers, ready to do their part in defending the ranch.

"Can you see anything?" John called out.

"Only the dust . . . No, there they are. Two riders," Rose shouted down, shading her eyes. "And one of them's carrying a white flag."

"I see Uncle Poke," Rachel said excitedly.

Poke had left on his own hours ago. Had he given up the search, found something or been found? The sun warming his back, John haltingly made his way toward the porch steps. His pulse quickened. He stood there anxious, begrudging each interminable second he waited.

At last Poke Tyler and an unknown vaquero with a square of dirty white cloth wrapped around the barrel of his Spencer carbine rode in through the gateway of the hacienda courtyard. They slowed to a walk as Poke led his mysterious companion down the path, past the madrone tree and garden and up to the hitching pillars in front of the porch.

"He's got somethin' to tell you," Poke said, jerking a thumb toward the man.

The stranger was an elegant-looking gentleman with silver hair and goatee. His features were leathery, but he sat straight and stiffly erect in the saddle. He bowed and swept the sombrero from his head.

"I am Aurelio Bustamante," he said in a deep and textured voice. "I ride under this flag of truce, Señor Anthem. *Sí*, I recognize you from long ago. And I bring greetings from an old, ah, not friend . . . let us say, acquaintance."

John Anthem frowned. The old man looked familiar, but the name meant nothing. He struggled to place the face. "An acquaintance? Who might that be? Don't play games with me, *viejo*, or that peace cloth will be your shroud. Now if you know something about the whereabouts of my son, you better talk. Talk and save your life," John said. He hooked a thumb on the hammer of his Colt Dragoon.

"If I do not return across the Río Bravo in four days' time, my master, your old *compañero*, will send your son back to you a piece at a time."

On the balcony, Rose gasped and lifted a hand to her mouth to stifle the sound. Billy was alive. Alive!

John Anthem stiffened. His eyes narrowed and his hand dropped over the gun he wore.

"No younker," Poke said, cautioning his friend. The tone of his voice hung in the sun-drenched air.

John kept his hand on his gun but reason returned to

his expression. "Just who is your master?"

"Andrés Varela," Aurelio replied.

The name struck John Anthem like a shotgun blast, a name from the past. Memories returned. A nightmare recalled. After the Mexican War, back in 1849, Andrés Varela had captured John Anthem as he was returning home to Texas from service in the Texas Rangers. Hostilities had ceased, and a proclamation of peace drafted in Mexico City had been signed by both countries. But for Gen. Andrés Varela, the war continued. He took John Anthem prisoner and held him prisoner for a year. Anthem toiled along with the other prisoners, some Anglo and other Yaqui or Mexican peasants, in the silver mines above the general's hacienda. John had survived his ordeal and escaped with his newfound friend Poke Tyler. Varela himself had tried to stop the Texan and lost his right hand for his trouble. Anthem had cut off Varela's hand with the general's own saber.

"My master has several wooden hands," Aurelio said. "But none is as good as his own right hand, which you cut away and left in the dust."

"Where's my son?" John said in a quiet, ominous tone.

"Safe," Aurelio answered, keeping his hand away from his sidearm. "My master will hold him. Until you meet his price."

"They want us to ransom him, Johnny," Poke said.

"How much?" Rose said from above. "If we can pay it, we will. As long as not one hair of his head is hurt." If they killed Laura, then Billy was in no less of a predicament.

Aurelio stroked his neatly trimmed beard and glanced about at the ordered garden, the outbuildings, the corral, where a couple of fine colts pranced and played in the October light.

"A dollar. A single silver dollar, *Señora*," Aurelio said aloud, his voice carrying in the stillness. "And your son will be released and sent on his way. I will escort him personally to the Río Bravo and see he safely crosses into Texas."

"You're mad. Varela is mad. You kill Billy's fiancée, kidnap him, then demand a dollar ransom," John blurted out, leaning forward on his crutch.

"A silver dollar. My master is sure such a rich man as you have become can afford that."

Another rider appeared in the gateway. It was Chapo Almendáriz. He noticed Aurelio and Poke and reined in. The segundo sensed trouble. Yet he waited and wisely continued on toward the bunkhouse, where he tethered his dust-caked Appaloosa and quickly ducked inside.

Aurelio nervously glanced over his shoulder and studied the segundo. Then, as Chapo disappeared, the bandit returned his attention to John Anthem.

"A silver dollar, Señor Anthem. Surely the price is not too great for a rich *haciendado* like yourself. But there is one thing more." Aurelio folded his arms across the pommel of his saddle. Leather creaked and the gelding pawed twice at the ground as the old bandit leaned forward, grinning, taking his time.

"You must deliver the ransom, Señor Anthem. And personally give it to Andrés Varela," said Aurelio, mimicking the act, his right hand clasping an imaginary coin extended out to Anthem where it hung poised and vulnerable. "And, *Señor*, you must come alone."

8

The Varelas and their prisoner had crossed the Rio Grande without mishap. Safe from pursuit now, the children of Andrés Varela made camp high upon a rocky slope beneath a massive ledge of volcanic rock. There two days passed as they watched. And waited.

Twenty yards from the campfire, a cluster of boulders offered a good vantage point. From these rocks, Natividad studied Texas across the river. Her eyes were red-rimmed from watching their back trail. Only now, in the country of her birth, had she begun to relax. She lifted a spyglass and for what seemed the millionth time scoured the wind-eroded landscape for a wisp of dust, a flash of sunlight on metal, anything to indicate an approaching rider.

"See him?" handsome, proud Rafael Varela called out as he dropped an armload of mesquite wood by the fire and dusted off his coat.

Natividad looked at him and shook her head. The young vaquero turned toward Billy, who squatted by the embers of the campfire. Hector Varela, a mountain unto himself, reclined on a blanket, opposite the remains of the fire. He began to add kindling to the hot coals, one stick at a time.

"I don't see why I have to gather the wood every morning." The rising sun had yet to leach the night's chill from the countryside and the bad-tempered young man's remarks clouded the air as he spoke.

"Because, my little brother," Hector explained in a gritty voice, "the last time I left you with Señor Anthem, I came back to find him with blood on his cheek and knocked unconscious."

"He attacked me," Rafael said, patting the ivory grip of the Colt revolver slung from his silver belt.

"And you baited him," Hector replied. "I take no pride in the woman's death. Yet you boast of it again and again to this one. Your words are like salt in his wound." The big man brushed the hair out of his eyes as he leaned over to blow on the coals. He exhaled softly, coaxing life into the embers. A tiny flame sprang into being and he sighed with satisfaction, a look of tenderness gentled his brutish features. Billy found it difficult to accept that one so ferocious in appearance would exhibit compassion. Of course, being able to appreciate the simple beauty of a flame did not make the likes of Hector Varela any less a cutthroat. He was Billy's enemy and could be nothing else, not with this kidnapping and Laura's death unaccounted for.

"You stare at me, *señor*," Hector said, his features near the budding flames, his gaze direct and studious as he evaluated his prisoner. "You wish your hands were free, no?"

"I wish I had a gun so I could kill the lot of you," Billy answered in a cold voice.

"Give him one," Rafael said, his whole frame tense.

He held his right hand out in front of him, then swept
it back and palmed his revolver. He snapped off two
quick shots, and two branches of a nearby ocotillo were
blown away.

Natividad dropped her spyglass, stood, and whirled
around. A six-shooter seemed to materialize in her hand.
Billy took note that brother and sister were equally adept
with a handgun. Natividad searched the terrain for someone to shoot at, then realized it was only Rafael showing
off.

As the gunshots echoed down the hills and reverberated in the dry air, Hector crawled to his feet and with
amazing quickness closed on Rafael, seizing him by the
coat and shirt. Hector lifted his brother off the ground
and shook him, then tossed him aside like a sack of
potatoes.

"Idiota," Hector roared.

Rafael landed in a crumpled heap. His ivory-handled
gun went bouncing down the slope. The youngest Varela
flattened against the ground. The last thing he wanted to
do was further provoke his bear of a brother. "The gringos have not followed us," Rafael lamely protested.

"You think I worry about the men who ride for John
Anthem?" said Hector. He grimaced and raised a hand
to slap his brother again, held the pose a moment, then
lowered his arm in disgust and walked back to the campfire.

"This is not our land, little brother. We'll survive in
these border mountains only as long as the Apache do
not know we are here," Hector explained. "I hope your
stupidity has not announced us. Or when Aurelio returns,
he will only find our remains."

Rafael stood, straightened his disheveled attire, retrieved his sombrero, and started down the slope after

his gun. Hector watched him a moment and then shook his head again.

"You might have a long wait," Billy said. "My father has a quick temper. And he doesn't like people demanding anything of him. Your companion, Aurelio, might be dead." He looked down at his bound hands where the leather strings had worn a pair of bloody welts encircling his wrists. "What, then?"

Hector shrugged and filled a coffeepot with water from his canteen. He added a handful of grounds to those already in the pot and set it on the edge of the fire. He drew a broad-bladed carving knife from a belt sheath and began to carve a side of salt pork into thick strips for frying. The knife was razor-sharp and slid effortlessly through the meat.

"Aurelio Bustamante has served my father many years. They fought your country's invasion of Mexico, they fought the French and the forces of Juárez as well," Hector explained. He tugged at his beard and reflected on the past. "Aurelio is like a second father to us all. If harm should come to him, I would . . ." Hector's expression became gravely serious. He touched the point of the carving knife to Billy's throat. "I would . . ."

"*Madre mía*, I see him," Natividad blurted out, and she leapt upright and focused the spyglass. "How did I miss him before? It is Aurelio. By the river, there near the bend. I see him. Aurelio is coming!"

Hector relaxed, his threat left unfinished.

And Billy Anthem decided it was for the best.

"We will give Aurelio a day to rest," Hector said, adding a few extra slices of salt pork to a skillet and placing it on the fire. "Tomorrow we start for home."

Rafael scrambled back to the campsite, his boots scuffed from his hill climb and his gun holstered. He was obviously anxious to leave today but refrained from arguing his point. "In a few days more we will dine in comfort at our father's table and sleep on soft feather-beds." Rafael grinned. "And we'll be safe."

Billy stared at the flames. His stomach growled, but he was much too proud to ask for food. His bonds hurt—well then let them. He'd show these bandits nothing but defiance, though his spirits plummeted with the prospect of being carried deeper into Mexico. Rafael's words echoed in Billy Anthem's mind, returning to mock his helplessness. "A few days more and we'll be safe."

Safe . . .

Late-afternoon sunlight burnished the walls of Luminaria Canyon burnt umber, and the subtle kiss of a cooling wind stirred the dust. John Anthem stood alone on the balcony outside his bedroom. He looked a bleak and solitary figure propped on his crutches, like some sorely wounded monarch overlooking his domain. He stiffened as he glanced over the wall and saw his daughter leave the house, mount a horse, and ride up the canyon road. John wondered what she was up to so close to supper-time, but he shrugged. It was futile to speculate on his daughter's intentions. He returned to his own troubled thoughts. John wanted to be left alone, to work out for himself the dilemma Aurelio Bustamante had left him with. Four days had passed since the bandit's visit to the ranch. Andrés Varela had sent his ultimatum. John Anthem must come to Varela's fortress by Christmas or Billy would suffer the consequences.

John wondered why Varela had waited such a long time for revenge. Perhaps the general had only recently learned that the lord of Luminaria was the same John Anthem who had been his prisoner long ago. No matter. Varela had Billy now, and was willing to trade him for the one who had maimed the general so many years past. Time heals some wounds, but others fester. For whatever reason, now was the time of Varela's revenge.

Aurelio had agreed to tell the general of John Anthem's broken leg and that Anthem could not travel until the limb was mended. But Varela had given Anthem until Christmas, and that was almost ten weeks away. In less than two months John intended to be well enough to ride, and then he had a rendezvous with death.

Rachel entered without knocking. The front door to Chapo's cabin swung back and crashed against the wall with resounding effect. Chapo sat at a table stowing the last of his gear into his saddle-bags. An assortment of weapons was arranged before him on the table. A sawed-off shotgun and burlap sack of shells, a Henry rifle, and a long-barreled Colt .45, broken down and freshly oiled. He looked up at Rachel standing in the doorway, suddenly disarmed by her forceful entry.

"It's true," she said. "You are packing to leave. Uncle Poke thought as much. He was going to my parents, but I told him to wait. I wanted to see for myself."

"Ah . . . Poke cannot be trusted," Chapo replied, scowling. He was glad to see her but hoped to avoid another confrontation, especially with Rachel. "Yes, I am going after Billy. Charlie Gibbs can be segundo until I return."

"Why wouldn't you tell us?"

"Big John would try to stop me. It is better this way. I will leave alone with no one the wiser."

Rachel stepped into the room. It was a humble

cabin, but clean and warmed by a cheerful blaze in the fireplace. Serapes were draped from the walls. A buffalo robe covered the featherbed in the back room. Coffee bubbled in a pot by the fire. Strips of jerked beef filled a paper packet along with a stack of corn tortillas waiting to join a sack of Arbuckle's coffee in the saddlebag. Chapo wanted to travel light and was taking only the most basic provisions. He reassembled the six-shooter and worked the .45-caliber cartridges into the cylinder.

"Well, since you're home, do you still remember how to roll me a smoke?" Chapo asked with a glint of amusement in his expression.

Rachel—her anger defused—took the fixings from the stone mantel and rolled tobacco in a paper. "You're as stubborn as Prometheus' old mule," she muttered.

Rachel poked the cigarette between Chapo's lips and lit the tip with a burning twig plucked from the fire. He grinned, inhaled, and blew a cloud of smoke in the still air. He took her hand in his, ran a finger across her palm, but whatever future he saw, Chapo kept to himself.

"When are you leaving?" Rachel asked.

"Tonight. I'll slip away, and no one need be the wiser until sunup," Chapo said. "Can I count on you?"

"I don't know. I ought to try to stop you," Rachel said. She tossed her hat aside and ran a hand through her bright copper curls. Her jeans clung provocatively to her lithe figure.

Chapo began to study her with renewed appreciation. She noticed his interest. "What is it?" she asked.

"Nothing. Except you've grown up," Chapo said.

"I've been grown up for a while," Rachel answered, blushing. Then she gave him a worried look. "You never noticed until now, 'cause maybe you think you won't be coming back. Oh, Chapo, they've got Billy and you'll be next."

"Varela doesn't know me," Chapo said. "I'll just be another lone rider of the barrancas to him, just a hard case looking for work. Once inside Varela's hacienda, maybe I can find Billy and free him." Chapo stood, buckled the gun belt around his waist, and hurried around the table as Rachel headed toward the door.

"Father ought to know," she said.

Chapo caught her and pulled her to him. His lips covered hers in a heated kiss. Then he released his hold on her.

Rachel stood still, caught completely off guard. They had been raised as brother and sister, but that had certainly been no brother's kiss, and the desires it awakened in her were not exactly sisterly either.

"Why did you do that?" Rachel stammered.

"I had to stop you, *chiquita*," Chapo said. "And besides, a kiss is much more fun than shooting you in the leg." He laughed and sauntered over to the door to close it. At the click of the latch his humor faded and he grew deadly serious.

"When he is able to ride, your father will go alone to Varela. I know he will. But Big John will not be alone if I am already there. If I can free Billy somehow and bring him home before Big John is able to ride, so much the better. Don't you see, either way I have to try to help. John Anthem has been like a father to me, for him I ride to hell if need be." Chapo walked up to the girl and put his hands on her shoulders. "For Billy, too," he said. "And for myself. This is something I must do. *¿Comprendes?*"

Rachel frowned and pulled away from him. She crossed the room and stood by the hearth and warmed herself by the fire, but the chill would not leave her limbs. First Billy, now Chapo, and soon her own father.

"My whole world is falling apart," she said. "How do I hold it together? What can I do?" She sensed Chapo moving to her side. There was warmth in his nearness and it gave her comfort even as it aroused her.

"You can wait with me awhile," Chapo said. He put an arm around her, flicked his cigarette into the fireplace. He was as confused as Rachel, discovering emotions in himself he had not expected to find.

"I'll stay," Rachel said. She leaned against him. "But I don't know why," she added.

"I think you do," he said. Her mouth tilted up to his. They kissed. Her supple form pressed against him. Desire grew, shattered restraint. Fingers tore at buttons, hands swept clothes aside. Moments later, the two stood naked, caressing, exploring each other, caught in the wonderment of sudden passion—yet somehow, innocent. And right.

Rachel arched her back as his lips traced a path across her small breasts. Her fingers dug into his shoulders. And when it seemed her legs would no longer support her, Chapo lifted her into his arms. He hesitated, his eyes questioning. He needed Rachel with him. But he wanted her to be certain as well.

Rachel understood then that for all his bold talk Chapo was as uncertain and even as frightened as she. His world, too, had fallen apart.

"I want to stay with you," she whispered.

"Until I go," he said, reminding her. "We have so little time, *mi querida*."

"Time enough," Rachel replied, and buried her face in the crook of his neck as he carried her to bed. In the dying light, in the lengthening shadows, two became one. They clung to each other and found completeness and strength.

And the world didn't fall apart.

PART TWO

9

They called him Yellowboy. He was a bounty-hunter, a hunter of men. A rangy, big-boned man with keen, piercing blue eyes, he studied the morning mist as it rose over the Red River. When he judged the shore to be free of threat, he left the cold ashes of an earlier campfire and led a dun stallion down to the water's edge and let the animal drink its fill.

The bounty-hunter knelt on the moist sand and, leaning on his Winchester '66, cupped a handful of water to his craggy features. A pair of mallards exploded from a nearby cluster of reeds twenty yards farther along the bank. He straightened and the Winchester spun in midair, its brass casing gleaming in sunlight. He caught the weapon, shouldered it, and brought the rifle to bear on the reeds. The Winchester was like an extension of the man himself. In fact, the rifle, with its shiny yellow frame, had given the bounty-hunter a name to be known by . . . Yellowboy. He thumbed the hammer back and waited.

A doe stepped out of the bushes and froze at the sight of the man with the gun. The bounty-hunter took his finger off the trigger, eased the hammer down, and cradled the yellowboy in the crook of his arm. His stomach growled, but he let the animal live.

The irony wasn't lost on him: if the doe had been a man with a price on his head, the bounty-hunter would not have hesitated for an instant. He knelt in the sand, set his rifle aside, and dunked his head beneath the surface of the water. When he straightened, gasping from the cold, his dark-blond hair was matted to his skull and neck. He bowed forward again, droplets spilling from face and hair and chin, rippling his reflection in the sluggish waters of the river, disfiguring his solemn, blunt features. There was sorrow there, a glimpse of hidden tragedy in the face of this solitary man.

Memories returned, unbidden, like a bad headache—only the pain they brought was centered in his soul. Men dying on a battlefield, their bodies ripped by minié ball and shrapnel. "Here, boy, take a pistol, ride to the sound of the guns . . . ride, boy, ride to glory." Where was glory? In the bodies swollen with rot beneath a Carolina sun. Where was glory? Being captured and packed like wretched beasts into freight cars and taken north. Where was glory? In the years spent aboard a prison ship in New York Harbor, living and dying in filth, unable to walk the land and being reduced to worse than an animal longing for freedom while haunted by memories of all he had lost.

The war faded in his mind. Imprisonment, too, and the shame of his failure and disillusionment. He drifted west, a boy in a man's body, working when he could, earning enough to eat, to barely live. And then one day in a little Kansas town he had crossed the wrong side of a local tough and the boy had killed in self-defense. It turned out the man was wanted, and the boy was paid a bounty of more than five hundred dollars. More than

enough for clothes, a horse, a good rifle, the yellowboy
Winchester, and a little extra for the trail. Sure, it was
blood money. But it beat starving. Honor and glory had
been a boy's foolish dream. Gold was real. Gold was
the difference between the prison of the past and the
freedom of the future.

The boy left that Kansas town with all the wanted
posters the sheriff could spare, and went to work. He
hunted men in Missouri and Kansas; he ranged from
Colorado to Texas, following the posters and the prices
on those who escaped organized law. He brought men
in alive when he could, but dead men were less trouble
and it made no difference to him if they chose to fight.
He'd shed his share of blood and earned a name along
the way that outlaws learned to fear while honest folk
kept their distance and voiced contempt for him in private.

They called him Yellowboy, a hunter of men. But his
name was Cole Tyler Anthem.

Blind Pete's was a tavern on the banks of the Trinity
River about five miles northeast of Fort Worth. Blind
Pete offered a decent glass of rotgut at a fair price, not
to mention clean rooms to bed down in, a bath to cut
the dirt, and local gossip concerning the lot of any number of hard cases. Pete had a standing offer of a night's
free room and board for whatever information and out-
of-county hearsay a traveler might pass along.

Blind Pete liked to brag he was hated by men from
Natchez to Santa Fe. He had no use for the outlaw ele-
ment; a robber had braced him years ago and fired a
load of birdshot into Pete's face, blasting away half his
sight. So he took pride in gathering information on desperadoes and enjoyed the patronage of peace officers and

bounty-hunters anxious to hear what Blind Pete had to say.

Cole Anthem, a dust-caked and saddle-weary figure, rode into the clearing and paused—his stallion pawing the earth in protest—to study the long low-roofed log building that blended into a canopy of post oaks and cottonwoods. Smoke trailed from the chimney. Lanterns burned amber in the windows. There were three horses tethered to the hitching rail in front of the tavern, and another four were loose in the corral. Cole recognized a feisty brown mare with a spattering of black on its rump. Cole grinned and glanced down at the stallion he rode.

"Looks like she beat us here. Hope the wait didn't foul her temper." He nudged his heels against the dun and the animal started forward at a brisk gallop, hardly needing any urging. Cole reckoned the smell of oats was in the air. Or maybe the dun had an eye for that black-rumped mare.

The western horizon across the Trinity wore a golden glow dotted with pastel purple-and-pink clouds. Gray squirrels scampered out of the path of the stallion while at the edge of the forest a coyote made a quick appraisal of the new arrival before slinking off into the trees. Cowbirds darted and spiraled up over the corral, black birds swooped home to nest among the willows down by the river, which flowed barely twenty yards from Blind Pete's back porch.

Cole rode over to the corral, dismounted, and peeled the saddle off the stallion's back. Anthem opened the gate and the dun trotted through. Favoring appetite over romance, the dun continued past the mare and headed straight for the trough of oats set against the outer wall of the stable. The trough was never empty and a horse could eat its fill. A black handyman stepped around the

corner of the barn. He'd heard the gate creak open and
noticed Anthem standing by the fence. The stableman
had seen the bounty-hunter before and waved. Cole
waved back and started toward the tavern, having
worked up a thirst, a powerful hunger, and enough curiosity to choke a dozen cats.

Pete was only blind in one eye. But the patch he wore
to cover his scarred face lent him a piratical look that
he purposefully reinforced. He garbed himself in black-
and-gray-striped breeches tucked into thigh-high leather
boots. A black silk shirt open to the waist revealed a
necklace of shark teeth around his neck, courtesy of a
gypsy merchant up from Galveston. A yellow sash encircled his narrow waist, a bandanna covered his balding
pate, and a gold ring pierced his earlobe. Blind Pete
grinned as Cole entered the tavern.

The bounty-hunter took in the room at a glance and
dropped his saddle off to the side of the doorway where
a number of other patrons had left their tack as well.
Half a dozen men looked up from their dinner and as
quickly lowered their gaze. Conversation was muted and
the men at the table returned their attention to plates of
food and cups of steaming hot coffee. As Cole crossed
the room, Pete ducked behind the bar and came up with
a bottle and shot glass in his hands.

"Yellowboy, I heard you were up Kansas way. Something about some work for the railroad, wasn't it?" Blind
Pete filled the glass and slid it across the bar to Cole.
He left the bottle in easy reach for the man to manage
his own refills.

"I finished the job," Cole said. Normally he would
have minded such prying questions, but Blind Pete was
an exception. A man had to be willing to give infor-

mation if he wanted to get the same. Cole glanced around the room again, none of the men there looked familiar. He guessed they were drifters like himself. A blond, solidly built individual wearing Eastern attire stepped away from the table. Lamplight glinted off the watch chain draped across his vest.

"Looking for anybody in particular?" Blind Pete asked.

"I saw Glory Doolin's mare out in the corral," Cole said, turning his back to the Easterner.

"Funny thing, she asked about you when she first showed up. That was about three days ago. Been keeping to herself mostly. Walks along the river or stays in her room. Number six at the end."

Cole downed the contents of the shot glass and tightened his hold on the bar as the liquid burned a hole clear down to his ankles. "You been experimenting with the whiskey again?" Cole gasped.

"You like it, huh?" Pete said, fingering the patch covering the left side of his face. "I call it Trinity River Busthead."

"The jalapeño juice is a nice touch," Cole said in a strangled tone. He dropped two bits on the bar.

"You gonna spend the night?" Pete asked. Cole shrugged. "Well, if'n you do, I hired me a new girl to work with the Gila Flower." Pete handed the bounty-hunter a wood token with "Good for One Screw" burned into both sides. "Her name's Coffee and she'll ring your bell in more ways than the Gila Flower ever dreamed of. The girls are busy now, but I reckon anything worth gettin' is worth waitin' for."

Cole slid the token back over the counter. "No, thanks, Pete," he said, his voice returning. "I'm a might tired. It's been a long trail." Anthem blanced his yellow brass-framed carbine in his left arm, turned from the bar, and walked into the Easterner. Cole read "law" in the man's eyes.

He flashed a silver badge beneath Cole's nose and identified himself as a Pinkerton agent. The detective wore a gray frock coat and gray woolen trousers. The hem of his coat was tucked back to reveal the smooth wooden grip of a Colt revolver. He adjusted the round wire-rimmed glasses perched on the bridge of his nose. His eyes were red-rimmed and betrayed his lack of sleep. He cleared his throat and tugged at a neatly waxed mustache that curled upward toward his cherubic cheeks.

"I'm Kenneth Dane," the detective declared. "You are Mr. Yellowboy, I believe." Dane twisted the curled tips of his mustache and straightened his posture in an attempt to look Anthem in the eye—a hopeless task as Cole's six-foot-six frame towered over the detective.

"What do you want?" the bounty-hunter asked impassively.

"Just to tell you what I've told the other men here. The Reilly brothers are Pinkerton business. We have tracked them to the Fort Worth area, and as soon as my lieutenants arrive, we'll hound them out and bring them to justice. They killed a Pinkerton man, and by heaven a Pinkerton will bring them in and any bounty-hunter who tries to interfere for the sake of a reward will suffer the consequences. So, if you don't want to find your own face among the wanted posters, you'll ride clear of the Reillys."

"I don't know what you are talking about," Cole said, touching the brim of his battered hat as he stepped around the detective.

The windows were thrown wide and an evening breeze gusted through the spacious room. The flames in the hearth leapt merrily and danced upon the mesquite logs. The smell of fresh corn bread and snap beans cooked with ham hocks wafted among the tables and filled the tavern with a mouth-watering aroma. Cole couldn't help himself. Like his dun stallion, hunger got the better of him. He sauntered over to the fireplace and, grabbing a plate from the stone hearth, placed a couple of inch-thick squares of corn bread in the center of his plate and smothered the golden-brown bread with snap beans and chunks of pork. Balancing plate and carbine, he retraced his steps and walked out the back door onto the porch. He sensed Dane's cautious, crafty stare boring a hole between his shoulder blades, and he didn't like the feeling. But discomfort faded at the sight of Glory Doolin. She wasn't in her room. She was standing down by the banks of the Trinity, a lone and lovely woman watching the dusk breed fire-flies among the willows.

Glory Doolin, Missouri-born and -bred. Her chestnut hair was shoulder-length and parted in the middle to frame features that on first glance a man might call plain, until he saw the myriad emotions, the ethereal and even haunted changes reflected in the still pool of her shy blue eyes. Plain, yes, until a man heard her laugh or whisper his name in a wise and earthy voice; until such a man clasped his hands about her narrow waist or rode in furious lovemaking between her strong, thickly muscled thighs.

She could be bold or feign demureness or mock some wide-eyed cloyingly sweet lass with the expertise of a skilled actress. Cole knew and liked the woman no matter what her role. Perhaps he sensed a kindred spirit in her moments of silence, in those brief, rare times when she exhibited an almost vulnerable self. Their paths had crossed before and the intersections had been both stormy and passionate.

Yes, Glory Doolin was one of the few people who knew a name for the man called Yellowboy.

She spied Cole watching her from the porch and made no move toward him. Cole shrugged, willing to play her game. He wolfed down his food, then put the plate aside and descended the steps to the grassy slope. Glory backed out of sight and vanished among the hanging branches of a willow whose leafy tendrils swept the surface of the river and formed a canopy.

Cole followed her. "Hello, Glory," he said. "It's been a while." Cole hooked a thumb in the cartridge belt circling his waist and moved closer to the woman. A gun belt circled her round, shapely hips. She wore buckskins that were smooth as suede, and a black cotton shirt that seemed a size too large, concealing her small bosom.

"You still favor that Navy .36," Cole asked.

"I do," she replied.

"Hmm. Then I better not try to kiss you."

"Maybe it isn't loaded," Glory said, cocking her head to one side, a note of daring in her voice.

"I wonder if it would be worth the risk?" Cole said.

"You've always thought so, Cole Tyler Anthem," Glory purred. She knew he was touchy about anyone using his real name. That was precisely why she used it.

Cole reached out, pulled her into his arms, and covered her lips with his. He felt the cold octagon-shaped barrel of a Navy Colt press against the side of his throat. He stiffened. The hammer clicked down on an empty chamber. He took his kiss, then released her.

"*Tsk tsk*. Empty. It must be terrible to be so forgetful." He grinned.

"It's terrible to be a lot of things," Glory said, holstering her gun.

Cole nodded and peered out through the leafy canopy at Blind Pete's Tavern. A figure obscured in the shadows darkening the porch was suddenly caught in the amber halo of an oil lamp placed in a nearby window. It was Dane, the Pinkerton man, and he was more than a little intrigued by the couple along the riverbank. He darted out of the circle of light like a fish from a predator and backed toward the far end of the porch.

The breeze changed and carried the fragrance of rose water and vanilla as Glory drew near.

"Poor Mr. Dane . . . I worry him," Glory said, "ever since I rode in from San Antone."

"You worry a lot of people." Cole turned and reached in his vest. He took a letter she had written him out of his shirt pocket and placed the rain-spattered piece of paper in the palm of her hand. "This was waiting for me at end of track up on the Kansas, Missouri, and Texas line. Your letter said urgent. The way I figure there's only two things worth getting urgent about: love or money. Coming from you, I figured either way I couldn't lose."

Glory frowned. In the fragile moonlight, for one brief instant she dropped her defenses and started to unbutton her shirt as if to remove something tucked away against her flesh. Then her hand suddenly dropped away.

"What is it? What's the matter, Glory?"

"Nothing," she said a little too sharply. "You're right. It's money."

Cole studied her face until she turned away. He did not believe her and suspected she was hiding something from him. But Glory had her own way of doing things and he wasn't about to press the matter—she'd tell him in good time. As for the subject of money, he was ready to listen.

"How much?"

"Twenty five hundred dollars. We split it down the middle," the woman said, recovering her composure.

"It isn't like you to offer to share."

"I need your help," Glory explained.

"That isn't like you either," Cole added.

Glory smiled and stepped around him, peering out through the branches. The Pinkerton man was no longer visible on the porch. Perhaps he had gone inside, or he might have crept to within earshot. She'd have to take the chance.

"You ever heard of Bone Reilly and his brother Tate?"

"I heard the Pinkertons want them," Cole said.

"Dane thinks he knows where they are, but he's wrong," Glory said, in a self-satisfied voice.

"But you know right where the Reillys have gone to roost?" Cole said.

Glory laughed softly and put her arms around his neck. She kissed him, offering that as her answer.

"Why do you need me?" Cole asked, liking the feel of her sweet curves in his arms. She was probably setting him up, but right now he didn't care.

"They're holed up on a hard scrabble ranch over on Seco Creek, beneath the limestone rims. I've totaled a thousand apiece for Bone and Tate and another five hundred for Jim Peaster, who owns the place. He's wanted in Fort Griffin for raping a schoolmarm and burning down the school."

"The man has plainly got no use for education," Cole said. He propped his carbine against the tree trunk and sat with his back to the tree. He stretched his legs out and yawned, and folding his hands behind his head. "Why do you need me?" he repeated.

"Because they are on the lookout for lawmen and bounty-hunters. Any dumb sod packing a gun who rides up out of the breaks will catch a bullet between the eyes." Glory knelt down and sat back on her haunches, putting her hand on his leg. "But how dangerous would a pair of young newlyweds be, who might drive up in a carriage all lost and helpless like. Real tenderfoots."

"You mean lambs," Cole corrected. "And I'd imagine if Peaster and the Reilly brothers are hard up for spending money and a good-looking woman, why, they'd welcome us to the slaughter with open arms." He tried to find fault with her plan. But dammit, Glory was so blasted close and Cole wasn't feeling nearly as tired as he had been. "When do we leave?"

"Tomorrow," Glory said. She leaned forward. Her warm breath caressed his cheek. "I brought along some city duds. But if we're gonna do this right"—her eyes gleamed wickedly—"maybe you better propose."

10

"I don't like this one bit," Cole complained, running a finger around the edge of the stiff white collar that threatened to choke off his breathing. "Damn it to hell," he said.

"Such talk, and from a preacher," Glory said. She rode at his side in the carriage. Her chestnut hair was gathered in a bun at the back of her neck. She wore a yellow silk bonnet with white lace trim and a full high-necked cotton dress the color of buttercups that accentuated her pert bosom and rounded hips. She leaned over and straightened the hem of her dress, then adjusted the parasol to cover the yellowboy carbine hidden at their feet.

Cole cursed again and tried to work the tightness out of his shoulders without tearing his coat. He shaded his eyes and studied the cabin and outlying buildings at the rear of the canyon just ahead. He judged they had another half-hour's ride to Peaster's ranch and flicked the reins in his hands. The dun stallion started forward. The horse seemed to resent pulling the carriage as much as Cole did wearing the ill-fitting somber garments of a minister.

"I am beginning to regret I ever let you talk me into this," Cole grumbled to his attractive companion.

"I did more than talk," Glory said, looking aside at him, her eyebrows arched and her lips pouted provocatively.

"You could have at least found some duds that fit. The bible-thumper you stole these from must have been a midget."

"Most men are, compared to you, Cole Tyler honey," Glory said. She untied the drawstrings of her purse and brought out a pair of wire-rimmed glasses. The Navy Colt she kept in the purse had bent the frames, but Glory managed to straighten them enough to hook over Cole's ears.

"There. Now you may be big, but at least you look harmless," she said, laughing at his appearance.

He endured her humor without comment. The lenses were clear glass and only slightly distorted his vision.

They rode in silence then, feeling the weight of the day and the business at hand rapidly approach with every jarring turn of the wheel. He glimpsed movement in the underbrush and a hundred yards down the trail a wiry little man on a brown horse rode out of a thicket of scrub oak. He whipped his horse across the rump and spurred the animal on toward the ranch.

"Tate Reilly," Glory muttered.

"I hope this works," Cole said. He didn't like having the Winchester on the floor of the carriage. And he felt like a sitting duck in the preacher's garb and shiny carriage. He wasn't afraid of death. He just didn't want to die looking like a fool.

"It already has," Glory said. "Tate Reilly could have opened up on us. Instead, he's run off to tell his brother.

I'll bet he fell in love with me at first sight," Glory added in a flippant tone.

"You watch yourself. Things are liable to get real nasty from here on out," Cole reminded.

"I can keep my powder dry," Glory snapped, her impatience betraying her worried state. Her flippancy was merely bravado, Cole now knew. She bit her lower lip and tightened her grip on her purse and the gun within. She jumped, started, as Cole broke into song with an off-key rendition of "Amazing Grace." She glanced over at him as if he were mad, then realized the man-hunter was warming to his part. She joined him in song. Her voice was sweet and clear and free of tremor. Cole patted her arm and flashed her a grin that radiated far more confidence than he felt.

Peaster's homestead consisted of a dogtrot cabin, a dozen scrawny chickens scratching around a pen, and a lean-to shed large enough for half a dozen horses. The limstone bluffs and boulder-topped hills provided ample cover for a small army. And a small army is exactly what stepped off the slanted porch of the log cabin. Tate Reilly was in the lead. He wore a faded pair of Levi's and brown shirt and vest. The Henry rifle he carried and the revolver holstered on his hip seemed too big for his diminutive frame. The other two men were of average height. One wore a duster and battered high-crowned hat and carried a pistol in either hand.

"Bone Reilly," Glory softly said. "And that's Peaster with him."

"The man with a taste for education," Cole remarked, and reaching up, he adjusted the bowler hat that dug into his forehead. He smiled and waved to the men in front of the cabin.

Jim Peaster, a sallow-faced, bearded man in overalls and a plaid shirt, spat a stream of tobacco and, keeping his hand on the gun holstered high on his right hip, took the lead. Bone held back, searching the settling dust in the wake of the carriage. Though he saw no one on the trail, Bone remained suspicious and kept his brace of Colt .44s in plain sight. A big brown flop-eared hound stood at the corner of the cabin and barked in a deep and threatening tone.

Glory sat erect, posing in the sunlight so the outlaws could fully appreciate her figure. She assumed an attitude of proper appeal, head held high, spine stiff, and hands folded demurely in her lap.

"Am I pretty?" she asked in a whisper.

"You just keep your purse close to hand," Cole replied, waving to the menacing trio as they closed in on the carriage. "Good day to you, brothers," Cole called out. He nudged the Winchester under the umbrella, but its proximity gave him little reassurance. Jim Peaster caught the bridle of the dun stallion to keep Cole from trying to leave. Bone looked at Glory, who flashed him a flirtatious smile and fluttered her eyelids. Bone gulped and tucked both pistols back in his waistband. The hound continued to bay and strain at the chain that kept him prisoner.

"Lucky we got that dog chained," Tate said, bringing the Henry to bear on Cole's midsection. "He's part wolf and bred to tear into trespassers like you and the pretty lady here."

"I am thankful," Cole said.

"Forgive our intrusion—" Glory began.

"We ain't forgivin' sorts," Bone called out. He grinned, revealing a row of broken teeth. All three men needed a bath. The stench of sweat, grease, and lived-in

clothes was enough to make a man retch. Only fear kept
Cole and Glory from emptying their stomachs.

"We might just make an exception, you being a
preacher an' all," Jim Peaster said.

"You travelin' alone?" Tate asked.

"The Good Lord goes with us wherever our path
leads," Glory said.

"He don't raise much dust, though, does he, Brother
Tate?" Bone said, satisfied there was no one on the
wheel-rutted trail leading up to the homestead.

"You see, we're on our way to minister to our new
flock over in Granbury," Glory explained.

"I must confess, I am absolutely lost," Cole said.

"You and your missus just step down and we'll set
things aright," Tate said. He reached out a hand to Glory.

"Yeah, I ain't been set aright for nigh on a month
'cept what five-finger Sally's been able to do." Bone
chuckled.

Tate glared over his shoulder at his brother, and
Bone's humor abruptly faded.

"I don't know . . ." Cole said.

"Darling, I wouldn't mind a glass of cool spring water," Glory said, and she allowed Tate to help her out of
the wagon.

"A girl as pretty as you can have a whole pitcher
full," Tate said. He turned and tossed the Henry rifle to
Peaster. Tate motioned for Glory to start toward the
homestead. "Me and Bone'll take her to the cabin. You
draw the preacher here a map to Granbury," he added.

"I could plumb use a drink myself," Bone said.

"Why me? I'm as, uh, thirsty as Bone or you," Peaster
said, frowning.

"We'll save some for you," Bone offered, unable to
take his eyes off Glory's hips as she walked past him.

Bone all but tripped in his haste to catch up to his brother, who had caught Glory by the arm and was hurrying her toward the cabin. Cole watched them go and made a mental note of the distance to the front door. He judged the structure to be about eighty feet away.

"Step down, sky-pilot," Peaster ordered, brandishing the Henry rifle. "Your woman just might be a spell."

It was obvious Jim Peaster did not like being left behind while the Reillys enjoyed themselves at his expense.

Glory was walking into a hornet's nest, Cole thought, and if she did not watch out, she might just get stung.

As if sensing his concern, Glory looked over her shoulder at Cole and waved as Tate Reilly all but pulled her inside the cabin.

"I ain't got much use for bible-beaters. My pa was one, but the only thing he ever beat was me," Peaster said as the bounty-hunter climbed out of the wagon. "The best day of my life was when a horse fell on him and killed him dead. I rode out a Mississippi and didn't look back."

A gust of wind swirled through a pile of brittle brown leaves and then chased them down the wheel-rutted road. The hound continued to bark and howl from in back of the cabin. The shadow of a vulture swept across the sunlit canyon, becoming two shadows, then three. A fourth joined the prospective feast; something had died among the jumble of boulders that littered the mesquite-choked slope behind the homestead.

"A man is not made perfect when he dons the vestments of salvation, my son," Cole reverently replied. He wanted to rip off his coat and jump the outlaw. He never liked working a bluff, not in cards and not in life, and he regretted more and more having agreed to play Glory Doolin's game.

"Meanin' the only difference between you and me is that collar, huh?" Peaster said, walking around the carriage. He noticed the empty leather straps and trunk rests. "Where the hell are your bags? You traveling mighty light, preacher. 'Course maybe that sweet piece of fluff riding with you is all you need." Peaster balanced the Henry on his shoulder and started back toward Cole.

"Our luggage was to be sent along," Cole said in a flustered tone. "We hardly had room for ourselves." He edged closer to the floorboard of the carriage. "What ever could be keeping my Millicent?"

"She'll be well taken care of, as long as she lasts," Peaster replied.

"What do you mean by that?" Cole asked.

"Better get your bible, preacher, and start to readin' 'cause I think you gonna have use for them holy words." Peaster thumb-cocked the Henry as it rested on his shoulder, his finger tightened on the trigger. He expected no trouble from an unarmed preacher.

"Maybe you can help me with the words," Cole suggested. "What did the teacher in Fort Griffin say after you beat and raped her?"

Peaster stopped in his tracks, staring in complete confusion. Realization was a slow dawn, but when it came, he burst into action. He jerked the rifle from his shoulder. Cole stepped inside the arc and drove his knee into Peaster's groin. The outlaw groaned and sank to his knees. Cole leapt back and reached inside the carriage as Peaster struggled to raise the Henry. Cole snatched out his own weapon from the floorboard.

"Drop it," Cole said, and aimed the yellow parasol at Peaster's heart.

Peaster, on reflex, dropped the Henry. Then he saw what Cole had trained on him, grabbed for the repeater again, and brought the rifle up.

"Oh, shit," Cole said, disgusted. No time for the yellowboy now. He opened the parasol in the outlaw's face and knocked the Henry in the air. The rifle spat flame as Peaster staggered and tripped over his own feet. He shoved himself upright, stood, and levered another shell. A shiny copper casing ejected from the breach. Cole rammed the wooden tip of the parasol into the muzzle of the rifle and dived for the dirt as Peaster squeezed the trigger. Cole hit the ground and covered his eyes as a sharp explosion split the air and shards of metal and pieces of parasol whined away in every direction. Chunks of clay stung his cheek, flame burned his neck. His ears were ringing from the blast.

Cole struggled to stand and managed to face Peaster, who staggered backward from the Henry rifle with its shattered breach which lay at his feet. Peaster held his blackened hands high in front of him. Two fingers of his left hand were completely blown away and the bloody stubs cauterized by the escaping flame.

"Gawddaaaammm," Peaster shouted. His hands were smoking, his eyes widened with pain and horror.

Gunfire erupted from inside the cabin, sparking Cole to action. He ran to the carriage and dragged out his carbine, taking comfort at last in the familiar feel of the gun.

"Gaaawwwwdddd," Peaster howled. He clawed in agony at the gun butt protruding from the holster on his hip, but his hands were so burned he could hardly move the fingers. "Oooowwwww," he shrieked. "I'll kill you sonovabitch . . . you ain't no preacher."

"Peace be with you," Cole said, and he slapped the

wooden stock of the yellowboy up against Peaster's skull. The outlaw sagged to the hard-packed earth.

The gun battle inside the cabin reached a furious pitch, as though a war were being waged in the humble confines of the shack.

Cole trotted across the yard and reached the porch in a matter of seconds. He veered to his right and battered through the rough timbered doors blocking the entrance.

Makeshift cots were overturned, a table lay on its side, plates were scattered, a puddle of beans and salt pork spread over the center of the floor. Tate Reilly sat propped against the wall, his pants off and tattered red long johns pulled to his ankles. A three-legged stool lay on its side under his scrawny thighs. His Colt revolver was nowhere to be seen, but two bright patches of blood spread out from puckered black wounds in both his shoulders.

"Don't shoot," Tate cried. "Your bitch has already crippled me."

The cabin had a second room. It was another bedroom, as torn up as the first, and beyond it a back door hung open.

"Cole!"

The bounty-hunter stared at the back doorway and heard Glory call his name. But the sound of her voice was cut off by the savage howl of the hound. Cole leapt the wreckage of another bed and darted past an overturned cast-iron stove, kicking a pile of ashes. He emerged, choking and nearly blind, to stumble toward the doorway, where he nearly fell into the slavering jaws of Peaster's wolf dog.

"Kill 'em, Diablo," Tate shouted from the cabin, his voice distorted with pain. "Kill 'em." The hound snapped at Cole, then leapt toward Glory as she tried to crawl away. The woman had lost most of her dress and petticoats and had them rolled around her arm to shield herself from the animal's attack. Glory's revolver had wound up in the dirt where she dropped it when the dog had first lunged for her.

A bullet fanned Cole's cheek and was embedded in the inside wall. Bone Reilly stepped out of the shadows of the lean-to barn and fired both of his pistols. Wood flew from the doorsill and another slug ricocheted off the stove and thudded into the ceiling. Cole stepped into the doorway and levered a shot into the barn as Bone dodged out of sight.

The shot had been high and wide, Cole realized, and cursing, he grabbed the spectacles off the bridge of his noise and threw them to the floor.

"Cole, for Chris'sake," Glory shouted. The hound had caught its teeth in the woman's garment-wrapped arm and was dragging her inch by inch into the sunlit yard, directly into Bone's line of fire. The man in the duster darted out and leveled both his pistols at the woman.

Cole fired. The man in the barn doubled over, straightened, lifted his guns once again.

Cole fired. The man in the barn flew backward and slammed into the horse behind him, rebounded, and stumbled out of the shadows. He dropped one pistol and blasted the earth with the other and tried to raise his gun hand.

Cole fired.

Bone Reilly spun, kicked his right leg up, and toppled over hard on his shoulders, arms and legs outstretched and still.

Cole stepped out of the cabin and walked toward the hound as the animal tore loose from the tattered dress, a flap of cotton in its bared fangs.

Cole headed straight for the dog. The bounty-hunter raised the carbine and sighted down the barrel, centering the rifle on a spot between the dog's ears.

"Nice . . . dog . . ." he said in a murderous tone.

The wolfhound panted, its tongue protruding. Its sharp canine eyes focused on the carbine, flickering with recognition. The animal lowered its head and stretched out. Cole swung the rifle to the left and squeezed off a round. The wolfhound yelped and leapt back before realizing Cole had shot away its chain leash. The hound scampered off toward the boulders and made for a deer trail that wound up the side of the canyon.

"You just have to know how to talk to them," Cole explained. The bounty-hunter sighed and sat down in the doorway. His shirt and coat were torn all the way down the back. Glory was damn near naked. She had a bruise on her forehead and a swollen lip. Cole's face was lacerated from half a dozen cuts and the left side of his neck was blackened and powder-burned.

Glory coughed, wincing with pain, and dabbed at her lip with a strip of petticoat. "I told you it would be easy," she said.

11

Cole Anthem peered out the window of the El Paso Hotel on Fort Worth's Main Street and watched a mule-drawn streetcar work its way past the hotel and on up the street. The car paused to allow a couple of men to disembark and saunter into the Exchange Office, then continued on its slow steady course through the burgeoning community on the banks of the Trinity. Eventually it would pass the stockyards and holding pens where stock was bought and sold and range feuds were settled as peacefully as possible. Then it would continue to the north side of town, where the saloonkeeper was king and wild drovers squandered the last of their savings before heading the herds north to Abilene.

"What do you see?" Glory asked from the four-poster bed. She raised up on an elbow, allowing the sheet to fall away from her small rounded breasts. Her hair was tousled and her eyes puffy from lack of sleep. She and Cole had spent a day and night sequestered in the hotel room "catching up on old times," as she liked to put it. She had drunk too much, made love too much—if there were such a thing—Glory silently wondered, having lived a week's worth of celebration in a single day and a night. She liked Cole; he was good company and asked nothing from her other than that she be as good company to him. If there was indeed room in her heart for love, then perhaps she loved him. Either way, she did not want to lose what they had together. Yet when Cole found out the real reason she had written him . . .

"I said what do you see?" she repeated, trying to shake those thoughts from her mind.

"Civilization," Cole said, making no effort to hide the contempt in his voice.

"Honey, if it wasn't for civilized folks, there wouldn't be any outlaws and you and I would be twenty-five hundred dollars poorer," Glory reminded.

"Maybe we'd be better off," Cole said, turning back to the room.

The El Paso Hotel was the best Fort Worth had to offer, and the Stratford-on-Avon Suite was the finest room in the place, generally reserved for cattle kings and visiting politicos. This weekend it housed a couple of bounty-hunters, Cole reflected as he took in the handsome end tables and elaborately japanned dresser, the love seat and easy chair set apart in what passed for the parlor. He studied walls adorned with chromolithographs depicting various scenes from Shakespearean tragedies as staged by the New York Theatre Guild. Beneath a print of Macbeth and the Ghost of Banquo, a roast beef cooled on a platter of congealed gravy. Cole sighed and fixed his gaze on Glory.

She smiled at him and moved a naked leg out from under the sheet, sliding it back and forth. Her eyes lowered demurely and her fingers lightly traced a circle around her nipples. Cole drifted, barefoot, back to bed. The springs creaked as he sat beside her and propped himself up on the pillows. He was naked and his arousal was plainly evident.

Glory snuggled against him and allowed her dancing fingers to entice him further. It was like this, after the chase, after the danger and the killing. Her desires and her wants were demanding, insatiable. She was a storm-tossed sea and Cole was here to ride her out. Glory knew his loneliness, knew she had the power to keep Cole with her for as long as she needed him. But now, instead, she rolled away and stared at the ceiling, pausing to summon the courage in herself to tell him the truth.

Cole watched her, trying to fathom what exactly her intentions were. She had lit a fire and now was content to let the ashes cool. He didn't need her peculiar behavior to add to his worries. Being back in Texas was uncomfortable enough, even though they were a good seven to ten days' ride from San Antonio. There was always the chance someone might recognize him even after all these years. Why, his own father probably drove his herds up to Fort Worth to join one of the large outfits pushing their stock northward over the Chisholm Trail.

Cole closed his eyes and tried to picture Rose and Big John. Billy must be full grown by now, and Rachel a fine lady.

Glory crawled out of bed, stepped over the quilt piled in a heap at the foot of the bed, and pulled on a scarlet robe embroidered with white roses the length of the hem. She helped herself to a brandy off the food cart and gulped it down for courage.

"I guess you've decided its time." Cole chuckled.

"What?" Glory asked as she searched through her buckskin coat which draped over the back of a chair.

"Time you told me why you really sent me that letter."

Glory spun on her heels and glared at him. "You think you know me so well," she said. Glory looked at the folded sheet of newspaper in her hand, her anger cooling. "Maybe you do," she added. "I was going to tell you about this, maybe I should have sent it . . . but then, I figured you wouldn't take time to help me with the Reillys. And you got to admit, twelve hundred dollars to your name is better than being a ragtag beggar, especially when you go home."

Cole frowned, his temper souring. Home was a dream at night, a sense of loss perhaps, but nothing he could redeem. The war and imprisonment and bounty money had blooded him, had marked him forever. No doubt his parents thought him dead. That was better, he decided than to have them discover the nature of their son's unsavory profession.

"Who says I'm going home?" he snapped.

"This does." Glory replied. She handed him the sheet of newspaper. It was the front page of the *San Antonio Light*. A headline set in bold type on a lower-left column read:

BORDER ALERT Mexican nationals kidnap William Michael Anthem, sole surviving son of John Anthem of Jeff Davis County. Laura Prescott, Billy's bride-to-be, foully murdered. Bride's father recounts the tragedy . . .

PART THREE

PART THREE

12

Rosarito was a sprawling cluster of adobe houses and humble jacals that dominated a broad valley in the heart of the Sierra de Calavera. At the westernmost end of the valley, at the base of a broken line of foothills and loftier peaks, rose the sun-bleached battlements of the fortress Andrés Varela called home.

Billy Anthem had seen towns and villages like Rosarito before, although such communities were few and far between in these sparsely settled reaches of the sierras. He closed his eyes and breathed in a variety of familiar scents, that of drying hay and distant pines, of tortillas baked on heated stones, pungent chilis and simmering stews and frying squash prepared for evening meals.

Children scampered out of the way of the horsemen. Dogs joined the parade, barking and nipping at the hooves of the horses. Farmers and storekeepers, laborers on their way back from the fields, paused to watch as Varela's children led their prisoner through the town. Half a dozen men, arm in arm with as many whores, emerged from a nearby cantina. The soldiers laughed and shouted and fired into the air. The whores struggled to lure the men inside, but the soldiers laughingly resisted. Then all commotion ceased at the sight of the procession and the big bearded individual who rode at the fore. The drunken soldiers quickly holstered their guns and attempted to stand at attention while the prostitutes scampered out of sight, balancing bottles of tequila and jugs of *pulque* as they hurried off the street and away from the stern glare of Hector Varela.

Billy glanced aside at Aurelio Bustamante, who made no effort to hide his own disapproval of such conduct. Up ahead, Hector looked over his shoulder at Bustamante.

"Our brave *soldados* have become a rabble in our absence," Hector said.

"You cannot expect an eagle when you tame a pig," Aurelio replied with a shrug. He brushed a leathery hand across his silver goatee and sadly shook his head.

"Do not be so harsh, Hector," Natividad spoke up. She walked her mount over to her older brother. "It will be night soon and they have a right to enjoy themselves."

"*Sí, señorita,*" one of the soldiers spoke up. "We have been relieved from duty. Your father himself sent us down from the hacienda."

"If we had been the gringos who ride for Señor John Anthem, you would be dead," Hector told them. His voice was deep and sonorous and carried a tone of gravity to sober even the drunkest of his men. "I tell you and you tell the others, your *capitán* has returned, and any of my soldiers who cannot stand at attention by morning will have no further use for his legs. I see to this personally. *¿Comprende?*"

The soldiers nodded in unison and hurried to straighten and button their uniforms.

Natividad started to protest but Hector silenced her with a stare.

"After all, Hector," Rafael called out. "The men do have a right—"

"Enough," Hector bellowed. He did not bother turning to look at his younger brother but continued down the main street that wound through the village.

Rafael reddened at being so publicly humiliated. He rode up alongside Billy and Aurelio. Detecting a glimmer of amusement in young Anthem's expression, Rafael lashed out and slapped Billy across the face.

"Such a temper, worse than a child," Aurelio scolded.

"Mind your own business, old one," Rafael angrily replied. "Remember I am the son of Andrés Varela. I must endure my brother's disrespect but not yours!" Rafael spurred his horse and the animal bolted away at a gallop, hurling clods of dirt in Hector's face as the gelding sped past.

Hector called to him, but Rafael ignored his brother and raced pell-mell toward the open gates of the fortress at the base of the mountain.

Billy studied the talus-littered slope and the yawning black openings to vacant mine shafts. Once there had been active mining here.

"The silver is gone," Aurelio said as the fortress drew ever nearer. "But *el jefe* has discovered another source of wealth. Power. And land. And the people who farm it. Andrés Varela is king of northern Chihuahua. And who is there to depose him?" Aurelio chuckled and hooked a thumb in his gun belt. "The soldiers at the cantina were once sent by Juárez to garrison the village. Andrés hung their officers and gave the soldiers the choice to ride for him or follow the example of their leaders." Aurelio slapped the silver-inlaid pommel of his saddle and laughed aloud. "They lost no time in becoming loyal Varelistas. They may be pigs, but not stupid pigs, sí?"

Billy Anthem wiped the blood from his lip. His face stung from Rafael's blow, but he endured the pain in silence and vowed one day to see just how brave Rafael was. He glanced over at Aurelio, sitting arrow-straight and confident in the saddle.

"That's a good story," Billy said. "Join up or die, huh? But tell me, what happens when someone comes along and hangs Varela?"

The hacienda of Andrés Varela was built like a fortress. Walls ten feet high and eighteen inches thick surrounded a broad compound a hundred yards across. There were barracks for the vaqueros and soldiers comprising Varela's little army, and a massive, two-story hacienda for the general, whose word was law in these northern reaches of Chihuahua.

Andrés Varela stood at the top of the front steps, resplendently clad in a scarlet satin robe that concealed his sparse frame and bony physique. He wore red woolen long johns and shiny black boots and carried a saber in his left hand. A scarlet turban covered the general's thinning silver hair. His features were hawklike, shrewd and predatory. His were the eyes of a man who had weathered wars and political storms, who had seen regimes rise and fall and the country change governments; they were eyes of wisdom, at times shimmering with the madness of a man with one final burning ambition before the grave claimed him.

Varela raised his right hand, a wooden hand, to shield his eyes from the sun's glare as Hector brought his prisoner into the fortress. Burned into the back of the

wooden hand was a single word, *venganza*, so that Andrés Varela would never forget the man who had
maimed him.

Vengeance! *¡Venganza!*

"What did I tell you, Father," Rafael said at Varela's
side. "The son of John Anthem, as we promised. I myself captured him. Natividad was of some help, of
course." Rafael's chest swelled with pride and he looked
at Andrés, hoping to find he had gained his father's favor.

A crowd of soldiers, vaqueros, their mistresses and
whores, filed out of the barracks below the walls. Men
in uniform guarding the walls paused on their rounds to
watch the horsemen ride through the gate.

"Bring him inside," Varela called out in a hoarse
voice. He sneezed and spat phlegm and then pointed the
tip of his saber at Billy. "Untie him. Let him enter the
house of Varela unbound." Varela swung around and
started back toward the front door of the hacienda.

"Free his hands," Rafael sputtered. "B-b-but, Father,
he might try to escape, or worse, do you harm."

"I have my sons and daughter to protect me." Andrés
chuckled, anxious to return to the warmth of the hacienda.

Rafael went with him.

Hector heard his father's command and ordered Billy
to hold out his wrists. Hector reached behind his neck
and drew a double-edged throwing knife from a sheath
sewn into the back of his shirt. He sawed at the leather
cords; they dropped almost on contact with the razor-
sharp steel.

"*Sí*, the blade is keen enough to cut your heart out if
you do not behave yourself while you are my father's
guest," Hector warned.

"Guest?" Billy repeated. His voice was thick with contempt. As he climbed down from the horse he searched the dark-brown faces studying him with a mixture of curiosity and relief that they weren't in his shoes.

Hector gave him a nudge and Billy sauntered toward the hacienda with the large bearded son of Andrés Varela at his arm. Natividad watched the two of them start up the few steps to the veranda. She slowly climbed down from her horse and signaled a nearby vaquero to take her mount. Aurelio Bustamante groaned and dismounted then walked up to the attractive young woman and offered her his arm in escort.

"The gringo acts brave, but I think he is frightened," Natividad remarked.

"Not so, *querida*," Aurelio said to her. "This Billy Anthem ceased to be afraid the moment he woke and found his bride-to-be dead in the rain."

"So he grieves," Natividad said with a shrug. "If not afraid, then, his spirit is broken."

"Neither fearful nor broken, *señorita*, but . . . waiting. Yes, waiting." Aurelio nodded. He stroked his silver chin whiskers and pursed his lips in thought as he suffered a premonition of dire events to come. "Better to have killed him along the way."

"Aurelio Bustamante, you who hunted the bandits in the passes and raided the Apache in his own *ranchería* and drove him from my father's lands, you talk like an old woman, frightened of some gringo's whelp." Natividad drew away from her father's old friend and shook her head in disgust. She stepped out into the compound for all the men to see. "Let there be a fiesta this night, for we have avenged the disgrace, we have raided the gringo and spilled his blood. The children of Varela have returned."

She drew her gun and emptied it into the air. Six shots reverberated among the thick clay walls, followed by a deafening reply as the soldiers and the vaqueros comprising Varela's personal guard fired their rifles and pistols in cheerful salute.

"You see, *viejo*," Natividad shouted above the din. "These men have not lost their spirit. Señor Anthem may rule north of the Río Bravo but here, my father is king." Natividad swaggered past Aurelio and vanished inside the hacienda.

Aurelio watched as the men and women of the fortress gave themselves to the coming celebration. Two goats were killed, men hurried off to procure casks of tequila and *pulque*. Women carried armfuls of wood to a central pit where the cabrito would roast over leaping flames. The fortress was suddenly alive with merriment and the hasty arrangements of a celebration.

Maybe time *has* made me timid, Aurelio thought. He sighed and walked out into the compound, working his way through the rapidly increasing crowd of rough-looking Varelistas, the majority of whom he no longer knew by name. A comely woman twenty years his junior hurried past. Aurelio caught the woman by the arm. She spun about, recognized authority in the bearing of the older man, and bounded into his arms. Her pendulous breasts crushed against Aurelio's chest and her fleshy brown arms encircled his neck as she smothered him with kisses. A young woman, newly arrived from an outlying farm, the *señorita* was eager to please one of such lofty station.

Aurelio didn't know her name. And tonight, he didn't care.

*   *   *

Varela slouched in a high-backed leather chair like some mad king upon his throne, watching as Hector brought Billy into the living room. The windows were shuttered and only a single oil lamp burned in the center of the room. The lamp and burning logs in the fireplace cast a pool of fluttering light about the ruler of the Sierra de Calavera.

He motioned with his wooden right hand for Billy to approach. Hector waited by the door. Young Anthem entered the room, his boot heels clicking on the tile floor. The walls around him were bare, except for an arrangement of sabers and percussion pistols that adorned a space alongside the hearth. Billy remembered his father's account of Varela, how the general had imprisoned Anthem years ago. Varela's wooden hand was Big John's legacy.

As Billy stood in front of Varela, the general held the younger man in a gaze of brutal triumph.

"I am Andrés Varela," the general said. He raised his left hand and leveled a Confederate-issue revolver at Billy. He squeezed the trigger and Billy flinched as a resounding click broke the stillness.

Varela chuckled. "I always keep one chamber empty," Andrés explained. "To guard against accidents." He smiled, placed the revolver in his lap, and reached for a crystal decanter of French cognac. The general filled two long-stemmed glasses shaped like tulips. He offered one to Billy, who made no move toward the general on his throne. Varela released the glass. It shattered at Billy's feet. Varela drained his, swirled the liquid around in his mouth, and swallowed.

"Too bad," Varela said, "it is an excellent brew. Perhaps you are not thirsty. But you will be." Varela stood in his scarlet robes, his revolver clutched in his left hand once more, his hawkish features exaggerated by the fire-light. He raised his wooden hand and brushed it against Billy's cheek.

"Your father's legacy," Varela said. "My flesh is rough, no? And without blood." Varela stepped closer, his breath fanned Billy's face. The general lowered his voice to a whisper. "A son is like a good right hand, eh? I have John Anthem's hand, but he can have it back. For a price. His life for his hand. I cut you off." Varela backed away. "I cut you off!" He fought for breath and staggered back to his chair.

"You're dying," Billy dryly observed.

Varela slumped in his throne and continued to strug-gle for breath. "We all are," Varela gasped. Slowly the color returned to his features. "Death is an ardent mis-tress, but before I succumb to her embrace, I will have my revenge."

"My father won't come for me," Billy said. "So Laura's death, all of this, has been for nothing, you mad old bastard." Billy lunged forward and Varela raised his gun hand, stopping his youthful attacker in his tracks.

"Then you will die," Varela snapped. "But not now." The general glanced past his prisoner. "Take our guest to the place we have prepared for him." He looked at Billy. "The silver has played out. But the mines have their use. I think your father will appreciate the irony."

Billy heard footsteps behind him and turned as Hector caught him by the arm. Rafael and Natividad slipped soundlessly into the darkened room. Even their bragga-docio was tamed in the presence of their father. Almost as if they feared him themselves.

"Ahh, my children," Varela purred. "Brave Rafael and my sweet Natividad. You have brought honor to the name Varela, though your mothers be whores, it is my seed that fathered you, my blood in your veins. I chose you for my own, set you above all the rest."

Hector hurried forward, forcing Billy to quicken his pace. He all but dragged the youth the last few steps into the hall. Before Hector slammed the door behind them, Billy looking over his shoulder, caught a glimpse of Rafael and Natividad approaching the scarlet-clothed figure on his throne in a pool of firelight.

"Come with me," Hector said. The bearish man seemed embarrassed by his father's revelation of their illegitimacy. Hector shoved Billy forward and motioned for him to continue down the hall. Billy did as he was told, passing doors that led into a dining room, a pantry, a study, and at the rear, a winter kitchen, where a portly *mamacita* and her two daughters worked near a great stone fireplace. The older woman was kneading bread dough while her daughters patted dollops of the mixture into round flat wheels to be fried in a skillet of grease.

"Keep moving," Hector ordered gruffly.

Billy shrugged and stepped through an open doorway and onto the rubble-strewn hillside. A trail wound its way upward, skirting around one hill and continuing up the slope. The walls of the fortress extended partway up the hill, leaving the rest of the landscape to form a natural barricade.

Beyond the hill rose a rugged series of ridges dotted with mine shafts. Billy remembered Big John's account of having toiled in Varela's mines long ago.

"Where are we going?" Billy asked.

Hector stabbed a calloused finger toward a yawning hole that loomed like an open wound in the belly of the ridge rising over the fortress.

"Your journey is ended," Hector said. He drew his

Colt and prodded Billy in the back. The two men continued up the winding narrow trail. With every step the cave mouth seemed to widen, revealing a blackness in its depths that rivaled Billy's own despair.

13

Early morning, Luminaria slowly came to life. The Mexican vaqueros who rode for the brand filed past the hacienda and the solitary figure of John Anthem, who stood on crutches under a tree behind the main house, staring down across his vast property. The vaqueros averted their eyes so as not to intrude on Big John Anthem who appeared to be deep in thought.

There was a ranch to run, cattle to be herded down from one meadow, boundary lines to be ridden, and missing stock to be accounted for. John Anthem didn't need men to suffer with him; he needed men to take up the slack while he waited for his leg to heal. And waited to avenge the loss of his son and the murder of Laura Prescott. The vaqueros did not stop to offer condolences, but showed their concern by continuing on up the canyon and getting on with the jobs they were paid to do.

John Anthem watched his men ride down the canyon trail, past a lone horseman working his way toward the ranch. Probably looking for a handout. No stranger ever left Luminaria hungry. That was Anthem's law, set down by Rose and John from the moment they began their lives together here in the desert mountains.

The wind gusted; John shivered. It was turning cold as a gambler's heart, he muttered to himself. Anthem dug his hands down into the pockets of his heavy flannel coat. He braced himself on his makeshift cane as the mischievous north breeze tried to steal his hat. John pulled his sweat-stained stetson down tight on his head, and the wind tugged to no avail.

He closed his eyes and tried to swallow away the thickness rising in his throat. He had fought for this harsh and lovely land, given everything. And for what? So he could wait alone while his one living son, Billy, paid the price for his own captivity long ago. Hell, "everything" was too damn much to give.

He thought of both his sons, twin boys, though hardly identical. Two different boys casting two different shadows.

"Ahh, Billy," John said suddenly to the rising wind. "You never had a chance. Your brother Cole and I were too much alike. We understood each other, and when he left, well, maybe I tried to shove Billy into his mold." John glanced around, suddenly self-conscious of his dialogue with a memory. But he was alone. Even the line rider was gone. A dog trotted over to the back door of the bunkhouse, hoping Prometheus would make an appearance with a bucket full of scraps. The black cook never let the pup down.

John half-smiled, turning back to face the hacienda.

"Billy, I lost your brother, and there's nothing I can do about it. But you're another matter entirely. I'm not gonna let you down again." John rubbed his forearm across the moistened eyes.

"Damn, I'm turnin' into an old woman." He sniffed and cleared his throat. If only he had reached out to Billy before the boy had set out with Laura, none of this would have . . . No! John clenched his fists and willed away the self-recrimination.

He couldn't snare the past and bring it back; it was easier to catch the wind. A man could go mad trying.

John sighed and started down the path to the hacienda. He heard a familiar cry echo over the land and shaded his eyes as he searched the morning sky and espied, against the cold blue dome of heaven, a formation of geese winging southward. Another flock followed the first and a third V formation of the wild and lovely creatures glided over the western rim, regained their bearing, and followed the others. John Anthem's soul soared with them, for this was a sight he never tired of. John glanced toward the sky, suddenly reminded of the son he understood so well. "I know, Cole. You love them too." Somehow he didn't feel so empty.

John continued down the path and went into the hacienda through the kitchen door, entering Rose's domain, fragrant with the smell of rising bread dough and fresh-brewed coffee. He started toward the coffeepot on the cast-iron stove and froze. The house seemed unnaturally still. Rose and her daughter had been kneading the dough and working it into bread pans. Now everything seemed so quiet . . . not completely, though. The sound of a stifled sob from the living room.

Trouble?

John Anthem limped out of the kitchen and into the hall.

"John," her voice reached to him. "John!" urgent now, crying out to him.

John slapped his right hip and realized he wasn't wearing a gun. By heaven, the cane would do. He hurried as best he could, taking great lumbering strides that propelled him quickly, if awkwardly down the hall and around the stairway to the living room. He brought up shortly at the sight of both wife and daughter in the arms of a tall, rugged-looking drifter. He was a hard and dangerous-looking man—and a stranger, to boot, until he raised his head. Two ice-blue eyes peered out from beneath the brim of his battered campaign hat, Confederate issue.

Uncertain of his reception, the stranger made no move but waited where he stood.

"Hello, Pa," the stranger said.

Rose turned a tear-streaked face toward her husband, waiting for him to speak, hoping his heart wasn't hardened to this, his prodigal son.

John couldn't speak, words failed. He limped forward, reached out like a doubting Thomas, unable to believe his own eyes. Finally he spoke, though his voice was barely a whisper.

"Welcome home, son."

Cole Tyler Anthem was in the living room as night wrapped its velvet cloak about the hacienda. He slouched comfortably in the cushioned embrace of the leather-backed chair and stretched his long legs toward the blaze in the fireplace.

He had slept through the afternoon and scrubbed a week's worth of dirt from his lanky frame. No one had pressed him for his story.

Rose and Rachel were too busy making a fuss over his homecoming, and Big John seemed surprisingly patient. He had ruined his relationship with one son by being too damn overbearing, and he wasn't about to repeat the mistake.

Cole devoured the hearty supper his mother and sister had hastily prepared, and over coffee, he listened quietly

as John Anthem recounted the kidnapping of Billy and
the murder of Laura Prescott.

John had given up any notion of appealing to Col.
Rex Colby and his company of Texas Rangers. They
couldn't legally cross into Mexico. But John Anthem
could, and every day he was getting stronger.

Evening came, and Uncle Poke Tyler rode in from
the Bend country with a few of the ranch hands. Poke
nearly fainted at the sight of the young man seated by
the fire, despite the fact that a vaquero had already
passed the word to him of Cole's return.

Evening and a warm fire and the close circle of family, however marked by tragedy, tempered Cole's resolve. A liberal dose of tequila helped to loosen his
tongue. Cole talked through the evening, his story spilling forth in a stream of emotions too long pent up.
Where to begin? The war, perhaps, that dreadful time of
carnage. He stared into the heart of the leaping flames
and saw again the bloody face of battle. He was a boy
of thirteen. He had thought he was a man, made a man
by the blood of a deer. Like so many young men Cole
had harbored fantasies of brave feats and honor won on
the field of battle. As a bugler and courier for the Third
Texas Volunteers, Cole discovered the realities of war.
Men blasted apart, brought forth to butchery, led to the
slaughter in the wilderness. No ideals, only survival,
only waste and more waste. Dreams fouled with blood,
bodies heaped like cordwood, smoldering flesh, shred-
ded flesh, ruined flesh.

Cole spoke of the war through a boy's eyes. He spoke
of capture and imprisonment, of filth and disease, of men
reduced to the primitive, where glory was a kind word
from a guard and an extra ration of cornmeal gruel.

And then, after a year in the federal stockades, the

war ended and he was set free, nearly sixteen years old and a hundred years wiser.

"Why didn't you come home, then?" Rose asked. "We're your family. How could you be hardened against us?"

"Hardened?" Cole repeated, sipping his coffee. He eased back in the chair. "No, I love you. But . . . I couldn't come home."

"Why?" Rose pressed on, reaching toward him, her hand on his arm.

"I wanted to return from the war with a chest full of medals, riding a fine charger, a silver saber at my side, a pouch of gold on my belt." Cole laughed softly to himself. "And there I was, ragtag and penniless . . . and dead inside." He squeezed his mother's hand. "I was too proud to let you see me. So I rode the rails west, stealing food when I had to, working odd jobs when I could."

Memories again, of life on the rails, of the worn and weary faces of other Johnny Rebs, hiding out in boxcars, scrounging for food, dodging the rail men and Yankees still bearing a grudge.

"I could talk all week if I had to." Cole chuckled. He rubbed a hand across his craggy features. He returned his coffeecup to an end table and settled back into the hand-stitched cushions.

He searched his memory and settled on a sunset that had changed his life forever.

Cole was a big rangy lad for sixteen and as down at heels as a young man could get, clad in a homespun shirt and overalls—both stolen—and boots a size too small for his growing feet. He had hitched a ride with a freight hauler to Dillon, Kansas, a busy little town on the fringe of the frontier. Cole walked down Main Street, drawn to the western end of town, as voices called to him from passing carriages and horsemen ordered the raw-boned youth out of the middle of the road. Cole ignored them. He followed the length of the wheel-rutted lane through a haze of dust, past storefronts advertising "Eats" and clothing, baths and a barbershop, a laundry, saloons. A doctor's shingle swung to and fro in the breeze.

Oblivious to the world around him, he walked at a slow defeated pace that carried him to the edge of town in the last lingering hours of the day. Main Street ended and limitless prairie began, stretching as far as the eye could see.

He looked out on the vast expanse of wilderness, watching the sun draw slowly to the horizon. It was a treeless plain with only a wheel-worn path to mark its passage through the tall and shimmering tableland of buffalo grass.

The world waited, poised with the setting sun, and the sun was a beacon challenging a man to take hold of his life and make the best of every moment. The once-golden sun turned burnt orange as it burned through a veil of cirrus clouds and bathed the solitary figure in its light, resurrecting in the young man a sense of purpose, a reason to call himself alive. The war had stripped him of every illusion; he had come of age in battle and in suffering. But he was alive, and that meant something. If the world was a choice of endless possibilities, why not his life, why not Cole Tyler himself?

"I don't know," he muttered to the sunset. "I don't know." He turned as shadows crept along the length of Main Street and cloaked the alleys of the town. Lights set in windows reached out onto the boardwalks. Some shopfronts darkened, others came alive.

Cole Tyler Anthem, still wrapped in his own

thoughts, didn't hear the horse approach. The animal collided with the lad and sent him sprawling face forward in the earth.

"Son of a bitch! Get the hell out of my way!"

Cole landed in the dirt and looked up in time to see a pair of flashing hooves slice down toward him. Reacting just in time, he rolled out of the way and crawled to his knees. The rider, a burly man with a patch over his right eye and a brace of pistols holstered high on his waist, spewed a stream of tobacco juice that barely missed Cole. Then he wiped his mouth on his sleeve. Cole noticed the remnants of a blue uniform. That and the ruffian's scarred features beneath the black patch branded him as a veteran of the recent war.

"Damn-fool place to be blocking the street. You think you own this town?" Patch bellowed.

"Maybe I deserved to be knocked down, mister, but trying to trample me underfoot was the act of a bully and a coward," Cole said. He looked about and saw the confrontation was slowly attracting attention.

"Listen to that," Patch bellowed. "The boy knows manners. Speaks just like a reb." He uncorked a brown bottle and tilted it to his lips, managing all the while to keep his horse under control. He drained a quarter of the bottle and popped the cork into place. As he tried to return the bottle to his saddlebag, he managed to drop it in the street. "Dammit," he muttered. "Get me that bottle! Yes, you!" He pointed a finger at Cole, who stood and dusted off his ragged clothes.

"Get it yourself," Cole retorted, and started toward the nearest boardwalk.

More people had gathered, some shopkeepers, a few farmers, men in frock coats, and painted ladies of the evening on their way to work. Cole figured that someone was bound to know what work there was to be had.

"Come back here," Patch yelled as the young man walked away. "You son of a bitch, I'll take you down from your high and mighty!"

Cole saw the people on the walk scatter and instinctively ducked. The roar of a gun sounded behind him and a bullet whistled past his skull, fanning his battered gray felt campaign hat from his head. Cole took off at a dead run for the saloon in front of him. He swerved to the right, cut left, as Patch fired twice and missed.

"Run, you jackrabbit," the horseman yelled.

Cole reached the boardwalk. A lead slug splintered a post and ricocheted off toward the crowd. A woman screamed and fell, clutching her shoulder. A window crashed, a chunk of the wall erupted into wooden fragments as Patch opened up with both guns.

Someone slammed the saloon door closed in Cole's face. Bullets chipped the wooden facing. Young Anthem darted for the alley and heard the gunman's horse keeping pace as Patch continued to blaze away.

A lone horse was tethered to a rail at the side of the saloon just at the mouth of the alley. Cole dived off the boardwalk and rolled underneath the startled animal. Patch momentarily held his fire, waiting for a clear shot. Cole glanced down the alley, then back toward Patch.

"I'll learn ye manners, jackrabbit. Come on out."

"Boy," another voice called, this from the alleyway. Cole turned to face what he thought was a new threat. Instead, something was tossed to him from the shadows: a brass-plated lever-action carbine landed in his hands.

"Jackrabbit, show yourself. Don't make me kill a good horse," said the gunman in the street.

Hardly pausing to study the gun, Cole worked the action, levered a shell into the chamber, and stepped out of the alley. He raised the carbine and sighted on the gunman's shirt pocket.

"Leave me alone," Cole said. "I'm through running." From everything, he added mentally. The wooden stock felt smooth against his cheek. He was conscious of a warm autumnal breeze, the stillness of the town. And his own sense of utter calm.

Patch grinned, snapped up both his guns, and fired. Cole squeezed the trigger, the carbine kicked into his shoulder, the rider flew backward out of the saddle and landed in the middle of the street. He groaned, shoved himself upright. Cole shot him again. Patch stiffened and settled on his side, one gun discharged in the dirt.

"Good shot," said the voice from the alleyway. A gray-haired man sporting a silvery handlebar mustache and goatee stepped into the light streaming from the saloon window. People were already crowding out to view the corpse. The gray-haired man waved the carbine aside when Cole offered to return it. The gentleman was slight of build and nattily dressed in a black frock coat and tailored, pin-striped trousers. He opened his coat and revealed a silk-brocade vest as he removed a deck of cards from his pocket.

"I won the rifle last night," the gambler said. "I have no use for it. I prefer to do my fighting on the tabletops of life. Keep the carbine. You'll need it." He patted Cole on the shoulder. "That's Big Boy McShannon out there in the dust. His kin is worse than him. Better light out when you collect the money."

"What money?" Cole asked.

"The five hundred dollars," the gambler explained. "I'll take you down to the town marshal. Hell, Big Boy's wanted from here to St. Louis. Five hundred dollars dead or alive. Now, if you feel at all charitable, once you've bought some duds, I'll be glad to win what's left of the reward. Just ask around town and someone'll know where Doc Bodine is dealing cards."

"Five hundred dollars," Cole said, his blue eyes drifting over the faces of his family. "If McShannon was worth that much, I figured there had to be others. And there were. Before I knew it, I had gone and found me a way of life." Cole patted the Winchester '66.

"You're the one," Poke blurted out from his corner off to the side. Smoke curled in lazy tendrils from the bowl of his pipe and collected in a billowing wreath among the rafters. "It's you . . . I mean. You're the one they call Yellowboy. The bounty-hunter."

"Yes," Cole said. He reached out and took his mother's hand in his. "I was dead to you, and I figured it would be easier for you if I just stayed dead."

Rose shook her head "no."

"But you came back," John gently corrected.

"Because you need me—and what I do better than anyone else in this world." Cole smiled at Rose, patted her hand, and touched Rachel's close-cropped hair.

She grinned at him, her eyes open wide with sympathy and honest acceptance.

"You're right, son, we need you," John said. He eased back in his armchair and made a steeple with his fingertips as his expression narrowed with thought. "I need you," John added.

"Cole's going to rest and be with us," Rose firmly replied. "I want my son to get to know us. And I want to know him."

John started to argue but threw up his hands in disgust and waved the whole discussion aside.

Cole got the distinct feeling no one ever won an argument with his mother. "Tomorrow I am your slave," he retorted.

"Good. Then first thing, come morning, we'll climb the hill," Rose said. "There's a headstone I want to tear down." She smiled.

"And break into a thousand pieces," Rachel said.

John nodded in accord. For once the Texas Anthems were of a like mind.

14

Chapo Almendáriz waited beneath a granite ledge and studied the ramshackle building nestled in the shadows of the mountain pass. It was a humble structure built of adobe bricks, whose walls were chipped and pocked with bullet holes. The word CANTINA had already begun to fade above the open door. A burly-looking man draped in a serape appeared in the doorway. He moved outside and rummaged among a much-depleted wood-pile, straightened, and carried an armload of dry timber into the cantina.

His voice carried across to Chapo as he spoke to someone inside. "Manuel, you have no money. Go away! There is nothing for you here."

Chapo guided the Appaloosa up the last few yards of incline and around the cantina to a rope corral. He dismounted and ground-tethered his Appaloosa next to a hammerheaded brown gelding.

A side door opened and the man Chapo had seen earlier stepped out to study this latest arrival. "This is not a mission, I am no *padre*," he called out in warning.

Chapo walked back to the corral and kicked a mound of pale-green straw toward his horse, then he headed for the side doorway. The man in the serape was middle-aged, heavyset, with thinning gray hair and weathered features that made his face look as if it were carved from wood. He rubbed a hand across his jaw and retreated as Chapo drew closer.

Just as the owner of the cantina raised a shotgun, Chapo reached inside his shirt, brought out a leather pouch, and picking out a single gold coin, held it up. The owner smiled and lowered his shotgun. Ten-dollar gold pieces were few and far between these days.

"Ah, *señor*, a man of substance. My home is yours. Enter . . . enter my good friend. Drink and eat your fill. I am Jesse Gómez and you are . . ." Gómez stepped aside to permit Chapo to slip past.

"Your good friend," Chapo replied, and dropped the ten-dollar gold piece into the owner's outstretched hand.

The interior of Gómez' cantina was as badly in need of repair as the exterior. The walls needed rechinking and the earth floor needed repacking. The roof consisted primarily of dried sotol roots woven into a mat and sealed with clay. The single room was furnished with three crudely made tables, an assortment of three-legged stools, and a couple of recently repaired ladder-backed chairs. A slight, ugly little man leaned against the bar, which blocked off an entire wall, behind which were pine-board shelves crowded with clay jugs and brown-glass bottles. The little man wore a loose, ragged coat and worn patched clothes. His cheeks were pockmarked and stringy black hair hung to his shoulders. Though dirty and unkempt, the ragged man commanded respect—he leveled a single-shot percussion pistol at Chapo. In his other hand he clutched a clay jug. He kept trying to pick up a burlap sack from off the bar while keeping Chapo and Gómez covered.

"By the mother of the saints, what are you doing?" Gómez roared. "Manuel, you put down the *pulque* or pay me what it costs."

Chapo stepped out of the line of fire and was relieved to find Manuel kept his pistol trained on Gómez.

"Bastard!" Manuel managed to lift the sack, and he held it aloft and shook it in the owner's face. "Varela will pay me plenty for these scalps. They are as good as gold. I will give you your damn money then."

"I will have my money now," Gómez repeated.

"You will be dead; just try to stop me and you will see," Manuel shouted, and backed toward the door. "Drop your shotgun!" He reached behind his back and worked the latch. The door swung open, shoved inward by the wind's invisible hand.

Thunder rolled across the deepening sky and a cold wind gusted through the open door, scattering the ashes in the fireplace. Gómez raised the shotgun and thumbed the hammers back; he meant business. Manuel stifled a gasp and dropped the clay jug. The vessel bounced in the dirt but didn't break. As the smaller man dodged out the front door, he managed to keep a tight grip on his percussion pistol and the sack of scalps.

Chapo glanced out the window and watched the ragged thief make his way up the hillside to a cave among the rocks.

Gómez cursed and walked across the room to retrieve the jug.

"You are a brave man, *señor*," Chapo remarked, turning back to the owner. "To confront a man who has hunted the Apache."

"Who?" Gómez asked, laughing. "Manuel the mouse hunt Apaches?" The owner set the jug on the table by Chapo and gave a hearty chuckle. "There are ruins, houses in the cliffs back in the passes. Sometimes the Apaches use them to live in. And sometimes the earth trembles and stones give way and the places collapse." Gómez walked around the bar and found the two cleanest cups and brought them over to Chapo's table. "That is where Manuel found his Indians. Men, women, and children all dead under the rocks. He dug the bodies out and lifted their hair. I am surprised he had the courage to touch even a dead Apache. But he is right about one thing: a scalp is worth gold to Andrés Varela. But I think it is bad luck to desecrate the dead."

Gómez sat down at the table and poured a drink for Chapo and one for himself. He held up his hand to listen for a moment as the rain started to fall in a gentle but chilling downpour. "Spirits of the dead walk these mountains. Red men, Mexican, gringos too." Gómez downed the contents of his cup. "I make this *pulque* myself, there is none better. Drink enough and maybe you shall see the ghosts, eh?"

Chapo took a swallow of the bitter and fiery liquid. It lit a glow in his belly. "To Manuel, the scourge of the Apaches," he toasted.

Gómez broke into laughter and allowed Chapo to pour him another drink. And another. And another.

The wind howled. The downpour continued, masking any noise Chapo might make. He glanced over his shoulder at the cantina in the distance. It was after midnight and no light showed in the window. Gómez was asleep. Chapo peered around the edge of the cave entrance where shadows danced in flickering firelight. Mesquite wood cracked and sizzled, tree limbs settled into the bed of ruby coals that filled the fire pit. A blanketed figure was curled in a fetal position by the campfire. A loud snore issued from the man. Chapo noticed a brown-glass bottle gripped in Manuel's hand. Manuel might be a mouse, but he was a clever one. He had probably hidden the bottle under his baggy coat and only made a show of attempting to steal the jug. Gómez hadn't thought to search the would-be thief.

Thunder boomed in the distance and reverberated off ridges and lonely summits. Manuel stirred, muttered some unintelligible phrase, and resumed snoring, clutching the bottle and the sack close to his huddled form.

The scalps were the key. Fate had provided Chapo with the perfect excuse to enter Varela's fortress. He might even gain a position among Varela's personal militia. But first, Chapo reminded himself, he had to have those scalps. But how? Manuel would probably put up some kind of fight and Chapo didn't particularly want to hurt the little man. The wind-whipped rain continued to fall, the voice of the wind rushing like some invisible cataract poured through crevice and crack and howled like the spirits of the dead.

The dead!

Chapo grinned. He removed his serape, unbuttoned his shirt, and stripped to the waist. He unbuckled his gun belt and hid it in a dry pocket among the rocks. A bracing gust left him shivering. He questioned the merits of his plan but dug into the rain-soaked ground and stirred the mud into a thick paste with his knife. Standing just inside the cave, he smeared his face and torso, taking special care to mat his hair with mud and powdered limestone. He tore a strip of cloth off his shirt, ripped it into four approximately even lengths, and stuck these to his face and cheeks. He scratched about on the floor of the cave and found a couple of sharp pointed stones and

fit them under his upper lip so they bulged the flesh and protruded like the fangs of a wolf.

He lifted a stone about the size of a man's head and entered the inner chamber of the cave. Chapo raised the stone overhead and slammed it down into the center of the fire pit and loosed a blood-curdling scream that roused Manuel from his stupor. The Mexican bolted awake, gasping, and peered, awestruck, through bleary eyes at the figure striding toward him through a shower of gleaming sparks.

It looked dead and rotting. It looked hairless and horrible. It was fanged and brandished a lethal knife blade that glimmered with a life of its own in the firelight.

"Hair for hair," Chapo moaned as he shambled forward. "You took the hair of my children, now I will have yours. Revenge! Revenge! Blood for blood! Hair for hair!"

Manuel's eyes grew wide with horror. His mouth dropped open; he tried to scream but no sound issued forth. He tried to crawl backward. His fingers touched the sack of scalps and instantly drew away, as if burned. Thunder crashed. Lightning lit the mouth of the cave, framing Chapo in its lurid glare.

"Blood for blood! Hair for haaiiirrr," Chapo wailed.

Manuel's eyes rolled up inside his head; he managed a strangled kind of cry and fell over on his back, arms outstretched. His skull bounced off a chunk of limestone.

Chapo hurried to the thief's side and listened against Manuel's bony chest and heard a heartbeat. Chapo nodded, satisfied, and scrambled back to the fire. He caught up the sack of scalps and worked his way out of the cave, taking care not to leave any tracks. He retrieved his clothes and gun belt and headed back down the slope.

The rain had washed the mud from his torso and face

by the time he reached the door of the cantina. He cracked open the door, peered inside. Gómez was sound asleep, sprawled on a makeshift pallet by the fireplace. Chapo entered and padded across the floor to his own bedroll a few feet away from Gómez.

Chapo stuffed the pack of scalps in his saddlebag and, after drying himself off, pulled on his shirt and crawled under his blankets.

Rain fell, thunder boomed, and without the weathered walls of the cantina, the wind continued its unceasing cry, mimicking the voices of the dead, fueling nightmares.

Poor Manuel would no doubt have quite a story to tell, come morning, Chapo thought. The segundo of Luminaria pulled his blanket up around his shoulders and yawned, drifting off to a sleep troubled not by ghosts of the dead but by a man named Andrés Varela who waited, sure as life and death, only two days' ride away.

15

Miranda danced. She was young and beautiful and men lusted at the sight of her brown slender body, at the way it moved, every motion seeming to flow into the next, the movement of her hips and waist and long, lovely legs and rounded bosom, the way her eyes gazed out in jaded innocence at the men around her, the way her smile seemed at once virginal and the tempting invitation of a whore.

Faces skimmed past. Miranda did not favor one over the other, yet pretended to dance for each and every man, enticing men with the sensuous language of the dance, with the play of her fingers and languid arms extended as if beckoning to embrace. But a woman did not resist in the court of Varela. That is how Miranda had come to think of it—and of Andrés Varela as the monarch of the sierras. He was seated on his throne at the far end of the ballroom, dressed all in burgundy, in waistcoat and flared trousers adorned with black silk stitchery. His ruffled blouse served to set off the splendor of the silver chain and medallion draped around his throat.

Miranda arched her body and swirled until her flowing skirts fluttered up about her hips, revealing her naked

flesh. She searched the exuberant throng for Rafael.
Women called him cruel, but he was one of Varela's
chosen sons, a prince then, and attracting his interest
meant riches and power. After all, what prince did not
need a princess?

Natividad seemed to read Miranda's thoughts and
locked her arm in Rafael's. Her eyes shot daggers as
Miranda swept past.

Miranda darted away and found herself in front of
Hector, the bear, or so men called him. He was seated
in the center of a table, ignoring the festivities. More
than a week had passed since he had returned with Billy
Anthem. And Hector would rather have spent his Sunday
afternoon patrolling the passes.

Miranda thrust a hip in his direction and bent over
the table until her head was beneath Hector's. She found
him ugly, frightening, but this bear, too, was a son of
Varela, and a prince was a prince. She ran her fingers
through her hair and moistened her lips and looked up
into his leaden eyes. Droplets of sweat clung to his
bearded cheeks, glistened in the folds and creases of his
flesh. Miranda swayed, her eyes closed, her lips parted
as she waited for his kiss.

Hector stuffed a forkful of sliced beef into the
woman's mouth. Miranda staggered away from the table,
gagging on the fatty meat to the delight of the revelers
and the complete hysterics of Andrés Varela. Varela
laughed so hard he fell out of his throne and landed on
his knees. His wine goblet crashed to the floor. An underling hurried to bring him another on a silver tray.
Varela drew a pistol from his belt and fired into the air.
The noise was deafening in the confines of the ballroom
and gained the attention of every guest. He placed the
revolver on the tray and hoisted his goblet in salute.

"To Hector, my son, who has as big an appetite for life as I." Andrés gulped his wine and slumped back in the chair.

As Miranda managed to cough the last of the meat out of her windpipe, Hector hoisted his silver tankard of *pulque* and acknowledged his father's compliment. He emptied the contents of the tankard in one long drink.

"Dance, my dear," Varela said. "Dance while the sun streams through the windows and the beauty of the day graces your every movement. Dance and then you can eat," Varela added with a chuckle. He gave the musicians near him a stern look of admonishment, but the guitarists were staring straight ahead. Sensing some new distraction, Varela wiped a hand over his features and peered unsteadily down the ballroom as Aurelio Bustamante and three of Varela's own militia led a man into the center of the room and up to the self-appointed governor of the sierras.

"Corporal Sancedo and his men caught him trying to sneak into Rosarito," Aurelio explained.

"I surrendered to them," Chapo Almendáriz announced.

"What is the difference?" a portly young soldier dressed in the tan-and-white uniform of the army asked.

"I would have killed you otherwise," Chapo explained.

Hector, Rafael, and Natividad closed in to stand on either side of their father. There was an aura of danger about this newcomer, an undefinable presence that reeked of deadly possibilities.

Chapo stood proud and erect, sweeping the room in a single glance. It was a broad spacious chamber jutting out to the side of the main hacienda. Massive hearths dominated two of the walls and housed blazing fires to warm the revelers. Smoke from oil lamps and cigarillos gathered in thick clouds and clung in an amber haze to the rafters. Silk banners streamed from the walls to the huge wooden chandeliers overhead. The tables were laden with slabs of beef and pork, tureens of peppery chili, platters of tortillas and roasted ears of corn.

The Varelistas, even in their drunkenness, looked to be a hard and wily lot, and far more capable than the soldiers Chapo had surrendered to only an hour ago. He recognized Varela, though Chapo had only been a boy when the vaqueros had come to claim his father's land and drive the Almendáriz family into hiding. Chapo suppressed his own revulsion and hatred for Varela. Determined to play out the ruse and win the general's trust, Chapo boldly approached the man on his throne. Varela watched the segundo's every move, noticing how Chapo seemed to study those around him.

Chapo discounted Rafael at a glance, then thought again. Here was a nervous yet prideful youth, a proud man who could be dangerous. Natividad was a fiery-looking beauty with just a hint of cruelty to harden her passionate expression. She seemed equally intrigued by Chapo. As for the huge bearded man who dwarfed those around him, even his own father, there was a man who exuded raw power and carried himself with dignity. Hector stood as immovable as granite, yet ready to spring into action if Chapo proved to be a troublemaker.

"I have come to collect what is due me," Chapo said, and reaching in his coat, he brought out the sack of scalps and tossed it toward Varela. Hector snatched the sack out of the air and Chapo noted the big man's quickness. "Ten dollars gold apiece or so I've heard," Chapo added.

Hector opened the sack and examined the contents

while the rest of the vaqueros crowded around, curious about the sack and what it held.

Hector provided the answer when he dumped the scalps out on the table in front of his father. Seven scalps in all, lengths of black hair sprouting from pads of dried flesh that once belonged to three men, a woman, and three children.

"You have had good hunting," Hector said, examining the scalps. "A lucky man. What is your name, señor?"

"I am called Chapo and I always have good hunting," Chapo said, hooking his thumbs in his gun belt as he strode up to the table.

Cpl. Sancedo stepped forward, carrying Chapo's Colt revolver, sawed-off shotgun, and Henry rifle, which the soldiers had confiscated earlier. Hector motioned for the corporal to leave the weapons on the table.

Andrés Varela reached over and inspected each firearm, his shrewd old visage revealing nothing of the inner workings of his mind. He examined the shotgun, saw it had been fired, the Henry too. "Where are the bodies?" he asked.

"I thought you only paid for the hair," Chapo said.

"A gun could be fired for a number of reasons. Where are the bodies?" Varela replied.

"In the bellies of vultures," Chapo answered peevishly. "I'll bring you the bones for another hundred dollars."

An audible gasp escaped from the corporal and the soldier quickly retreated from the table. He wanted no part of his general's wrath; no one spoke in such a disrespectful tone to Andrés Varela. But to the surprise of everyone in the room, the general merely eased back in his chair, folded his hands beneath his chin, and continued to study the man before him.

Chapo wore a coarsely woven cotton shirt, fleece-lined waistcoat, and wool pants tucked into knee-high leather boots that showed wear but were hardly down at heel. Varela could find no softness in the man. He glanced down at the scalps, then reached inside his coat for a leather pouch and removed seven gold pieces.

"*Señor*, I think you are a bandit. And I am pledged to protect my people and rid the mountains of bandits."

Chapo stiffened. He had ridden into a hornet's nest; now he was about to get stung. He readied himself, gauging the distance to the table. He would have to leap for his guns. He might be able to get off a shot . . .

"But I make you a bandit no longer," Varela continued. He added another three coins to the stack on the table. "So you ride for Andrés Varela. I think you will find honesty has its benefits." The general broke into laughter and those around him joined in. The irony wasn't lost on Chapo. They were all bandits here, but they were bandits in the service of law and order—Varela's law and Varela's order. Chapo walked up to the table and collected his money and weapons.

"I ride for you, *jefe*," Chapo said.

"Good! Good." Varela replied. He waved a hand toward his children. "This is Hector. The bear, my men call him. But he is my rock. And here is my youngest, Rafael. He hungers for power, my power, and one day perhaps he shall have it. If he is man enough." Varela turned to Natividad, who stared boldly at the newcomer. "And this is my daughter, Natividad. She needs a firm hand on the reins, she has much spirit. She is too wild, too wild."

"I like wild things," Chapo said, meeting Natividad's

hungry gaze. A hint of a smile touched the corners of her mouth.

Varela chuckled and watched them both and sighed. Natividad had a way with men. But she used them up. Andrés had need of men with Chapo's talents, men with courage enough to hunt the Apache and kill them. A man who could take seven scalps ought to be able to handle any of the men Anthem brought with him when he came.

"Know that my children speak for me. They are to be obeyed," Varela cautioned.

"Gladly," Chapo said, his eyes twinkled and never left Natividad's. Behind him, the guitarists began to play. The vaqueros returned to their places, the fiesta continued, and Miranda danced.

In the late afternoon, as the bordering mountains were draped in purple shadows, Chapo received his tour of the fortress that Varela called home. With the silver mines looming behind, the hacienda was set at the western end of a valley. The walled fortress dominated the valley and held the sprawling collection of cabins and business establishments of Rosarito hostage in its proximity.

Aurelio Bustamante led Chapo beneath the walls to the barracks where men took their siesta while their compatriots paced the walls. The compound boasted two nine-pounder cannons, one at the corner of the entrance wall. Chapo noticed the gate was open. He made no effort to hide his interest in the place. Curiosity would only be natural. He turned and faced the slope rising behind the hacienda.

"I have heard the mines of Varela were some of the richest in Mexico," Chapo said.

"Once, but no more. The seam played out," Aurelio said with a sigh. He wagged his silvery head and gazed at the mine openings dotting the mountainside. "All the good things end. Still they have their uses. You have heard of the gringo Varela took from across the border."

"There has been talk around the campfires," Chapo replied indifferently. "He has taken the son of some gringo *haciendado*, eh?" Chapo noticed how Aurelio's gaze seemed to fix on one cave in particular and filed it in his memory. "I am more interested in a cup of *pulque* and a plate of *frijoles* and beef than some damn gringo."

Chapo turned and started toward the horse he had left tethered by the barracks. He watched several Varelistas ride through the gate. They appeared to be leaving the fort for the night. Aurelio sensed Chapo's curiosity.

"Some of the men have wives in Rosarito," Busta-mante explained. "They have jacals in town." Varela's lieutenant gestured in the direction of the barracks. "Come. We will find you a bed with the rest of the men."

"No," Chapo said. "I will ride for Señor Varela, fight for him, and bleed for him if need be. But at night, here, I am my own man."

"I think you should stay here," Aurelio said, scratching at his goatee. "I like to keep an eye on all the new men we take on."

"Fine." Chapo nodded. "You do that, all day, tomorrow." He started toward the horse he had ridden in on, a sturdy little brown mare that wore no brand. Aurelio watched the younger man, then started after him and caught up to Chapo as he slid the Henry into his saddle boot and untethered his mount.

"You would be wise to heed my words," Aurelio said. "The people of Rosarito are a troublesome lot. They will rob you blind and put a knife in your ribs at the first opportunity." Aurelio sighed and shook his head in exasperation.

Chapo feigned surprise. "They threaten us, their benefactors and protectors?" he asked, incredulous. He slung his shotgun over his shoulder. "Whats has become of gratitude in this world?" He mounted and pulled back on the reins, guiding the mare past Aurelio, who retreated a few paces to watch as Chapo rode out of the fortress.

There was something familiar about this newcomer. It disturbed Aurelio not to be able to put his finger on it, but given time, he knew he could dredge a name or place up out of his mind.

Until then, this Chapo Almendáriz bore watching by day. And night. Aurelio glanced over to the front of the hacienda and saw Natividad standing in the doorway, her attention fixed on Chapo as he vanished through the gate.

Day and night, Señor Chapo, Aurelio repeated to himself. He grinned and formulated a plan.

Chapo walked his mount through the narrow streets of Rosarito, past cantinas and rowdy brothels, past shops and crudely lettered storefronts, and homes both humble and mirroring their owner's prosperity.

His stomach growled at the smell of fried beef and tortillas that permeated one alley, but he didn't stop. A couple of farmers lurched out of the shadows and paused to stare at him. A prostitute, standing naked in a lamplit doorway, tugged at the dark nest covering her crotch and called Chapo to her bed. He touched the brim of his sombrero and rode on, suffering a savage display of abusive remarks from the harlot as he continued on up the alley. He rounded the corner of a burned-out jacal and

reined in, taking a moment to consider his options. He
didn't remain there for long.

It was night now and a stone flew out of the blackness
to his right and bounced off his elbow. Chapo grimaced
in pain and dragged the shotgun, slung over his shoulder,
to bear on the ruins. A pack of children, wild as wolves,
burst from concealment and showered the segundo with
stones and broken bricks. Boys and girls clad in torn,
dirty garments attempted to surround the man on
horseback. A ten-year-old girl wielding a length of wood
as long as she was tall scampered up and cracked Chapo
over the shin.

Chapo dropped the hammers on his shotgun, yelped
as his youthful attacker hit him again, and did the only
thing he could do. The segundo spurred his horse and
ran like hell through a gauntlet of children, cleared the
last *enfant terrible* in a single bound and headed at a
gallop out of town.

With a silvery plume of moonlit dust settling in his
wake, Chapo walked his skittish mare up a gentle rise
to the town cemetery. Five worn crosses reflecting the
temporal nature of man were scattered over the hillock.
There were planks of wood as a flat-sided chunk of stone
marked an occasional gravesite.

Chapo tethered the mare to a cross made from sotol
roots and fed the mountain pony the last of the oats he
had brought from Luminaria. He unrolled his blankets,
ate a cold camp meal of corn dodgers and beef jerky,
and inspected his trail for anyone who might have followed him. When he was sure of his back trail, Chapo
returned to his camp, unsaddled the mare, and rubbed
the animal down. A half-hour later he was stretched out
on his bedroll, the shotgun and revolver lying within

easy reach, his saddle a makeshift pillow. He lifted his eyes to the caves dotting the mountain slope and thought of his last encounter with Billy.

John Anthem's son had learned to take a punch that day, Chapo thought, ruefully grinned. Memories of home and Big John's children seemed to just naturally gravitate to Rachel.

Chapo sighed and shook his head. He was too old for love, and especially too old for Rachel. Mother of God, what had he done? She had always been like a sister to him. But he'd certainly forgotten kinship on the night he had left. Chapo thought of her copper curls shining in the firelit cabin, her white slender body cradled in his arms. He knew instantly that he loved her—Rachel was a part of the mystery that was Luminaria, a part of the mystery that had become his only home. He rubbed a work-hardened hand over his dark handsome features and closed his eyes, handing his troubles over to the star-scattered sky.

He had found Varela. And Billy. So . . . first things first. Chapo was alone and the likes of Andrés and Hector Varela were no fools. Chapo remembered Aurelio as the man who had ridden in, to present Varela's terms to John Anthem. Now if Aurelio Bustamante had a good memory . . .

No, Chapo could not worry about Rachel, he could not worry about love. For now, there among the graves of Rosarito, in the stronghold of Varela's cutthroats, Chapo Almendáriz had only one concern.

Staying alive.

16

John Anthem didn't have to go to San Antonio. On a cold day in mid-November, San Antonio came to him. Ten days passed, and Rex Colby, at the head of a column of Texas Rangers, rode into Luminaria Canyon around noon on a Wednesday.

John Anthem heard the warning bells sound from the east rim as the rangers first trailed into view. He and Cole shoved away from the table just as Rose was filling their coffeecups. As the men hurried out of the house, Rose set the pot on the table near the platter of doughnuts she had just made. She walked to one of the unshuttered windows at the front of the house and waited to see who would arrive.

Father and son stood on the porch, waiting. John leaned on his cane; Cole stood ready, his rifle at hand. Across the yard, Prometheus stepped out of the back of the bunkhouse. The trail cook wore a flour-covered apron over his jeans and carried a revolver in one hand, a meat cleaver in the other. Several of the ranch hands had just ridden in for grub. Soon all five men, leather-tough and loyal to the brand, sauntered outside into the cold light to lounge against the walls of the bunkhouse.

Although the very picture of inactivity, each man held a Winchester.

"Rangers," John Anthem whispered, and then called out to his men in a much louder voice, "Rangers!" He waved the ranch hands back inside to their meals. Prometheus, the last to leave, looked almost regretful that there wasn't to be trouble.

"Captain Colby," Cole said. He cradled the Winchester '66 in the crook of his arm and shaded his eyes. "Who's that with him, a preacher?"

"Everett Cotter," John replied. "The adjutant general himself."

And more, Cole Anthem silently added, remembering the stories his father had told him. There had been bad blood between the Anthems and Cotters and blood shed between the familes. What had once been strong family-like ties between Everett and John had turned to hatred and jealousy, betrayal and revenge. Cole wondered if time had healed the wounds. This was the first time Everett Cotter had visited Luminaria.

Capt. Rex Colby led his men up from the tree-lined creek onto the road to the hacienda, which crowned a knoll between the steep walls of the canyon. The captain fished in his coat pocket for his pipe, brought it out, and clamped the stem between his lips. He cupped a match over the bowl and soon had the tobacco lit.

Cole noticed changes in Rex Colby. A patch over his left eye was the legacy of a gallant charge at Shiloh. The thinning gray hair could be attributed to age. He was a man of small stature like Cotter, but reedy and thin, not barrel-chested like the adjutant general. And the elderly Cotter had his hair, a thick white mane. As the men walked their horses into the yard, John strode down the steps and waved to the rangers. There were six men in all.

"Grub's on, boys," Anthem said. "Drop your reins and sit a spell. You are welcome here."

The rangers, most of them hardened veterans of the war between the states looked to their commander. Colby nodded and the men headed for the bunkhouse. As the ranger captain's security glance covered the barn and corral, he noticed there were a half-dozen rangy mustangs circling the inside of the oak fence.

"The boys have been saddle-breaking some mounts. I have to deliver thirty head over to Fort Davis by the end of the month," John said as Colby dismounted. Anthem stepped around the ranger's gelding and walked up to Everett Cotter. Time had worn none of the roughness out of the man, nor softened any of the edges. Cotter climbed down out of the saddle and patted the dust from his frock coat. John offered his hand in friendship and Cotter accepted it out of politeness, but there was no warmth in his handshake.

"It's been a long time," John said. He looked over at Colby, who made no effort to explain why the adjutant general of the state had traveled all the way to west Texas.

"Yes, a very long time," Cotter replied. Other than the extra wrinkles crisscrossing his features, the rancher-turned-politician looked much the same as he had twenty years ago—square-jawed, stubborn, and full of fight.

"My God, is that you Cole?" Capt. Colby exclaimed, heading toward the man on the porch. The ranger halted, glanced toward the family cemetery and then back to Cole.

The young man wore a gray wool shirt, faded blue jeans tucked into shotgun chaps. His boots were scuffed and the leather was scratched. Dust caked his clothes, the legacy of a bronc rider.

"Yep. I ain't dead, Captain," Cole said.

"Where you been, lad?" Colby approached with his hand extended.

"Around," Cole replied flatly, revealing as much as he intended. He stepped aside and allowed Colby onto the porch. Everett Cotter and John Anthem remained in the yard, coolly appraising each other.

"You are welcome here, Everett," John said. But Everett seemed to suddenly stare right through him. He turned and surveyed the canyon, the sunlight dappling the creek.

"We'll see," Cotter said. "We'll see."

"Bear sign!" Colby exclaimed as he espied the sugared doughnuts on the table. The ranger captain stuffed his now-extinguished pipe in his pocket and glanced at Rose, who greeted him and bade him enter her house and help himself.

Cotter paused in front of Rose, bowed slightly, and lifted her hand to his lips.

Rose, unable to hide her astonishment, stumbled through a "hello" and "welcome." "Papa Rett . . . I can't believe it's you."

"I can believe it's you," Everett said to the woman he had taken into his house as an orphaned girl and helped raise. "You haven't changed a bit, my dear." Cotter allowed Rose to bring him into the dining room.

Colby had wolfed down his first doughnut and was happily ducking his second into a mug of coffee when Cotter turned to him. The adjutant general cleared his throat, making a sharp unpleasant sound that commanded the ranger captain's attention.

"Before we take advantage of the Anthems' hospitality, perhaps you had better tell them why we have come," Cotter suggested sternly.

Colby looked around at his hosts and with great regret wiped crumbs and sugar from his mouth and set aside the half-eaten doughnut.

"Hell, I know why you're here," John said. "To ride with me when I go after Billy."

"Not exactly," Everett interjected, his voice silken, the very soul of civility. This was a new side to the man, and John's eyes narrowed as he suddenly sensed that he was in the presence of an enemy.

"You aren't crossing the border, John," Colby said.

John Anthem stared at the ranger, then shifted his gaze to Cotter, who maintained an air of professional detachment.

"What?" Rose asked from the doorway, unable to believe she had heard correctly.

"You are not going after your son," Cotter explained. "The governor is aware of your situation, but he insists you leave this matter up to the proper authorities." Everett cleared his throat again, picked up the coffeepot, filled a cup for himself, and lifted it to his lips.

Cole intercepted the adjutant's hand and returned the cup to the table, leaving the politician to stand embarrassed, his hand still raised.

"You are a rude young man," Cotter said.

"That's right. I am," Cole replied. "Rude enough to go after Billy."

"Cole . . ." John said.

His son acquiesced. Cole held up his hand, palm out, and started out of the room. "Rachel has a mare about to foal. Poke's with her. Maybe I can be of help there." Cole nodded to his mother and stormed from the hacienda, slamming the front door to punctuate his departure.

"What the hell's this, Colby?" Anthem turned to the ranger, knuckles whitening as he leaned forward on the oak surface of the table. His blue eyes flashed fire, he spoke in a voice that trembled with suppressed emotion. "Not go after my son? Captain Colby, the bastard Varela has my son."

"Look, John, this thing could explode in our faces," Colby said, looking again to Cotter for help. "We don't need an incident."

"The United States—and especially Texas—wish to show respect for the Mexican government," Cotter interrupted in a conciliatory tone that might have soothed in the Senate but not here in Luminaria. "Lerdo de Tejada is anxious to establish closer ties with Washington and of course the government in Austin. What better way to prove their sincerity, and the sincerity of Lerdo's administration than for him to arrange Billy's release and the punishment of those responsible?" Cotter folded his hands across his stomach and then hooked his thumbs in his vest pocket and smiled. "The whole thing is really cut and dried. You must admit, Johnny, it does make sense. The Mexicans have kicked out the French. Lerdo de Tejada needs to prove his administration is in control of the country."

Rose braced herself in the doorway, listening with openmouthed incredulity to Cotter's brief but startling explanation. It was something only a bureaucrat would think up. She put her hands in her apron pockets and circled the table until she stood at her husband's side. The hem of her paleblue cotton dress rustled with each step.

John put his arm around her shoulders, sensing she was about to explode in anger.

"Let me see if I have this right," Rose said. "It's in the best interest of our government that there is stability south of the border. Hence my Billy is to be sacrificed for someone's idea of a political ploy? Well, Mr. Cotter, you can go soak your head in the creek."

"Rose, look, we just have to give the Mexican authorities the opportunity to act," Capt. Colby spoke up. "I'm sorry, but that's the way it is. The word comes right from Austin." Colby propped a foot on the nearest chair and leaned an elbow on his knee. He tried to offer an apology, something to temper the situation. He didn't feel good about it. Surely John knew that.

"Well, take the word back to where you got it." John retorted angrily.

"No," Cotter interjected. "Captain Colby will keep his men in the area to see that the government's wishes are obeyed." The politician helped himself to the second cup of coffee now that Cole was no longer present to deny him.

The Anthems ignored him, their eyes on their old friend, Colby, who could not meet their gaze.

"I'm going after my son," John said.

"Don't make me have to stop you," the ranger responded sternly.

"And if John fails, I'll go," Rose said, her features as determined as her husband's.

John's grip tightened on her.

"Dammit," Colby blurted out. He slammed his fist on the tabletop, knocking a cup on its side and toppling the pile of doughnuts.

"Damn it to hell, but you Anthems are so bullheaded stubborn. You haven't heard a word I been saying." Colby wiped the crumbs from his mouth. "All right, don't make this any easier for me. You're a big man,

John Anthem, but not as big as the Texas Rangers. Try to cross the border and I'll place you under arrest." Colby brushed past the couple, tugged his hat down tight on his head, and headed for the front door. "Thanks for your hospitality," he added. "My men will make camp down by the creek." He touched the brim of his hat and left.

The ranger's departure seemed only to increase the tension in the room as the past came flooding in to fill the space left by his absence.

Everett Cotter sipped his coffee and smiled with satisfaction. "You always brewed excellent coffee, Rose, even as a young girl," the politician remarked. He carried his coffee into the living room and stood admiring the heavy hand-crafted furniture, the serape-covered walls, and the shelves displaying a collection of wood-fired pottery. "You have done well," Everett said.

John didn't reply. For all his forty-four years he felt a child again—the frightened, orphaned survivor of a massacre whom Everett had brought to his own ranch, and given a home. He had given Rose a home, too, and raised them both with Vin, Everett's own son.

But Everett Cotter's son had grown into a jealous, evil man . . . a man obsessed with Rose and driven to violence, until John Anthem put a stop to him.

Forever.

John Anthem followed Cotter into the living room slowly, so his limp was hardly noticeable, refusing to allow himself the slightest show of weakness before Cotter.

Rose was tempted to join her husband, yet she hesitated, knowing in her heart that this was a moment he must face alone. She moved quietly to the stairway and continued upstairs as unobtrusively as possible.

John Anthem was a towering presence alongside the politician. Yet power seemed concentrated in Everett Cotter.

"Where is my son?" said the adjutant general.

"Up on the hill beyond the house. In the family plot."

"Oh? An act borne of guilt."

"No," said John, "of pity." He gestured toward the hallway leading through the hacienda to the back door. "Come. I'll take you."

They walked to the graves, two men side by side in the afternoon.

John Anthem's heart was all turmoil, his confusion increasing with every step he took alongside Everett Cotter. Glancing over his shoulder, he saw the rangers file out of the bunkhouse and mount their horses, Capt. Colby in command once more.

"Don't make me fight you, old friend," John thought.

The rangers rode out of the yard at a clipped pace and on down to the tree-lined creek that undulated the length of the canyon.

Cotter reached the grave markers ahead of John. At the marker that held particular interest for him, the adjutant general removed his hat.

VIN COTTER

The cross had only a name, nothing else, no date of birth or death.

A cold wind ruffled the buffalo grass carpeting the canyon floor and climbed the hillside to harrass the men among the graves.

"Do you see how we are alike, Johnny?" Everett said. He ran a hand along the edge of the cross and received a splinter for his effort. He licked away the droplet of blood on the tip of his finger. "You drove your boy away from you like I drove mine. Isn't the similarity amusing?"

John Anthem stroked his stubbled chin and squinted at the afternoon sun, judging the time of day. He noticed a speck drifting against the cold cloudless heavens . . . a lone eagle in azure.

"Vin Cotter stole my horse and left me to die in Mexico. Only I didn't die. I escaped from Varela and came home to find your son had stolen the woman I loved by convincing her I was dead." John's eyes bore into the older man at his side. "I tried to walk away, because of you, Everett. But Vin wouldn't let me. He turned mean and vicious. He drove Rose out of your house, and when she came to me for safety, he tried to kill us both. He could not live in your image, but he tried, in his own warped way, and it destroyed him. And now you blame me?

"No. We are nothing alike, Everett. Because I know when I am wrong. And I intend to do something about it, just as soon as I bring Billy home."

Cotter knelt, using the cross to support himself. He grabbed a handful of dirt from the top of the burial place and held it up for John to see. "A man's child is his future," Cotter said. "This is all I have now. A handful of dust . . . God damn it but I wish to heaven I had left you in that burned-out wagon long ago."

"Let the dead bury the dead," John replied. After all, Cotter had rescued John and given him a home, and John owed the old man too much to want to hurt him.

Cotter stood and shook his head and sighed. "I tried to understand. I even blamed myself . . . for a while." He looked out over the valley and moistened his dry lips, his eyes taking on a dreamlike stare as if he were watching the past replayed before him. "I sold the ranch, I had to. Who was there to leave it to? But I invested wisely, made judicious loans to the right people and got myself elected to office. I have power now, real power, Johnny boy. And I shall use it to call in your debt to me."

John frowned, his mood darkening. Images of the past faded for him, memories dissolved along with gratitude and regret. And in their place came an instantaneous realization.

"It was you," John blurted out. "You put the rangers up to this! The governor is probably acting on your suggestion." John advanced on Cotter and pulled him up by the lapels of his frock coat. Dried, dead, brittle flowers crackled underfoot. "I'm right, aren't I? You want me to lose my son like you lost yours. It's all for revenge, for revenge!"

Cotter tore loose from John's grasp and stumbled out of the cemetery plot.

"Answer me, Cotter," John shouted.

Everett Cotter swung back toward Anthem. The adjutant general slowly, imperceptibly at first, nodded. He pointed at the cross bearing the name of what had been his only flesh and blood. "A son for a son," Cotter said, his tone bitter, yet triumphant. His hand trembled and dropped to his side. He turned and started back the way he had come, leaving a solitary man on the hill, and above, an eagle in the sky.

By firelight two men prepared for war. The lamps burned low behind tightly shuttered windows while within the hacienda John Anthem and Cole packed the last of their gear into saddlebags. They intended to travel light, carrying only a change of clothing, extra ammunition, and enough food to last them a couple of weeks if hunting proved too dangerous.

Big John holstered his Colt Dragoon and tucked another revolver among his clothes. Cole fed shells into his yellowboy. A Colt .44 rode high on his hip. Rose brought yet another packet of smokedbeef sandwiches wrapped in oilskin and shoved them into an already crowded leather bag.

"You can sling this around the pommel," she said defensively as John gave her a warning look. She was not supposed to load them down. "I know, you aren't going on a picnic, but it doesn't mean you have to starve," Rose pointedly explained.

Slouched in a chair near the fireplace, Poke Tyler sneezed, tried to clear his throat, and suffered a series of chest-racking coughs. When he finally caught his breath, he resumed the argument that had gained him absolutely nothing but a dry rasp for the better part of an hour.

"I ought to be goin' with you," the old man said in a raw voice.

"You wouldn't last a day's ride. And the grippe would probably turn to pneumonia by morning," John said. He glanced over at Rachel, who looked away sheepishly. "Bad enough my daughter drags you out of your sickbed to help with the foal. The last thing you needed was being in the damp barn."

"It were my idea, you stove-up bronc-buster! Anyway, with that limp you ain't exactly the picture of health," Poke grumbled. "Tell him, Rose. Talk sense, make him wait till he heals."

Rose looked from the old-timer by the fire to her husband. In her heart she dreaded John's decision to leave now. A growing fear gnawed at her soul: she had already lost one son, now she might lose the other and her husband. But the Anthems had not held on to Luminaria by surrendering to fear. She had seen the scars on her husband's back, the mark of Varela's whip in days long past. Now Varela had reached out to scar their lives once more. She stepped over the guns and saddlebags strewn around the floor, and took John's big rough hand in hers.

"I will wait until the first of the year, and then, winter or not, I will come after you," she said. "Poke knows the way."

"What about me?" Rachel said, standing, her voice full of defiance. "I can handle a gun as good as any of you."

"Better." John chuckled. He hugged Rose, held an arm out to Rachel, who hurried into his embrace.

Poke looked away, muttered an indecency, but dabbed at his eyes. He wondered if the family he had come to call his own would ever be together again. It galled him that he was too sick to go along. It was his right, he owed Varela too. The worst of it was, John made sense. Poke would only be in the way.

Cole stood off to one side, shifting uncomfortably. Here was the family he had abandoned in his pride, the family he had been too ashamed, or too wounded by the war to face. He had left as a boy; now he towered over his father. He had returned, a stranger, seeking to reclaim his past. Cole wanted to step into the circle of his family and even started forward, but he hesitated and the moment was lost.

John broke the embrace and gathered his saddlebags, his hickory cane, and a Henry rifle off the floor.

Rose leaned into her husband and kissed him on the cheek. They had made a more ardent farewell in the early evening hours while Cole tended the horses and

Rachel rode through the canyon issuing instructions to the vaqueros and ranch hands who rode for the brand.

John held his wife at arm's length, marveling at his good fortune that such a beautiful and resilient woman loved him and wanted to stand at his side.

"Yellow Rose," he said softly, and then looked over at the man warming himself by the fire. "I'll give Andrés Varela your regards, *amigo*."

"Don't be funny," Poke solemnly retorted. "The grave's for funny men. You kill the son of a bitch. Shoot him dead. That's what I give you my gun for."

John nodded, his own humor fading. He squeezed Rose's hand and patted Rachel on the cheek. "You two know what to do. But for heaven's sake, be careful."

"We won't gun anyone we don't have to," Rachel said, thumbs in her belt, her chest out. She looked every inch a tomboy now, the pretty young girl hidden behind a determination to prove herself.

Cole swung his saddlebag over his shoulder, gripped the carbine in his left hand. He folded the fleece-lined collar up to protect his neck, anticipating the bite of the cold night air. Rose and Rachel donned their wool-lined riding coats and followed John to the front door, extinguishing the oil lamps as they went so as not to outline themselves in the glow. Capt. Colby was bound to have posted a watch on the house.

Rose held back to walk beside Cole. "We've hardly been together," she said. "Now you're leaving again."

"Nothing lasts. Especially not the good times," Cole responded, a note of bitterness in his voice.

"You're wrong, Cole," Rose corrected. "They last forever." She placed her hand over her heart. "Here. In the love we keep, in the love we pass on, in the lives we live."

"Maybe if I had never run off," Cole thought aloud. "Hell, now I'm trying to change what's done. A man only knows what's in his possibles, everything else is just so much wasted time and suffering that doesn't amount to a damn thing. Like a fella who keeps bucking after the bronc is rode out."

"I love you, son," Rose whispered, stretching up on tiptoes to kiss him on the side of the neck. "Take care of yourself and don't let anything happen." She glanced ahead as John limped through the doorway and disappeared into the night. As she watched, her son held up the brass-plated carbine that seemed like an extension of the man. His features hardened, became strong and frightening in intensity, and she knew then there was no one better to ride with her husband. John Anthem was a rancher driven to fight, to become a manhunter. But Cole Tyler Anthem hunted men for a living. Violence was a way of life for him; he was a man who could kill without emotion, who walked a world of deadly trackers, of the hunters and hunted and survived.

In camp along the banks of Luminaria Creek, men huddled in exhausted sleep by crackling campfires. Everett Cotter, too, was curled in his blankets, but the old man knew no rest. He twisted and turned on his bedding of dry grass, his lips moving soundlessly.

First darkness, and in the void at last a face, pale and shimmering like gauze fluttering in a wind. Features disassembled, reunited, became recognizable at last. The face of Everett's son.

Father.

But Vin was dead. Of course, dead. And for all his misdeeds, he had been Everett's hope, his future, everything a man thinks of when miracles tremble and age robs sinews of strength and streaks youth with silvery hair and wrinkled countenance.

Father.

You brought it on yourself, boy. I tried to warn you.

Father. Avenge me.

Died on Anthem's land. Maybe at the hands of Johnny Anthem himself. I'll never know for sure.

Avenge me.

I will. I have to. My son, my only son.

The face came closer, the spirit widening the empty blackness of its mouth. Closer still as if to swallow Everett. Closer, and the ghostly lips engulfed the dreamer.

Everett gasped and bolted awake. He sat up sharply and winced, his back protesting such mistreatment. Cotter grimaced. Not as limber as I used to be, he reminded himself, and wiped the sweat from his forehead before he caught a chill.

A solitary figure hunched over the campfire, feeding mesquite wood to the flames. It was Rex Colby, his cheeks red from proximity to the fire. The captain sat back on his haunches and watched the flames feast on the branches. He helped himself to another cup of strong black coffee.

"I'll take some of that Mississippi mud," Cotter said, squatting down alongside the ranger.

Colby filled a cup and passed it to Cotter, who passed it from hand to hand, left to right to left until the enamel tin cup was cool enough to hold.

"Couldn't sleep," Cotter said. "Suspect that's pretty obvious, since I'm sitting here," he added with a shrug. He fidgeted with a button on his greatcoat and managed to fasten it after a couple of attempts. The ranger had wrapped a serape over his shoulders to break the night's cold grip. He glanced at the half-dozen snoring, sleeping souls circling the blaze.

"You post a guard?" Cotter asked, taking in the dark patches of foliage surrounding them. Clouds drifted across the moon, obscuring its sliver of light and leaving the surface of the creek an obsidian seam undulating out of shadow into shadow, its rippling surface barely revealed in the glow of the campfire fifty feet away.

"I am the guard," Colby sourly retorted. "Don't worry, Everett, you stick to politikin' and leave me to handle my job."

"Of course," the adjutant remarked with a reassuring smile. "We make a good team, Captain. I won't forget your scrupulous execution of duty, my friend."

Colby fingered the patch over his eye and cast a baleful look in the politician's direction. "Everett . . . we've known each other a hell of a long time, but that don't make us friends. Let's not start now." Colby gulped a mouthful of coffee, grimaced, and added a dollop of rye whiskey to the cup from an uncorked brown bottle at his side. "We ain't no team. If I got any friends, it's John Anthem. Trouble is, there's only one thing stronger than a handshake between friends, and that's the law." The captain tasted the contents of his cup and nodded. The blend of liquor and boiled grounds suited his taste.

Everett Cotter's disapproval was evident. He slapped the dust from his woolen trousers. It had been a long time since he had camped on the trail. Every muscle ached from the arduous ride out to these mountains. Well, he'd seen John Anthem and, in Cotter's own way, settled a score.

"Just so the law is stronger than the whiskey you're swilling," Cotter remarked offhandedly.

Capt. Rex Colby threw his cup aside and leapt to his feet.

Cotter fell back on the seat of his pants, caught off guard by the ranger's explosive response.

"Look, Mr. Cotter . . ." the ranger blurted out. But the phrase hung unfinished in the early-morning chill. Colby stared past the adjutant general at the woods behind them as eleven hard men emerged from the shadows and, led by Rose Anthem, stepped into the glow of the campfire. Every one of her men brandished a rifle or shotgun, and Rose leveled a Navy Colt at the two men by the fire.

Colby's jaw dropped in astonishment. Everett scrambled to his feet, saw what was happening, and reached for the derringer tucked in his vest pocket.

Rose fired a shot that blew away a chunk of dirt between the adjutant's boots. The gunshot sent Colby's already aroused command tumbling out of their blankets. Hands that reached for side arms as quickly fell away at the sight of Winchesters and scatterguns.

Cotter gingerly removed the derringer with thumb and forefinger and tossed it aside.

The vaqueros moved rapidly to gather all the weapons in camp, leaving the rangers to stand by their bedrolls, hands raised, sheepishly.

"Rose, what the hell do you think you're doing?" Colby exclaimed.

"Breaking the law," Everett said.

Rose wore an expression of mock offense. Her long hair was tied back by a scarlet bandanna. In her brown poncho and heavy wool skirt she looked more Apache than white. Her skin was dark from a life spent in the sun. Only the gold sheen of her hair gave her ancestry away. She certainly looked as dangerous as any Apache brave, Colby thought as Rose relived him of his gun belt.

"I'm just being sociable," she explained. "No law against that. You and your men will be our guests for a few days."

"Long enough for Big John to cross the Rio Grande," Colby finished. "Damn it all, guests nothing. You aim to hold us prisoners, Rose? The hell I say, saddle up men." Colby turned to his command. "I said saddle up! She'll have to shoot us to stop us." He faced Rose again, ignoring the Colt she held. "I know you, Rose Anthem. You talk bold, but you won't shoot."

"Of course I won't," Rose said, backing away to join the riders of Luminaria. "If you have no use for my hospitality, ride out whenever you like." She smiled, then turned to the men around her, men who rode for the brand and owed loyalty to John Anthem and his family. Rose waved and said aloud, *"Vámonos."*

Rose Anthem, the vaqueros, and ranch hands disappeared among the trees, making no attempt to conceal their departure as they broke a noisy path through the live oaks and cedar.

Cotter, his features livid with rage, turned on the captain. He shook his fists in Colby's face. "Mind your own business, you said. You were the guard, heaven, a goddamn child could have gotten the drop on you!"

"I was too damn busy listening to your palaver," Colby said. He shoved past the adjutant. "Hold that order, men." The rangers were already carrying saddles to their mounts; they paused and returned to camp.

"Now, what are you doing?" Cotter roared. "Anthem can't have that much of a head start. And it's two or three days to the border."

"I think we're staying here, boys," Colby said. "Looks like she's got us. This country isn't safe to travel in without guns." He noticed that his rangers, every one of them bearded and rough-hewn as new-cut timber, didn't seem too upset.

"A hundred-dollar bonus for every man who'll ride out now," Cotter said.

One of the rangers, a towheaded young man of nineteen, knelt on his bedroll and held up an empty holster. "What are we supposed to do if we catch the Anthems or run into a raiding party of Mescaleros . . . throw rocks at them?" The youth crawled into his blankets and rolled over on his side.

Another voice, this one gruffer, suggested that Cotter could probably make a speech to the raiding party. The six men chuckled.

"They'd scalp us and vote for Cotter," a third voice muttered, to his compatriots' amusement.

Cotter fumed and cursed, then flung his hands up in despair. He glanced at Colby, who had stretched out by the fire. "What are you doing, Captain? What in the name of Abraham and Moses do you intend?"

"I aim to sleep, Mr. Cotter, now that there ain't nobody to listen for. And come sunup, I reckon I'll wander up and eat me a passel of Rose's doughnuts I didn't get earlier today." Capt. Colby leaned back against his saddle, tilted his hat down over his eyes to block the glare of the fire, and allowed himself the luxury of trying to sleep. He thought of John Anthem and silently wished him Godspeed. Rose had certainly pulled a fast one, too. She'd beat the captain at his own game. Funny thing, Colby grinned, he didn't really mind at all.

17

Three men rode together in the dusk of new December, in the brittle cold that scoured the streets of Rosarito clean of stragglers and the lazy gatherings of crowds. No children darted among the horses and dared the retribution of the Varelistas, the merchants and farmers of the town hurried through the last of their transactions and sped on their way to home and hearth, however humble.

Chapo Almendáriz patted the dust from his nut-colored jacket. His knee-high boots were scuffed and scratched from the barb- and bramble-lined trails that crisscrossed the Sierra de Calavera. His horse, one of Varela's mounts, shivered and eyed the fortress up ahead with expectation, as the sight of home meant a rubdown and a bait of oats and sweet hay.

"Come with us," said Tomás, one of Chapo's *compadres*, a haughty, lecherous youth with a taste for bullying that belied his size. Tomás was rumored to be quick and deadly in a fight. The bandit jerked a thumb toward a cantina on his right. Its windows were shuttered against the cold wind, but the noises of celebration and good cheer drifted into the street.

"*Sí, amigo,*" the second man joined in. He was a short stocky cutthroat whose mottled features split in a broad grin, revealing a line of broken teeth. Esteban had lived the lonely life of a trapper and scalp-hunter before joining Andrés's militia. "Tomás here knows a girl who gives us much pleasure. She has Apache blood and never says no. Oh, she is a real tiger cat this one, eh, Tomás?"

Tomás nodded, tilted back his sombrero and chuckled. "We waste our time, Esteban. Anyway, I have heard none other than Natividad herself has sought our friend out. Sought but not found."

"Keep your breed woman," Chapo replied with a wave of his hand. "Maybe I have let the daughter of Varela suffer long enough; tonight I let her find me. *Adiós.*" Chapo spurred the horse beneath him, and the animal broke into a brisk trot toward the gate of the hacienda. Tomás and Esteban shouted farewell, walked their mounts across the wheel-rutted street, and climbed—bone-weary and tapped dry—down from their tired horses. They strode purposely into the cantina.

Once they were out of sight, Chapo changed his course in the darkness and rode quickly around the walls of the fortress. He angled out at a distance so as not to attract attention. In a matter of minutes he had reached the talus-strewn slope.

He dismounted near a cluster of dwarf piñon pines that seemed to be rooted in solid stone. Chapo stared up at the mountainside and judged the distance to the nearest cave mouth. He doubted it was the one. There were several mine shafts dotting the slope and Billy would have to be in one of them. The question was, which one? There was only one way to find out. He slapped the rump of his mount. The horse trotted back toward the fortress fifty yards away. It rounded the walls and a voice called out from above. Chapo imagined the men inside the fort would think the horse had simply wandered off from its hitching post in town and stranded one of their own in Rosarito. He doubted anyone would come looking.

Chapo Almendáriz worked his fingers and pulled his rawhide gloves tight. He slung his shotgun muzzle down across his back. The wind stirred the dust and brushed the clouds apart to reveal a half-moon suspended in space like a single silver tear. But the segundo had no time for poetic reflection. Precious minutes were slipping past and Chapo intended to find Billy Anthem. And escape with him if they could.

Andrés Varela paced the floor of his spacious bedroom. From time to time he paused by the fireplace and warmed himself before the blaze, impatiently retracing his steps anew across the tiled floor. He had discarded the affected dress of days before—the scarlet robes and turbans and other outrageous accoutrements taken from a French colonel during the war for independence, when the men of Varela had ridden with Juárez and brought down the French regime of Maximilian. Once these garments had been to his liking, a symbol of success.

Waiting had soured even that enjoyment. Now these same elegant bed clothes served to fuel the fire that warmed the general's buttocks. Despite his age, Varela looked much his old self, in burgundy breeches and waistcoat, his wooden right hand protruding from its lace-ruffled sleeve revealing its brand of vengeance in the polished wood. Varela tilted a crystal glass of brandy to his lips, drained the fiery contents, and doubled over in a savage spasm of coughing that all but brought him to his knees. The crystal shattered on the stoneware tile.

Hector, casting a huge shadow in the dimly lit room, rose from a wing-backed chair and hurried to his father's side. He draped an arm as sturdy as the trunk of an oak tree around Andrés' shoulders. The general tried to wave his bear of a son away, but Hector almost tenderly forced his father to bedside.

Varela continued to protest. "I'm not ill. Let me go. I have drunk too much, that's all. Take your hands away."

The general's efforts were no match for Hector's raw power. The big man easily maneuvered his father into bed despite Andrés' objections. Hector straightened and wiped the perspiration from his forehead. Andrés coughed and sighed, settling into the feather mattress. At last, the general closed his eyes.

"Does he sleep?" Aurelio spoke softly from the doorway. He stepped into the room and headed for the hearth. Varela's faithful lieutenant stopped to pick the shards of glass from the tile floor. "I was on my way to see him, heard the glass shatter and voices raised."

"He was drinking too much." Hector shrugged, joining the man by the fire. "Nothing more."

"He drinks to sleep," Aurelio said. The lieutenant stroked his silvery goatee and glanced around the room. Every article of furniture was the handiwork of an artisan, from end tables and thickly cushioned easy chairs to couches and cabinets of hand-blown crystal. A dozen golden goblets once destined for Napoleon III were arrayed across the mantel. A chest of silver ingots rested at the foot of the canopy bed. Andrés kept his treasures close at hand. It was rumored he slept with a Confederate-issue revolver, a nine-shot Le Mat, hidden beneath the sheets, and woe be to the man who laid hand to the silver or entered the general's room unbidden.

Aurelio had no reason to doubt such rumors, though he had been tempted from time to time to test them.

"Madness among riches," Aurelio said, a note of regret in his voice.

"Waiting breeds it," Hector gruffly replied. "We should have ridden in and killed Anthem and finished it off. You tree a panther, kill it, not tease the damn thing and wait for it to pounce."

Hector stretched, his immense physique swelling in proportion, strength, and power. He walked over to the wing-backed chair set well back from the fire. Hector Varela, because of his size, was usually too warm. He scratched at his hair-matted chest and tied his blousy shirt together again. He retrieved a brace of Colts from the end table, shoved them into the sash at his waist, and lifted a clay bottle of *pulque* in one of his pawlike hands.

"Come," Hector said.

"I must talk to Andrés. That new man, Almendáriz—something bothers me," Aurelio said.

"What has he done?"

"Nothing." Aurelio shrugged. "But I have seen him before."

"You are getting old, Aurelio. Everything worries you. Like an assayer in the city, you weigh all you touch." Hector grinned and gestured to the door. "A man who can kill Apaches can kill Texans, eh? We need more men like that one."

Aurelio hesitated and glanced toward the man in bed.

"Come, my father needs rest," Hector said sternly.

Aurelio colored, his hard eyes narrowing. Was he some underling to be spoken to, especially by this bastard son? They were all bastards—Hector, Rafael, Natividad—yet given power because Andrés Varela wanted to leave something of himself behind. Given power on the whim of a man suddenly faced with mortality.

"Come," Hector repeated.

Aurelio looked back at Varela, the past, then shrugged and followed the future out of the room. After they had left and the door swung quietly shut, Andrés Varela opened his eyes, reached under his pillow, and closed his hands around the Le Mat. He climbed out of bed and made his way around the room, extinguishing the lamps. He crossed to the window and, bathed in moonlight, looked out upon his valley. His gaze, benevolent now, drifted over the twinkling lights of Rosarito and beyond to the distant mountains.

A sense of achievement stirred in him. He nodded, as if all his domain had been arranged for his pleasure. He took what he wanted, gave when least expected. He had driven out the Apache and Yaqui tribes. Rosarito's farmers lived in peace. But the price of peace had been the loss of freedom.

He stared at the mountains and tried to picture John Anthem, making his way alone, cold and tired, filled with revenge.

Yes, let him be filled with revenge, let it eat at him like a cancer, let it gut his soul.

Andrés raised his wooden hand and placed it against the window. He stared at the word burned into wooden flesh. How much longer to wait? Soon, John Anthem, let it be soon.

Soon. Andrés' lips pulled back. Pain tore at his insides and he mouthed a silent scream. Soon. Soon. The window cracked beneath his hammering hand.

Madness among riches . . .

Serrated ridges against the night sky bordered a narrow
canyon choked with ocotillo, wild rose, and scrub oak.
Beneath a granite ledge a tiny flame flickered, a symbol
of life in the arid mountainscape. And by that tremulous
flame two men finished the last of their beans and jerked
beef and scrubbed their plates clean in the sand. The
aroma of strong black coffee drifted through the narrow
canyon. It was risky to have a fire, but with the temperature hovering near freezing, a little comfort outweighed
the danger of being spotted by any of Varela's outriders.

Big John Anthem stretched his boot heels to the fire
and leaned back against the stone wall. He stared up at
the smoke making its serpentine journey over the ledge
to be sucked away by the winter wind. Cole Anthem had
wandered away from the campfire and disappeared down
the slope to check on the horses tethered among the
scrub oaks. John Anthem listened—his trail-wise hearing followed Cole to the horses, heard him rummage
some extra feed for the horses, then traced him back up
the deer trail that led to the overhang. There came a
scrape of boot leather in loose shale and the sound of
cloth tearing as Cole discovered a bed of prickly pear,
a spiny plant whose oval pads dotted the mountainside.

Cole returned to the campfire nursing a torn knee, a
look of disgust on his face. He carried an armload of
firewood, which he deposited by the fire. He sat on his
bedroll and poured an extra cup of coffee for himself.

"You'd never make an Apache," John chided.

"I don't want to make an Apache," Cole retorted
sourly. He gulped the coffee, set the cup aside, and began to clean his yellowboy carbine. He ejected the shells,
wiped each bullet clean of sand, and arranged them on
the blanket. He worked the lever action and wiped the
inner mechanism free of grit. He proceeded in a me-

thodical way, like a surgeon performing his appointed
task, without a trace of emotion. His youthful face
seemed to age, growing hard as flint as he cleaned the
carbine. Suddenly, for a frightening instant, this man was
no longer John's son but a bounty-hunter, a man who
killed other men for the price on their head. His repu-
tation was as notorious as that of any gunfighter of the
time. John had heard of the man called Yellowboy. But
he had never guessed the manhunter whose name had
become part of folklore would turn out to be his own
flesh and blood.

"Cole?" John spoke, to try to break the transforma-
tion. The bounty-hunter glanced up from his work and
slowly, his harsh features softened. "Once we bring Billy
home, I'm hoping you'll stay on. Your mother and I . . .
Well, we figure what's past is past."

"For you, maybe." Cole chuckled. "But it's still a part
of me. It's what I am. I've been riding this trail a long
time." Cole fit the shells back into the carbine and inspected each bullet for anything that might jam the
weapon's spring-loaded chamber.

It wasn't only his deadly expertise with the carbine
that kept him alive, Cole realized. For years he hadn't
cared whether he lived or died. That was his edge. Here
in the high lonesome a man could think, a man could
see himself anew, clear and fresh and for what he was.
Cole looked at his father and remembered another mountain, another time when a boy of fourteen had killed his
first deer . . .

"I downed him with a single shot," Cole said
abruptly. "I was thirteen and the buck had come to drink
there in the canyon of Apache Lookout. I shot him
through the heart and washed my face in the blood and
thought that made me a man." Cole set the rifle aside

and waited for his father's reaction. He seemed to be carved of bedrock, solid as the land. And simple as nature itself, free of subterfuge and doubts. He was John Anthem—nothing else.

John crooked and straightened his sore leg. Though the bone was on the mend, it still pained the rancher. His cane lay within easy reach along with his holstered Dragoon Colt, a bowie knife, and Henry rifle. John had been a man of action all his life—action, not words. Yet here he sat, wanting to comfort his son, knowing only words would do.

"Wasn't the blood of that buck that marked you a man, wasn't even the damned war," John said, and laughed. "We're alike, you and I." John crawled to his feet, stood over his son, and patted Cole on the shoulder. Anthem's sun-browned face beamed with rough affection for his wayward son. "We both blooded late. You coming home to us when we needed you, Cole. And me . . ." John sighed and shook his head. "When I finally began to realize Billy had a right to follow his own star . . ."

John Anthem nudged a coal back into the campfire and turned from Cole's startled expression, retreating out of the circle of light to stand alone in the cold night. The mines of Varela were somewhere off to the west. It was difficult to remember exactly, to dredge from his memory the escape route he had ridden long ago.

He studied the harsh contours of the land. A swarm of bats rushed past overhead, a blur of black motion against the sky. The cry of a coyote lingered long on the wind, to be answered in echoes distant and mournful.

Somewhere in the night Billy waited, lost and dejected; somewhere Chapo was risking his life for Billy. Why? John lowered his head and tried to recall if he had given Chapo cause to think of himself as anything more than a hired hand. He was like another son to John and Rose; yet had they ever told him? John remembered the morning Rachel had revealed Chapo's absence and the purpose of his nightly departure. John's sense of concern and loss had been great. There was a lot to make up for, the rancher silently tallied with a shake of his head. Big John had only just begun.

"Pa?"

"Yeah." John glanced at his son, grateful his thoughts had been interrupted.

"How many men you reckon Varela has with him?"

"Who can say? Times change. Maybe twenty, maybe two hundred. One thing's for sure—they'll outnumber us."

"Have you got a plan?" Cole asked, settling down beneath his blankets.

"Sure. We'll ride in. Find Chapo wherever the hell he is, rescue Billy, and get the hell out."

"Good. I feel a lot better." Cole laughed. He reached out to make certain the Winchester carbine was within easy reach. The weapon offered a great deal of comfort here among the dark and lonely hills above the desert floor. He pulled the blankets up to his chin and closed his eyes. A few minutes later he was snoring.

The third cave was the charm. Once past the walls of the fort and the corner of the hacienda, Chapo angled over to the left until he was positioned directly behind the hacienda. He cut across a well-worn trail that wound its way up the mountainside and branched off toward the various mine openings where, years before, Varela had worked his prisoners. The first two mine shafts had proved barren and empty of life. But the third, now that

Chapo had scrambled up the remaining few yards, bore the faint emanations of lantern light.

Chapo stepped into the mine shaft. The stone ceiling rose about ten feet overhead and was braced with massive timbers that seemed to creak under the weight of the mountain as Chapo stepped quietly past. The segundo worked his numb fingers and stifled a sneeze, his limbs crying out for a warm fire and strong drink. And rest, plenty of rest. It was only a matter of time before Aurelio remembered him, or something else happened to give him away. Such were the premonitions of disaster that plagued him as he made his way into the heart of the mountain, through the angling course of the mine shaft.

The light grew brighter, and Chapo hurried despite himself and rounded a waist-high pile of rubble, entering a spacious chamber thirty feet across. At the rear of the chamber, in a natural cavern where stalactites hung from twenty feet above like stone icicles, an iron ring had been driven into stone. A heavy black iron chain was looped through the ring and tethered to the end of the chain was Billy Anthem.

His clothes were torn and filthy, his flesh was bruised and bore the mark of the lash. A serape served as an extra coat and blanket, but it was a pitiful excuse for either. He was hunched over a tin plate, hungrily finishing off the beans and tortillas that made his evening meal. He ate with his fingers, shoving food in his mouth like an animal. Gone was the dashing young son of John Anthem, first with the ladies, ever the gentleman. Though they had parted with animosity, Chapo's heart all but broke at the pathetic sight. He stepped into the chamber. Billy squatted at the end of his chain, about ten feet from the wall. He glimpsed movement and glanced up as Chapo stepped into the light.

Billy returned his attention to the food on his plate, scooped another mouthful to his lips, paused, and looked again. His jaw went slack and recognition warmed his bemused gaze. Suddenly his expression became one of alarm. Billy grabbed up his plate and lunged to his feet, hurling the plate at Chapo, who just managed to dart out of the way.

"What the hell?" Chapo said. He started to curse Billy by name, but the click of a hammer drawn back on a revolver diverted his attention. Natividad stepped out of the shadows to his left and leveled the gun at Chapo's midsection. The segundo realized Billy had quite possibly saved his life.

"What are you doing here?" she asked in a voice like that of a purring wildcat. The woman wore a coarse woolen riding skirt that accentuated her broad, rounded hips. A thick cotton blouse and fleece-lined coat hid her ample bosom. She wore a headband, like an Apache, a length of scarlet cloth that held back her long black hair. "I said—"

"I can hear, *querida*." Chapo grinned. He drew close to her until the muzzle of the woman's gun pressed against his chest. "I saw you carrying a plate up the trail and I wondered, What man does she go to? Who has won her heart? I must know. So I followed you. It was easy."

"I think you are a liar," Natividad hissed, in her own way enjoying the game. This was a bold one, all right, far different from the others who rode for her father.

"If that is the case, then there is only one thing you can do." Chapo brushed the barrel of the gun aside and lowered his lips to hers. "Better kill me, little wildcat. Before I get the drop on you and take your gun away."

"You think so, huh," Natividad replied, stepping out of his embrace. Her dark eyes mocked him even as the curve of her lips and the thrust of her shoulders offered invitation. "What would you have done if I had been with my lover instead of bringing food to such as this?"

Chapo's hand was a blur as it brushed across his holstered gun. He spun toward Billy, who flinched as the Colt appeared in Chapo's fist.

"No," Natividad blurted out, completely fooled by Chapo's intentions. "Kill him and my father will have your head. The gringo is for Andrés Varela to deal with." Natividad reached out and placed her hand on Chapo's extended arm. It lowered at her touch and holstered the gun. "You are *loco*," she said, arching an eyebrow as she returned her own gun to its holster.

"You are the only woman worth risking my head for in all the sierras," Chapo said.

"And beyond the mountains?" Natividad asked.

"There are others." Chapo shrugged.

Natividad's nostrils flared, her eyes glinted with fire, then she threw back her head and laughed aloud. "Come with me and maybe I will show you how wrong you are." She started out of the chamber, taking the lead. Chapo looked over his shoulder at Billy, who was standing now, looking thin and haggard. But not beaten. He stood defiant, and if Natividad had taken the time to notice, she would have seen his dull expression transformed. Hope burned in his eyes. Billy gave a slight wave of his hand, the chain rattled and he was lost from sight.

Brown limbs soft as doeskin, thighs the color of creamed coffee, drawing in his strength and his driving lust and the fire of passion into her womb. Full breasts the color of autumn leaves kneaded by his hands, covered by his kisses.

Natividad thrust against him, her nails raked his back, drew blood. She didn't care.

Chapo grimaced, drove against her with his fading strength, nearing his own peak but holding back. Images haunted him in the throes of this animalistic lust. Memories of a growing love that he might never know again, of Rachel coming to him in the night, no longer a girl, but a woman.

Lovemaking . . .

"Now," Natividad groaned. "Now." Her lips tightened. The muscles of her throat stood out in stark relief. Her ankles locked against his thighs, her black hair splayed out upon the silken pillowcase as she pressed into the pillow.

Both bodies trembled, forms entwined, feeding on each other's climax. Their union was a collision of energies, silent outcries, shuddering.

"Now," Natividad groaned, and eased her embrace, her legs straightening at last.

Chapo rolled off and lay alongside her in the bed, his exhaustion complete. He had gone to find and free Billy and wound up tumbling with one of his captors. There had been no other way. His lust was satiated, but his heart felt cold, his soul unclean. He couldn't will the feeling away.

Natividad chuckled at his side, propping herself on an elbow as she traced a line across his chest with a fingernail. The room smelled of rose water and musk. Beeswax candles burned at bedside on a table that held a tray of sweet breads and mulled wine. Despite the blaze in the fireplace, a chill crept up from the tile floor and cooled the sweat on Chapo's forehead.

"Aurelio does not trust you. He wanted me to keep an eye on you. He is a suspicious old man," Natividad said. Her fingers lowered to his belly, then cupped his manhood. "I don't think you will do any mischief as long as I have this. *¿Comprendes?*"

Chapo caught her by the hair and gave a sharp tug that pulled her onto her back. She yelped as he rose over her to settle between her legs. "I can be full of mischief. Maybe more than you can handle, *querida*."

"Show me," Natividad replied, and pulled him to her.

Lovemaking . . . No, thought Chapo. This was war. And Natividad didn't take prisoners.

18

Hector Varela finished the last of his rounds, riding through a miserably cold drizzle beneath a lowering gray sky. His brother and sister were at his side—not by choice, however. Andrés had insisted his three children ride to every outpost and lookout and judge for themselves whether the passes were adequately guarded. Natividad protested that she had better things to do than spend a couple of days and nights riding the wintry countryside.

"Yes, better things, and I can imagine with who," Hector said.

Rafael chuckled, then glanced quickly away when Natividad gave him an angry look.

"What I do is my own business." Natividad scowled, tying her serape in place with a loop of rawhide around her waist. Icy droplets of water rolled off the brim of her hat.

"You are foolish to be so close to a man you know nothing about," Hector cautioned. The moist air drowned out his voice as they walked their mounts through a narrow ravine that opened onto the mountain valley. The lights of Rosarito glimmered like ghostly amber blossoms in the diaphanous dusk.

"I know more about him than either of you," Natividad shouted merrily. She whipped her horse, raking its sides with her rowled spurs. The animal shouldered aside the two steeds and bore Natividad at a brisk gallop between her brothers.

"Natividad! You'll break your neck," Hector shouted. His admonition turned to a curse and he slapped the pommel of his saddle. He should have told her about Aurelio's misgivings, or better yet, simply ordered her . . . Ordered? *Madre mía*, and when had Natividad ever obeyed his orders? Easier to ask dry kindling not to burn, to tell the wind not to blow, to order rain not to fall beneath his collar and run down his back.

"She is going to him," Rafael said. "She has no pride, sleeping with some damn scalp-hunter." Hector's younger brother sniffed and dug his hand into his pocket for warmth. Despite his gloves, Rafael was certain his fingers were freezing.

What madness, to be out in such weather. Someday, perhaps soon, Rafael thought, I will never have to be ordered out again. Rafael glanced at his brother's massive silhouette and wondered if Hector was as weary and miserable as he.

Burrowing deeper into his coat and serape, Rafael ventured, "He's dying, Father is dying. Soon we shall be orphans, eh?" Then he brightened with an afterthought. "Or kings?"

Faces in the dark, silence, their two horses came to a halt on the hillside, at the crest of a slope broken by the trail to town, and Hector turned to face Rafael.

"You sound anxious, my little brother. Like the vulture who circles its prey, waiting to feast." Hector loomed over his brother.

Rafael shrugged. "He never calls me to his side. But I see enough. I see him in pain. I hear him when he cries out like one made *loco* with hurting and sickness." Rafael held up his hands in a gesture of innocence. "I do not think of myself, but of all of us. What will we do?"

"What generosity is this?" Hector exclaimed, his voice like rolling thunder. He shifted in the saddle, leather creaked, the horse started forward a step to be reined immediately. "Let me worry about Father," he said.

"Fine. *Gracias*," Rafael said, his anger rising. "My big brother shall see that Natividad and I are rewarded for all our work, maybe given our own special little troop of *soldados* to order around at your command! *¡Caramba!* I'm better off with the bastard alive."

Hector's right arm was a blur beneath his coat as, quickly, a Colt revolver appeared in his hand and he jammed the muzzle in his brother's side.

Rafael gasped at the force of the thrust that might have broken a rib were it not for the extra clothing that padded his thin frame. Even so, he doubled over and clung to the pommel of his saddle, gasping for breath.

"You will speak of our father with respect," Hector growled. "You would be nothing if it were not for Andrés Varela."

"I am nothing now," Rafael said as he eased away from the gun and rubbed his bruised side. " 'We are like dogs that jump to do his bidding."

"No, Rafael, you are wrong," Hector replied. He returned the revolver to the pocket of his bearskin coat. His horse pawed the moist ground, but the drizzle had subsided, moisture hung in the air without falling. Hector looked down at the valley, the town, the fortress. "We are his children. And children must be obedient to the father. Yes, he is sick, but not as sick as you think." Hector sighed, his breath clouded the air. "Andrés Varela is no god. He will die. And then will everything pass to us. If we are strong enough to hold it together, my ambitious brother, all this shall be ours." Hector indicated the mountains, the broad fertile valley, and all the lights, beckoning them.

"Come," Hector said, and started down the road to town.

Rafael held back, his hand ducking beneath his serape and woolen coat to the revolver holstered on his hip. He paused then, not for lack of courage. Hector Varela was no god either. A bullet in the back of the head would humble him. But he was Father's favorite, and Father was still alive. Rafael did not relish the idea of provoking the wrath of Andrés Varela. He brought his hand out of his coat and took up the reins, consoling himself with the knowledge that his day would come.

As Hector had said, Andrés would not live forever. Rafael smiled despite his discomfort. Fantasies of wealth and power warmed him on his way.

Natividad shouted for one of the soldiers in the courtyard to take her mount to the stable and give the animal a brisk rubdown. The soldier, a bad-tempered corporal who had been on his way to the barracks for supper, paused as if deciding whether or not to obey the woman. Natividad repeated her demand, this time with authority, and passed the reins to the soldier. He shrugged and reluctantly changed his direction. With a contemptuous toss of her long black hair the daughter of Varela bounded up the steps to the door of the hacienda.

Natividad turned into the hacienda and without thinking glanced to her side for a servant to take her coat. But Aurelio had dismissed all the servants with the onset of Andrés Varela's increasingly erratic behavior and worsening physical condition. He wanted to control the situation and keep rumors to a minimum. So Natividad found no one to take her coat, and she thought to herself that Aurelio needed to be put in his place. She just wasn't sure how. Recently she had begun to find his motives suspect and would not have put it past Bustamante to have designs on the power and wealth that by rights should soon fall to herself and her brothers.

The foyer was dimly lit by a feeble flame burning low in the tall glass oil lamp. Natividad shivered and started toward the stairs. She hoped a fire burned in her bedroom, but she knew better. Who would be there to prepare it?

"Come and have a brandy," a voice said from the stairway.

Natividad glanced up, startled. A shadow glided back into the hall. But she had recognized her father's voice. She climbed the stairs, gained the hallway, and found it empty. The door to her father's bedroom was open. Natividad reached down, removed the spurs from her riding boots, and continued down the hall to Varela's bedroom.

Andrés sat on the foot of his bed. He was dressed in faded long johns and boots and sat with his feet propped up on the box of silver ingots he kept there. A saber and scabbard dangled from a brass hook affixed to one of the bedposts, and Andrés nudged the tip of the scabbard with his toe and set the weapon swaying like a pendulum. He beckoned with his wooden hand, and Natividad entered the room. She removed her serape and the coat beneath. Her coarse cotton blouse clung to her breasts and her brown breeches molded to the shapely curve of her hips and thighs as she walked across the room to warm herself at fireside. She waited, hip cocked and thumbs hooked in the gunbelt circling her waist.

"I thought you were Aurelio, when I heard the front door open," Andrés said, his speech only slightly slurred. He had drunk enough that the pain in his belly was only a dull ache, yet not enough to render him unconscious. "Foolish Aurelio, still bothered by Almendáriz. Went into Rosarito to find out where he is staying and to find out where he goes. Aurelio, the worried rabbit . . ." Andrés lifted a glass of brandy in salute.

Natividad had also been doing a lot of thinking about Chapo, though not in the same way as Aurelio. She too wondered where he might keep himself during her absence. Maybe he was bedding one of the town harlots this very moment. She would cut the woman's heart out and make the bastard eat it if that were the case.

Andrés drained the last of the brandy and left his glass on the wooden chest. He walked over to Natividad, his gaze undressing her as he moved closer to the fireplace.

"You had a hard ride?" Andrés reached up and tenderly touched her thick black hair. "But everything was secure in the passes?"

"*Sí,*" Natividad replied, eyeing the man with suspicion.

"You have done well, Natividad," Andrés said. The smell of liquor was heavy on his breath. "One day it will be for you to rule this valley."

"You mean Hector," Natividad corrected.

"I mean whoever is strong enough to rule," Andrés said. He lowered his hand to her blouse. She brushed his hand aside. Varela frowned and tried to encircle her.

"No," Natividad sharply said. She retreated to the

center of the room; Andrés reached for her and missed.

"Stay here," he ordered. Then added gently, "It has been a long time for us. Be with me, tonight."

"No."

Andrés scowled, his mood turning ugly. "That was not your answer before."

"I was not asked then," Natividad snapped.

"I brought you into this house. I can cast you out," Andrés bellowed. The effort hurt him. He started coughing, then doubled over and clutched his abdomen. He staggered toward the bedside table where he kept a supply of brandy and other strong spirits as well as a tea brewed from cactus pods that helped him rest. He tried to fill a cup with brandy but could not manage the task by himself.

Natividad crossed to the table and poured a healthy measure of liquor into a stoneware cup. She added some of the medicinal tea to the contents of the cup and placed it in her father's hand.

"See, father, things have changed," she icily observed. "You need me as much as I need you."

Natividad left him at his bedside, a once-proud figure humbled by a racking cough and a pain knifing through his gut.

"Come back here," he called to her as the spasm subsided. "Natividad!" Her name echoed in the empty hacienda, his voice followed her down the darkened hall.

She quickened her pace, darting into her bedroom and closing the door behind her. Suddenly she gasped as arms embraced her and a mouth covered her lips.

Her room was warm from a fire cheerfully ablaze in the fireplace. Her bed was turned down and a platter of smoked meat and a loaf of bread had been set near her own bed. She struggled against the kiss, then softened as she realized the identity of the intruder. Natividad squirmed out of Chapo's arms.

"What are you doing here? Are you mad to come here before I returned? Father might have had you shot."

"By whom? He has sent away all the help." Chapo laughed. "You were expected tonight. I thought you would be cold and hungry. And since Aurelio kept following me in Rosarito, it seemed only appropriate I lose him and come here. You have been plaguing my thoughts, *mi amor*." Chapo leaned into her and nuzzled her neck and cheek. He did not bother mentioning that he had tried to visit Billy and found that Aurelio had tripled the guards around the cave. Chapo had resigned himself to the fact he would need Natividad's help to rescue Billy Anthem. Not that she would help him of her own free will. She would have no choice when the time came.

Natividad stared at him, then laughed aloud and pulled her shirt off over her head. Her mocha-colored breasts bobbed free. She held her arms out to him.

"You are mad," Natividad said, backing to her bed. She unfastened and dropped her gun belt and fumbled with the fastenings of her trousers.

Chapo, already half-naked, kicked out of his trousers and padded across a buffalo-hide rug to her bed. He pulled away the last of her clothes.

"Mad . . ." Natividad continued. "Or very brave. Which is it?"

"You tell me," Chapo said, and lowered himself atop her.

Andrés Varela paused outside the door to his daughter's room. He listened to hushed, feverish sounds of a man and woman joined in passion. Slowly, silently, he opened the door slightly. With the dark hall at his back, he remained invisible, but he saw what he needed to see. His features never changed, even as he watched. And recognized. He closed the bedroom door then and stood in the darkness, his left hand knotted into a fist.

The general closed his eyes, tried to remember the one of a dozen whores he had slept with who bore him this treacherous daughter. But faces of the past were specters of night to him, strange and ghostly silhouettes without identity. Andrés remembered only those who had caused him displeasure . . . those he had grown to hate . . . like John Anthem. Like this man, Almendáriz, and Natividad.

19

It was a mad game Chapo played. Perhaps it was his outlaw heritage that drove him to risk the animosity of Natividad's family. But the way he figured, a timid man had no business riding south of the border or joining Varela's militia. A timid man had no business bedding Varela's cruel, tempestuous daughter. He draped his gun belt over his shoulder, took up his shotgun, and crept from the room while Natividad slept.

His boot heels rapped a crisp cadence as he descended the stair, pausing at the bottom step to inhale the fragrance of coffee wafting in from the back of the house. It was early, almost six o'clock, and the eastern horizon had yet to wear the sun's first wintry blush. But someone was astir.

Chapo rubbed his empty stomach, straightened his coat, and running a hand through his black hair, decided to test his luck. The price of breakfast might be a bullet between the eyes. Then again, he might carve a niche for himself at the table.

Chapo was perceptive enough to sense that the structure of power ruling these mountains had grown brittle over the years. Now that the mines had played out, some of the more law-abiding inhabitants of Rosarito were anxious to be rid of Varela's "protection," finding his militia to be more trouble than the occasional Apache foray.

Stealing into the hacienda had been no problem. Chapo had considered trying to take Varela hostage, but the man was half-mad from illness and drink and therefore too unpredictable.

Varela's hacienda was certainly more spacious than Luminaria. Broad airy rooms, almost impossible to keep warm, opened onto one another. The walls were hung with the portraits of some noble lineage that bore no resemblance to Andrés (he had probably stolen them), the rooms filled with mahogany and walnut tables, armoires, china cabinets, japanned chairs, cabinets, thickly woven rugs, and porcelainware wrought with tender artistry by Parisian hands.

Chapo saw in these rooms a man desperate for the legitimacy of a noble heritage, something to possess, to mark his entrance into the passage from a world that all too soon forgets its common children. As he pitied Varela, Chapo's respect for John Anthem grew. Somewhere on the trail north rode a man to whom the word *prestige* was as useful as a tick, a hard man, but fair and easy to respect. John Anthem rode his land, worked his cattle, ate dust, and froze in winter alongside his vaqueros. And he asked no man to ride a trail that John himself wouldn't travel. Andrés Varela and John Anthem had founded their own private empires, but there any resemblance ended.

A winter kitchen dominated the rear of the hacienda. A plump, comely woman, dark as a Yaqui, middle-aged and oblivious to Chapo's entrance, was busy trimming the excess dough from around the edges of a meat pie.

She worked at one end of a broad wooden table, its
surface crowded with the tools of her trade. At another
table, Hector Varela leaned on his elbows, his head lowered over a stoneware mug of steaming coffee.

He glanced up, his red-rimmed eyes burning and
guarded. He sneezed, and a geyser of scalding brew
emptied from the mug and splashed his thickly bearded
jowls. Hector cursed and wiped a meaty forearm over
his features.

"Son of a bitch," Hector growled, and coughed. His
lungs were congested, his head felt as if there were an
avalanche loose in his skull. He looked at Chapo. "The
coffee, not you."

Chapo nodded, nonchalantly, dropped his gun belt
and shotgun on the table, and reached over to fill a cup
for himself. A platter of meat sat in the center of the
table. Chapo lost no time in filling a flour tortilla with
the stringy meat. A calf's head had been smoked over-
night and then stripped clean and piled high on a china
serving plate.

"Come to think of it, I think you're a son of a bitch,
too," Hector continued. He lowered his face again and
tried to breathe in the steam. A circle of oil lamps burned
overhead; the cook fire warmed the room slightly and
added to the illumination. Chapo started to eat. He
couldn't think of anything to say. He hoped the big man
sitting across the table mistook silence for unabashed
courage. Chapo didn't relish the idea of a confrontation.

"The damn place is too empty," Hector complained.
"If it weren't for Constancia we'd have to eat our own
cooking."

The big man turned his head from the cup and
sneezed again, this time a great bellow that filled the
room like a gunshot. Constancia glanced over and then

as quickly returned her attention to the pots and skillets hanging from a rack near the hearth. She choose a skillet suitable for searing several cuts of meat at one time and brought it over to the table closest to her. There she set to with cleaver and knife, chopping onions and spicy red peppers and carving freshly butchered beef into bloody cubes.

"Aurelio doesn't trust you," Hector said. "You trouble him, but he can't figure why."

"That is his problem, no?" Chapo said around a mouthful of meat. He sopped the juices with the tortilla and shrugged. "You want me to ride out of Rosarito, say so, I go," he added matter-of-factly.

Hector unfolded a bandanna, blew his nose, rolled the cloth back up, and tucked it inside his woolen coat. He wore a ruffled cotton shirt and brocaded vest beneath his coat, and his trousers strained to contain his huge thighs. He rose from the ladder-backed chair and it creaked with relief from the easing of his great weight. He leaned across the table, his fists knuckledown on the wood surface.

"Stay," Hector said in a hushed, heavy tone. And he brought his bearlike visage close to Chapo's face. "Stay. I like knowing where you are, *amigo*." The big man eased back into his chair. "I know why a man like you rode in when you did."

"Oh?" Chapo nonchalantly replied. Underneath the table, his hand stole toward a throwing knife secreted in the top of his right boot.

"A panther lies wounded, dying; only then does the coyote challenge his domain, eh?" Hector laughed bitterly. "But the panther has three cubs with teeth and claws. Three cubs only, and no more." The big man's eyes narrowed to slits. "What I'm trying to say is you came too late, *amigo*, to carve another piece of this pie. It only cuts three ways."

"Or maybe only one?" Chapo suggested. He finished the last of his coffee and studied Hector's reaction, an arching of eyebrows that seemed to indicate Hector might be thinking of just such an arrangement. Chapo doubted any sense of loyalty existed among Varela's children. If Andrés Varela died, Chapo guessed only the strongest would survive—Hector to be sure, and possibly Natividad. More sobering was the uncertain future Andrés Varela's demise would spell for Billy Anthem. The general's death might result in Billy's.

None of the Varela heirs had use for their hostage and would have killed him long ago, were it not for their father's instructions to keep John's son alive.

Andrés was enjoying his revenge and wanted to prolong it indefinitely, or so Natividad had revealed, lying in Chapo's arms, warm and satiated from lovemaking.

Chapo stood and gathered his weapons, the shotgun, his gun belt, and holstered Colt.

"Tell Aurelio I've gone to the stable to check on my horse. I think it threw a shoe the other night in town. The old one won't have to hide in the shadows as he follows me. And I shall build a fire so the old one can warm his bones." Chapo started out.

"I'll tell him," Hector conceded. He liked the man's bravado, whether or not it was misplaced. This "wild pony of the barrancas" still had much spirit and could be useful in a fight. Of course that depended which side he was on. "*Amigo*, I am no Apache. Do not make the mistake of trying to lift my hair."

Chapo turned in the doorway and faced the big man.

"I won't make any mistakes," Chapo said in a voice

as even and warm as the warning of a coiled rattler, a warning that Hector, in his misery, failed to heed.

"What is a man but jealousy and unspent rage? As for a king . . . a king can hate better than most. And I am a king, though a monarch without a crown," Varela declared.

Aurelio listened and stood before the east window, thinking how Andrés ruled the Sierra de Calavera without divine right—brute force had placed him on his "throne." A gun was his scepter of authority. And if time had left his power brittle, still he clung to it with all his strength. Power was survival. Power was the force that fed Varela's veins and kept him alive in his pain. Vengeance was one aspect of his power, like lightning to a storm. His rage was as inevitable as lightning.

Andrés Varela had waited at his window and kept this vigil until Chapo appeared in the courtyard. Then the general sent Constancia to summon Aurelio to the hacienda.

"I want Almendáriz killed," Varela said.

Aurelio spun around where he stood bathed in the golden beams of sunrise streaming through the east window. The old lieutenant rubbed a hand across his tired leathery features. He had been up most of the night seeking, and not finding, Chapo Almendáriz. Failure displeased him mightily, but his foul mood had only worsened at the sight of Chapo leaving the hacienda. The man had spent the night under this very roof, no doubt in better quarters than Aurelio kept for himself.

"What did you say, *jefe?*" Aurelio asked. He looked in open disbelief at Varela who sat propped up in his bed, a breakfast table across his outstretched legs.

"I said kill him. You wanted to be rid of him, no?" Varela repeated impatiently.

"I'll send guards to the stable and have him brought into the courtyard to be executed."

"No." Varela sipped coffee from an ivory-colored cup. He set the cup down and nibbled on a piece of bacon, his expression that of a man lost in thought. "It must be done away from here," he added. "Some of the men might misunderstand . . ." Varela did not want Natividad to know. He was also aware of the unrest that threatened his sovereignty over this mountain domain. Men now loyal to him might believe his hold was weakening and begin to question his judgment. Better to have as few men as possible involved. "You will ride with Chapo on patrol . . . say, as far as Jesse's cantina up in east pass. Kill him. Blame it on Apaches or old Jesse. I don't care. Just do this for me, Aurelio, *comprendes*?"

Aurelio Bustamante stroked his silvery goatee as his mind struggled with a plan. An *hombre* like Chapo was too dangerous to take on by himself.

"I may need help . . ." Aurelio pondered the matter and came up with a couple of names. Tomás and Esteban. They were good men, loyal to the general and the wages he paid. And they had ridden with Chapo before, so he probably wouldn't suspect them of mischief. "Two men," Aurelio said. "And a hundred dollars in gold or silver."

"To buy their courage," Varela contemptuously sneered.

"No, *jefe*. Their silence," Aurelio explained.

Varela shoved the tray aside and climbed out of bed. He padded naked to the trunk at its foot. He unfastened a pair of straps and raised the lid, but before Aurelio could glimpse the contents, he had closed the chest and fastened it shut. He handed Aurelio a small rawhide pouch, its contents jingling as he passed it to his faithful lieutenant.

"Count out a hundred dollars and keep the rest for yourself," Varela said. He shivered, his flesh stretched tautly over bony limbs. His ribs showed with every breath. There was a faint, sickish-sweet odor about him, the smell of decadence and decay. Gray hairs covered his thin chest, a scruf of the same covered his groin.

"We will ride out tomorrow morning," Aurelio said.

"No, this afternoon," Varela said. He clapped Aurelio on the shoulder and walked him to the door.

Bustamente knew better than to ask what had changed the general's mind about Chapo.

Constancia, the housekeeper and cook was waiting in the hall; she stepped dutifully aside for Aurelio, then entered the bedroom. The rotund woman appeared to take no notice of Andrés Varela. She crossed to his bed and began clearing away the remains of breakfast.

Varela walked barefoot to the fireplace and warmed himself before the flames. He ran his left hand over his bony chest and flattened stomach. This morning there was no pain. This morning he felt like a man, immortal, the center of the world.

He lowered his hand and stroked himself erect. Andrés slowly turned. The Yaqui pulled her blouse over her head and stepped out of the billowing folds of her skirt. Watery rolls of fat rippled as she crawled into bed and awaited his pleasure.

Andrés Varela rubbed his backside for a moment, rev-

eling in the warmth of the fire. When he felt adequately
prepared to cross the cold floor, he sauntered to his bed
and gazed with satisfaction at the banquet of dark flesh
opening to him.

20

Hector Varela had been drinking, but the fact that his belly rumbled with tequila and the spicy beans and beef Constancia had prepared for the afternoon dinner did not dissuade the big man from making his rounds. Normally the winding path to the cave held little challenge, even for a man of such impressive girth. Today, however, Hector's cheeks reddened with the effort and his breath in the cold air rushed from his lips like steam from a locomotive.

The sentry, a man named Miguel, seemed surprised to see Hector and snapped to attention, his carbine cradled in the crook of his arm. He hoped Hector had not noticed how the sentry had been dozing by a fire near the mouth of the mine shaft.

"Buenas," Miguel said with false enthusiasm. Hector's mood looked as somber as the line of clouds darkening the northern horizon. "I was expecting Aurelio or maybe your sister, Natividad. Those two have taken personal charge of the prisoner."

"Aurelio rode out at noon," Hector explained. "And as for Natividad. Who can find that one? I saw her this morning. Now she is gone, and the devil take her!" Hector shouldered past the guard and entered the mine. His boots echoed on the stone floor as he followed a corridor, pier-and-beam-defined passages, massive timbers set in place more than twenty years before and built to last. Unfortunately, the silver hadn't. And now we are reduced to banditry and kidnapping, Hector thought with a sigh. He liked none of it. Revenge was a fool's game. When he assumed Andrés' place, things would be different. First reestablish favorable relations with President Lerdo de Tejada. Then apply for a governorship. Now, there was a path that led to far more power and wealth than any fool vein of sliver.

Hector rounded a well-braced wall and stepped over the pile of rubble to follow twin lines of iron rail into a broad open chamber. There in a cell Billy Anthem lay on his side, curled beneath his ragged blankets on a bed of hay.

Hector paused, reached beneath his coat for a packet of sandwiches and a tin of warm coffee. He sniffed the stale musty air. Damn if he intended to empty any slop buckets, leave that task for Miguel.

Oil lamps set in pick-scarred walls cast their fluttering amber glow to rouse garish shadows. Years ago, Varela's forced laborers had tunneled through the rear of this natural cavern to a seam of ore running several yards into the mountain. But it had been a false lead and one soon abandoned.

Hector glanced toward the black maw of the tunnel blasted out of bedrock at the rear of the chamber. He shivered despite himself, for he dreaded those stygian corridors that ran through the bowels of the earth. This prison chamber marked the limit of his venture into this or any of the other mine shafts that were the legacy of earlier, more prosperous times.

Billy rolled over in his blankets and studied his visitor. His earlier elation at the sight of Chapo had long since faded, become a dull aching hope. Of all the people who might have come after him, Billy had never expected Chapo. But the segundo had not returned and Billy could only wonder whether Chapo had been discovered and murdered or was still planning some escape. He had simply resolved to be ready when the time came.

"I don't suppose it's chuck steak tonight," Billy said, scratching at the months-old scraggly blond beard that aged his features. "The gravy last night was a bit on the lumpy side. Let me out of here and I'll show the chef how to make it right."

Hector nodded and passed the sandwiches and coffee through the iron bars of the cell.

"Be grateful I am not Natividad. She would throw your food in the slops," the big man replied.

"Oh, I am," Billy said, and a spasm of chestracking coughs doubled him over, leaving him gasping for air.

Hector glanced at the straw at the back of the cell. The mound was smaller. A depression in its center served as mattress and insulation from the cold. "I will see Miguel brings you fresh straw."

Billy stooped down and retrieved the sandwiches. He gulped the warm coffee with obvious relish. "Be careful, your father will consider such kindness a sign of weakness."

"I do not want you here. You will bring us much trouble. Still, by my father's wish you shall live. But my father is dying. Soon you will answer not to vengeance, but necessity."

"Maybe we will both answer! I for the blind pride that drove me from my father and you for the foul murder of a defenseless girl." Billy's eyes locked with Hector's and there flowed an understanding between them.

Hector rubbed a hand beneath his chin and his gaze narrowed. He did not like the prisoner's tone of voice. It was strange. Why wasn't he broken yet? Any other man would be crawling for mercy after being kept in such a bitterly cold cell, with little water or food, with nothing but ragged blankets and straw for comfort.

"What do you know?" Hector muttered, studying the youth. "Have you dreamed of escape for so long you actually think it is coming to pass. Señor Anthem, your time is like dust in the wind. How you say, fleeting, eh? There is no escape."

Billy hurried back to the warmth of his straw, clutching his sandwiches to his chest. Hector turned and started back the way he had come. He had rounded the corner and entered the passage leading outside when the sound of Billy's voice echoed in the dark. The young man was laughing. Not loudly—no, more horrible: a soft low laughing that reverberated eerily down the corridor. Hector blessed himself with the sign of the cross and quickened his pace, anxious to put as much distance as possible between himself and the laughter in the dark.

Tomás fingered the pleasant bulge of coins in his coat pocket, thinking of all the bad women and good liquor his money would buy. Esteban squatted off to the side, scraped out a depression in the hard-packed earth, filled it with kindling, and started a fire. He performed his task out of habit, with the expertise of a man bred in the wild. It gave his hands something to do while he plotted Chapo's murder.

Chapo led the horses down to a shallow spring for a drink. Aurelio had kept the man company part of the way down the path but had returned to campsite under pretense of having a bad knee.

Tomás watched Aurelio's return, interested in the deed at hand. He wandered over to Esteban's side. "We kill him now?" he said aloud.

"Be quiet, you fool. He'll hear you," Aurelio cautioned.

"And what if he does?" Tomás sneered.

"He'll charge up that path," Esteban replied by the fire, "and blow your head clean off, *compadre*. What brains you have will be dog smear, eh?"

Aurelio nodded. "We made a plan, let's stick to it. We'll let him ride ahead up to Jesse's cantina and kill him there."

"While his mind is on a bottle of tequila and a warm fire," Esteban concluded. Esteban added more wood and held out his hands to the blaze. "Snow coming. I can feel it."

Aurelio glanced around at the mountainscape of ridges and bleak granite summits where the wind howled and Apache spirit demons could be heard wailing for the blood of intruders. These were sacred mountains once, Apache holy men came here to offer sacrifice and sing their prayer songs. There had been other tribes as well, cliff dwellers whose origins lay shrouded in the mists of time. Only the ruins of their dwelling places remained providing shelter for the wayfarer and wandering tribe.

Stars glittered overhead, but to the north their brilliance dimmed, obscured by an ever-widening onslaught of clouds, the vanguard of an oncoming storm. It promised to be a long uncomfortable journey to Jesse's cantina. Aurelio thought to himself, and he considered anew the idea of ambushing Chapo as he started up the trail. Do it and return to Rosarito before snowfall. But then everyone would know that Bustamante and Tomás and Esteban were responsible, and not Jesse. And that might lead to problems, and Andrés did not want problems.

Even as the lieutenant wrestled with his problem, his attention was suddenly diverted by Esteban, who reached for his breechloader and knelt by his saddle. His eyes were riveted on the trail they had ridden up barely an hour ago. Aurelio started to ask what the matter was, then heard the unmistakable sound of an approaching horse.

A revolver appeared in Tomás' hand as a horse and rider took shape in the pass. Aurelio dropped a hand to his gun butt and his body tensed, poised to spring into action. But apprehension turned to openmouthed amazement as Natividad Varela rode into the circle of light cast by the campfire.

She noticed with amusement the looks on the faces of the men and, swinging her firmly rounded hips down from the saddle, leapt lightly to the ground. She led her winded mare up to the fire.

"I was hoping for coffee. And I am hungry, but don't worry, Aurelio, I'll eat whatever you are having." She tilted her hat back on her forehead and looked around for Chapo.

"What are you doing here?" Aurelio gasped. "You have no business . . . Did your father send you?"

"I am not a child anymore. Or haven't you noticed?" She gestured to the other two men, who gazed appreciatively at the way her trousers clung to her hips and thighs. "*They* have." She laughed lustily. "Where is Chapo?"

"Watering the horses," Esteban replied. He set his rifle aside and began to rummage in his knapsack for flour and coffee.

Aurelio glanced at Esteban, then returned his attention to the girl and shook his head. "It is wrong what you do, *chiquita.* You cannot go with us. Stay the night, but tomorrow—"

"Tomorrow I will do what I want to," Natividad snapped. "Just like yesterday and today." She spun on her heels, her long black hair whipping across Aurelio's face. She had made camp here before and knew the way to the spring nestled among the rocks in the gully below. Her boot heels ground in the gravel, crushed a cactus pod, and telegraphed her progress as she vanished among the shadows of night.

Aurelio watched her leave. He smacked a fist into the palm of his hand and growled a curse.

"Now, what in hell do we do?" Esteban asked.

Tomás chuckled. "Maybe we ought to sneak on down there and shoot him while she's lickin' his ear."

"Shut up," Aurelio said. "You'll do what you have been paid to do. Tomorrow when we reach the cantina, Chapo Almendáriz dies."

"The girl won't like that," Esteban mentioned.

"That's too damn bad," Aurelio said.

"Maybe I could give her something else to think about on the ride back," Tomás added, and cupped his crotch. He stared enviously at the path stretching into the dark, speculating as to what the man and woman were doing down in the gully.

"You know, that Chapo, he is one lucky bastard," Tomás said. He knelt and began to unroll his blankets.

"Not so lucky, *amigo,*" Esteban reminded him. He was slicing thick slabs of bacon and looked up, knife in hand. Pointing toward the darkness with the blade, he ran the knife across his throat an inch from flesh.

Tomás nodded, understanding.

Esteban continued to slice the bacon, the razorsharp blade sawing smoothly through fat and flesh.

Chapo watched the horses toss their manes and dip their muzzles into the frigid pool as he kicked through the ice. He spoke softly to the animals in smooth and gentle tones that calmed the skittish beast. He enjoyed his solitude. It gave him time to think. He was suspicious of the way Aurelio had collared him for patrol. It was far more important that he remain in Rosarito with Natividad. She was the key to Billy's freedom. Chapo needed an ally in this den of enemies, and what better person than Varela's own daughter, who had easy access to the prisoner in the mine?

He loathed the Varelistas and all they stood for. Such men had terrorized his own village, murdered his mother, and driven his father into a life of banditry. Not that Andrés Varela or any of his lieutenants would remember the deed. But two names were etched in Chapo's memory: Andrés Varela and Aurelio Bustamante. In those earlier days they had ranged the mountains with their wolf pack, preying on the weak and unwary, robbing and kidnapping men to work in the mines.

Chapo rubbed a gloved hand across his features as if the gesture would free him from the tragedies of the past, free his memories of hurt as well. He could expect no miracle, though. But he thought of life at Luminaria, of hard work in the company of a man who was his second father, Big John Anthem. There was someone who judged men by their actions, not their color. He was fiery-tempered and stubborn as a mule, but a man to ride with in this harsh and violent land. Chapo hoped the same could be said of himself. He thought again of Rachel, missing her sweet beauty, the innocence of her touch. How far from Luminaria's warm embrace he had traveled! He wanted to think of himself as a man of honor and yet wondered just how much honor he would have left by the time his role-playing was ended.

He heard someone on the slope behind him and turned as Natividad led her horse through the weeds and cholla lining the dry wash. She headed for a cluster of scrub oaks by the spring, sensing Chapo's nearness.

Chapo recognized her. He fished a cigarillo from his coat pocket and struck a match. Natividad dropped the reins and her horse ambled off toward the spring. Guided by the glowing ruby tip of burning tobacco, the woman stepped in close, her dark eyes full of daring and promises.

"You are not surprised to see me?" she asked in a husky voice.

"Nothing you do surprises me . . . and everything you do," Chapo said. He grinned and exhaled a cloud of bluish-white smoke.

"You speak as if you were *loco*," Natividad replied, "Words with no meaning. Maybe I do better to talk to the horses."

"I mean you are like a storm, *querida*," Chapo said. He dropped the cigarillo. It exploded on the ground in a shower of embers soon crushed beneath his boot heel. "A man in a storm is not surprised to see lightning," Chapo continued. "He is only surprised when it strikes him."

Natividad smiled, enjoying the allusion. "You can say nice things. And do nice things too, like last night. But I will need more from you than what you carry between your legs." She leaned into him and brushed her lips across his. "I shall need someone I can trust in the days to come. Not just a lover but a man of courage. And strength. This is why I have ridden out . . . to speak to you. To tell you my father is dying, and when he does, what is left is for the strong to claim. I ride here to find out if you are such a man." She cocked a hip and studied his expression. "Tell me, my wild stallion, do you fear the storm?"

Chapo hooked a thumb in his gun belt and appeared to give her proposition some thought. If Andrés died, there would be hell for breakfast with any number of factions struggling to replace him. And he had heard enough talk to know those struggling for a share of money and power wouldn't all be named Varela. He met Natividad's smoldering gaze and his features hardened.

"I like storms," Chapo replied. "Lightning most of all."

21

In December, in an afternoon of stillness and brittle cold when it seemed even the stones threatened to shatter from the plummeting temperature, Chapo Almendáriz returned to a familiar mountain pass. He rode beneath towering ridges of wind-carved granite and followed a telltale trace of chimney smoke into the heart of the pass. The riders, even Natividad, were dressed much the same: serapes draped over wool-lined waistcoats, knee-high boots, and sombreros pulled low to block the wind.

To Tomás and Esteban, killing Chapo was simply a matter of economics, of silver coins and perhaps a place of trust and honor in Andrés' personal guard.

Chapos death to Aurelio meant that Andrés' trusted lieutenant could rest easier and enjoy his sleep. He would be free of a man whose presence had bothered him from the onset, a man with a strangely familiar face that Aurelio could not place. More than likely this Almendáriz was exactly who he claimed to be. If that were the case, then Aurelio would have made a mistake and Chapo's death would be unnecessary. But what was the point of speculation, now. Andrés, for whatever reason, had ordered Chapo's murder. So, then, the matter was closed.

Chapo had been riding point for most of the afternoon. His neck hurt and his spine felt cramped and tight. He didn't like turning his back on men like Tomás and Esteban. So it was with a sense of real pleasure that Chapo rounded a hillock and saw the crumbling facade of Jesse Gómez' cantina. Its battered facade and shuttered windows would offer relief from the terrible cold.

"Ride ahead," Aurelio shouted out. "I trust your instincts, my friend."

Chapo shrugged. What was the old bastard up to? Almendáriz studied the cantina. Everything looked the same. He couldn't see the corral from this angle. There certainly wasn't any sign of trouble, though the mountains were still home to roving bands of Apache braves who lived up to their name, which meant "enemy."

Chapo frowned, trying to put a handle on just what was bothering him. Then he knew, remembering how Jesse had stood in the doorway and offered a warning to ride clear if Chapo's pockets were empty. He was only a couple of hundred feet from the cabin and Jesse had yet to make an appearance. Maybe the old Mexican was stove up. Maybe Manuel had crept down from his cave and bashed the tavern keeper's head in and stole his tequila.

Chapo's hand drifted over to the Colt holstered at his side.

Aurelio reached out as Natividad started forward to join her lover in the lead. Her eyes flashed fire, but Aurelio took no notice.

"Humor an old friend," he said in a kindly voice. And nodded to the two men ahead of him. Tomás immediately began to angle off to the left and Esteban to the right. They held their animals to a slow steady walk.

Each man rode erect, poised, more alert now than ever before. Tension bridged the gap between them, tension that flowed invisibly back to Aurelio and the daughter of Andrés Varela and infected them all.

Natividad glanced around at the bordering ridges as if they were the source of her increasing anxiety, not realizing until the last instant that her uneasiness came from Aurelio Bustamante, who now held a gun. Tomás and Esteban quietly pulled out their guns and aimed them at the man in the lead.

"No," Natividad blurted out, half-choking.

"Your father's orders," Aurelio said, hushing her.

Natividad pulled free of his grasp. "Chapo," she shouted. She dug beneath her coat and pulled out a revolver. Aurelio slapped the gun out of her hand. Natividad cursed him and shouted again. "Chapo!"

The urgency in her voice spun him around. Chapo pulled hard on the reins and swung the horse to the right, gripping the saddle horn as the animal danced and pawed the air in a savage half-turn. Chapo stared at the barrels of three revolvers aimed at him. As they were fired, he threw himself off the skittish animal he rode.

The horse reared again as gunfire echoed through the pass. A bullet burned a path across the back of Chapo's hand and he lost hold on the reins. Another two slugs thudded into horseflesh, piercing the neck and shattering the animal's skull. The horse crumpled over on its side, with Chapo still caught in the stirrups. He tried to drag his shotgun free from its scabbard just below the pommel of the saddle, but the dying beast covered it.

Chapo worked on reflex, clinging close to his dying mount as slugs whirred past. Dust and grit filled his mouth, the stench of fresh blood assailed his nostrils.

The horse shuddered as bullet after bullet slammed into its belly and neck. Chapo clawed for his handgun and raked his fingers across an empty holster. He'd lost his damn gun. With his left leg pinned beneath a thousand pounds of horseflesh, he was trapped, trussed up for the kill like a hog in the slaughter barn. He craned his head around, espied his Colt revolver in the dirt, and stretched his arms, extended his fingers, reached till he groaned. His fingertips brushed the gun butt, fanned the weapon, but nothing more.

Gravel crunched under foot and a ghostly pale shadow of a man stretched across the ground to cover the pinned man and the gun just inches from Almendáriz' grasp. The horse kicked out in its death throe and the saddle's hard leather cantle dug into the pinned man's inner thigh. Chapo screamed, unable to contain the pain.

Tomás, whose cruel eyes betrayed the pleasure he felt at seeing another in pain, only laughed. The small, wiry youth sat astride his gelding, balanced his gunhand on the pommel of his saddle, and thumbed the hammer of his revolver.

Chapo did not ask for mercy, he expected none. He had drawn for an inside straight and come up one card short. His only regret was that he had lost the game for Billy as well as himself.

"I forbid this," Natividad shouted. "Do you hear? I will see each of you stripped naked and dragged through the streets of Rosarito until the flesh hangs from your bones." She tried to pull away from Aurelio, but the lieutenant had managed to snatch the reins from her grasp. Varela's daughter was helpless to interfere.

Esteban walked his horse back across the trail, blocking Aurelio and the girl from view. A few paces behind

Tomás, Esteban had a clear shot at Chapo but seemed less eager to actually do the killing, as if his heart weren't in it.

Tomás grinned at Chapo, then sighed. "You should not have turned your back on me, my friend. I thought you were an *hombre* of much experience. *Mi padre* used to tell me, "Tomás, never trust anyone, always watch your back . . . Then he would beat the hell out of me."

"Kill him," Aurelio shouted, his voice as brittle as the cold.

Tomás aimed at the pinned man.

Chapo raised up on an elbow and braced himself for the shock. But when the explosion came, he jumped. As the roar of the handgun reverberated in the stillness, Chapo listened to the echo and realized with utter amazement that he was alive. Even better, Tomás' handgun came bouncing off Chapo's dead mount and landed nearby. Chapo stretched to grasp the weapon. He twisted and clawed in desperation and inched closer . . . closer . . .

Tomás managed to stay astride his own gelding, though not without effort, for his right arm dangled uselessly at his side and a patch of blood spread over his right shoulder. Dazed and in pain, the bandit clawed at his breechloader and worked it from the scabbard.

Aurelio trotted forward on horseback. The old lieutenant's cheeks were flush from anger and the bitter wind gusting out of the north. He had glimpsed a flash of fire from within the cantina. The shot that disarmed Tomás must have come from Jesse Gómez.

"Jesse, you damn *loco*, you have no business in this," Aurelio shouted. "Maybe you don't see so good, eh?" Aurelio stood in his stirrups and brushed back his sombrero, revealing his silver hair and goatee. "You know me now?" He addressed the open doorway.

A tall rangy gunfighter with the look of a hard case about him walked his dun stallion around the corner of the cantina. For a big man he sat easy in the saddle. He wore a long black coat of heavy wool that hung below his knees. The coat was unbuttoned to permit access to the gun holstered on his hip. He cradled a Winchester yellowboy in his arms. The brass casing gleamed even in the meager light.

Aurelio started to speak, but a voice from the doorway cut him off.

"I know you," John Anthem said, and he, too, stepped into the yard, his Colt Dragoon trailing smoke from the barrel. In his heavy, fleece-lined leather coat the man from Luminaria seemed even larger than usual . . . big and solid as the mountain ridges behind him.

Chapo looked up in surprise and, his sense of hope renewed, reached again for Tomás' gun. Hell had come to dinner and the segundo wanted to be able to dish out his share.

Esteban glanced around at the boulder-strewn landscape, suspecting every shadow and natural barricade of concealing an armed horde. None of the Varelistas liked the looks of these two strangers. They decided it was time to turn Mother's picture to the wall and run. Even Natividad, who had regained control of her mount, paused. The daughter of Varela had a sneaking suspicion the big Anglo walking toward Aurelio meant real trouble. She glanced around at the way they had come. No one had moved to block her escape. Natividad noticed Esteban backing his horse away from the cantina and decided retreat made good sense.

Aurelio's jaw dropped as he stared in utter amazement and recognition. Slowly, Aurelio raised his gun hand, then hesitated. "You," he said in a harsh whisper. Then in a ringing outcry to alert the others, "John Anthem!"

Anthem, watching the lieutenant's every movement, lowered his own gun. His ice-blue eyes narrowed and a malicious smile tightened his lips. "Go ahead, you son of a bitch. There's no white flag today."

Aurelio cursed and made his play. His arm swept up. But not in time. Big John Anthem was quicker. He pointed the revolver, and fired. The Dragoon spat flame and bucked in his solid grip. The shot lifted the lieutenant completely out of the saddle and flung him head over heels over the rump of his horse.

He stiffened and plummeted into the blackness that swelled upward to engulf him.

Death and its sweet peace—and final judgment.

Chapo's fingers closed around the pistol grip and he raised up as Tomás leveled the breechloader at John Anthem. Chapo loosed a shot as the Dragoon bellowed in his ear. He squeezed off a second and third round and then collapsed on his back as Tomás' bullet-riddled body tumbled out of the saddle.

Esteban fired over his shoulder and spurred his horse to a gallop back down the trail, Natividad racing alongside him and the man called Yellowboy in pursuit. Natividad would have taken the lead, her mare was the fastest in all Rosarito. But its hooves caught in the loose shale and went down, throwing the girl into the rocks. She tried to roll and brought her arms up to cover her face. Her head glanced off a saddle-sized stone and knocked her completely unconscious.

Cole Anthem closed the distance between himself and Esteban. The bounty-hunter took note that the girl was either knocked cold or dead and rode past without stopping. The man up ahead was his prey. The bandit twisted around and tried a second shot, which went as wide as the first. Cole gripped the reins in his left hand and slapped the Winchester '66 to his shoulder and leveled five quick shots as the fleeing horseman neared a bend in the trail.

Esteban leaned forward and slid out of the saddle. He hit the ground feetfirst and even managed to run a few steps before his legs buckled and he fell faceforward in the trail.

Powder smoke clouded the air and dust churned by the horses obscured the field of battle. John Anthem knelt by Chapo's side. The big man's windroughened features split into a smile as he studied Chapo's predicament.

"You attached to that horse, are you?"

"You better watch out for Gómez. He's liable to shoot your ass off while you kneel here making a joke."

"The owner of that piss-poor excuse for a saloon? He's trussed up neat as a branded calf, him and some poor sod we found in a cave back yonder." John clapped Chapo on the shoulder and glanced up as Cole came riding back up the valley. He led Natividad's mare with Varela's daughter drapped across the saddle. A rope around her ankles looped beneath the horse and secured her wrists. Cole headed straight for his father and reined to a halt. He touched a hand to the brim of his hat as the light of recognition dawned in Chapo's eyes.

"Howdy, *amigo*. Been a while," Cole said.

"Mother of heaven," Chapo exclaimed, and blessed himself. "Cole . . . but you're dead!"

"I wish folks would quit telling me that," Cole muttered.

"Chapo . . . help me," Natividad moaned as John and

Cole worked Almendáriz out from under the dead horse. Chapo limped in a tight circle until the feeling returned to his leg. John freed the saddle from the dead horse while Cole fetched a canteen of water.

The daughter of Varela could not fail to notice the familiarity between Chapo and the Anglos.

"Mi amor," Natividad pleaded, "you know these men?"

John Anthem stepped in front of Chapo before he could reply. The older man touched the brim of his hat.

"He's my son," John said. Then, with a glance over his shoulder at the surprised younger man, added. "At least as much as he wants to be." He turned around and walked past Chapo, gave him a fatherly pat on the shoulder, and continued back to the cantina.

Natividad stared into Chapo's eyes and saw that John Anthem spoke the truth.

"You bastard," she spat. "I shall cut your manhood off and feed it to the coyotes. I'll carve your heart out and crush it beneath my boots. Liar! Bastard! May you rot in hell!" Natividad kicked and flailed and pulled against the ropes that bound her.

"Friend of yours?" Cole asked in a laconic aside.

"We were going to be married," Chapo answered.

Natividad heard him. And screamed, and cursed . . . until her words were a dry rasp in a tortured throat. Even then, her eyes continued to smolder with hatred.

22

Manual was on his third bottle of tequila and only a swallow from killing it off when he raised the bottle in salute to his captors.

"*Señor* . . . I, Manuel . . ." He rubbed his forehead. "*Caramba*, I have forgotten my last name."

"You had no father," Jesse Gómez retorted. His voice trembled with anger. Bad enough to be trussed up in this back room alongside Manuel, but to have to watch the bastard gulp down bottle after bottle of Jesse's own profits was a torture beyond imagining. Jesse raised his eyes in silent prayer to heaven, but he saw only Cole Anthem.

The tall, lanky bounty-hunter had already popped the cork on a fourth bottle.

"I am . . . No, no matter." Manuel shrugged, his speech slurred. "I am verrry happy . . . happy, *señor*, to be your prisoner." He nodded, raised the bottle in his hand, and slid over on his side, unconscious.

Cole grunted an "at last" and squatted before Jesse.

"I will not drink," Jesse firmly stated.

"Suit yourself." Cole chuckled and drew his Colt.

"Wait, *por favor*," Jesse exclaimed, eyes widening. "Maybe I could use a drink. Before Manuel bleeds me dry." He stretched out his hands, bound at the wrists, and accepted the bottle of tequila. He took a sip and Cole tilted the bottle and forced Gómez to drain half the contents before allowing him to breathe. The owner of the cantina lasted another half-hour and through most of another bottle before he slumped forward and began to snore.

Cole checked the man and, satisfied that Gómez was unconscious, walked out of the narrow confines of the storeroom. Behind the bar, he helped himself to a bottle of what appeared to be whiskey. Then he stepped around the bar and walked to the table where Big John Anthem and Chapo Almendáriz were studying a map of Rosarito and Varela's stronghold.

Chapo, charcoal in hand, sketched in the ridge behind the fortress and the various mine shafts dotting the mountainside. He circled one opening in particular.

"Billy's there," he said, looking up at John, who nodded and placed a finger on the rendering as if somehow he might contact his son by touching it.

Chapo glanced up at Cole and shook his head. "I figured I was seeing a ghost when you came riding out." The segundo chuckled. "I thought you were dead."

"I was," Cole dryly retorted.

"I know what you mean," Chapo said. "I've been dead a few times myself." He held out a tin cup of coffee for Cole to lace with a dollop of whiskey. The bounty-hunter complied, pouring a measure into his own cof-feecup before setting the bottle aside. He tasted the contents of his cup and shuddered. There had to be a better way of keeping warm.

Cole thought of Glory Doolin and sighed. Now, Glory was a woman made for a wintry night. He lifted his gaze to Natividad, now sitting upright and securely bound at the wrists. She sat on a blanket by the fireplace and, other than being angry as the devil, appeared no worse for the wear. Varela's daughter stared at Chapo, who sat with his back to her. Cole decided that Chapo was mighty lucky looks couldn't kill or there'd be nothing left of him but a puff of smoke and boots filled with ashes.

"I don't aim to take on an army, not just the three of us. If we can get in, free Billy, and get out, so much the better," John said, studying the map.

"What about Varela?" Cole asked, incredulous that his father had nothing in store for the general. "Chapo said he's dismissed most of his servants. He knows where the old man's room is. The house will probably be empty."

"Except for his two sons and whatever guests they might be entertaining," John replied. "No, I won't risk Billy's life just for a chance at revenge." He shifted in the chair and the ladder-back creaked beneath his weight. He unbuttoned his fleece-lined leather coat and leaned back in the chair, balancing it on the back legs. He hooked his thumbs in his gun belt. "I want as little trouble as possible. It will be difficult enough getting to the mine where Billy's kept. If we're seen . . ."

"I know a way." Chapo shrugged and sketched in the deer trail that circumvented Varela's garrison and wound its way up the mountainside to the point where it intersected the footpath to the mine. "We'll be on foot all the way. Leave our horses here." Chapo pointed to a spot near the walls. "And if something happens to alert the posted guards . . . we'll be under their guns."

"And they'll be under mine," Cole interjected. He pointed to a place on the slope where he might be adequately protected. "You two free Billy, I'll wait here."

"Might be more men than you can handle, *amigo*," Chapo cautioned, his dark eyes studying the tall, solemn son of John Anthem.

"Not hardly," Cole answered with cold confidence. The action today seemed to have only whet his appetite for more.

"What the hell you been doing all these years, Cole?" Chapo asked, chilled by what he heard in young Anthem's voice.

"This," the bounty-hunter replied matter-of-factly. He turned and walked over to his yellowboy Winchester. Cradling the rifle in his arms, he announced he was going to check on the horses. He pulled on his long black coat and stepped out into the still and frigid night.

Chapo watched Cole leave. Chapo could be as hard as any man and as dangerous in a fight as a cornered Comanche. But he never lost his feelings and he never looked for trouble. He was the segundo, a man who rode for the brand and fought for the brand if need be, but always with heart. Chapo had noticed the hard, emotionless professionalism in Cole's tone of voice. In a fight Cole Anthem might just have about as much mercy in him as a death's-head.

"I know," John Anthem said softly. John knew that Chapo had been like an older brother to Cole and Billy, that he knew as much about the twins and was as close to them as their own father. "He's a bounty-hunter."

John Anthem handed over a wanted poster he had borrowed from Cole's saddlebags. It revealed a crude sketch of a malcontented, dangerous-looking youth wanted for stage robbery, rustling, and cutting telegraph wires. A five-hundred-dollar reward was offered for his capture.

"Cole's been riding a rough trail," John continued.

"And he did not ride into Luminaria a poor man."

Chapo shook his head in disbelief and returned the poster. He had no use for bounty-hunters. They were no better than gunmen, just killers for profit to his way of thinking.

"We've all changed," John said, tucking the poster away in his shirt pocket.

"Yeah," Chapo agreed. He glanced over at Natividad, who instantly looked away. "I suppose we've all had to do things we never thought we would." He pursed his lips, his gaze gentling. Despite Natividad's part in the kidnapping he couldn't help feeling guilty about the way he had duped her.

"Maybe I'll step outside and freeze my ass off," John said. "If you can handle things in here."

John had lived long enough to appreciate another's need for privacy. He did not understand Chapo's relationship with the *señorita*, but no matter. Life was full of things he had learned not to worry about. Everything indeed had its season, as the Good Book said: a time to be born, and a time to die.

John opened the door and followed his son into the dark. Tempting folly, he left Chapo and Natividad alone at last.

"Cut me loose," the woman hissed. "Quickly now." She held out her hands and showed where she had worked at the thongs with her teeth. The leather was only slightly frayed.

"When we free Billy Anthem," Chapo said, crossing to the fire to warm himself.

"No, I cannot believe what you say," Natividad blurted out. Her eyebrows arched, the intensity in her voice reached out to him. "Whatever they pay you, I can pay more." She rose up on her knees, her eyes turning soft and seductive. "I can pay much more." Natividad stood and moved in close so that the firelight played on her dusky features and her shiny black hair. The heat radiating from her body matched the warmth of the flames dancing in the hearth. She reached up and slid her arms over Chapo's head and caressed the back of his neck.

"You love your Natividad," the woman purred. "You could not hurt me, no?" The words spilled smooth as sweet cream off her tongue, and her full lips, pouted and moist, awaited his kiss.

"I'll kill you if I have to," Chapo said.

Natividad's eyes widened. She sucked in her breath. Her cheeks flushed as the truth of his answer sank in and she recognized that Chapo was not merely a hireling but someone whose ties to John Anthem ran deeper than money. She had given herself to him, taken him into her house, and all the while he was one of Anthem's men, all the while using her. All the while, planning and plotting . . . A cry began deep in her throat, became a singular note of outrage uncontained.

"Aaaahhhhh!" She sprang at him and tried to sink her teeth into his throat.

Chapo cursed and backed away but pulled her with him. He lost his footing and fell, the weight of his body pulling the woman down with him. Her teeth raked across his shoulder. She butted him in the face with her head and blood flowed from his nose. She fought like a tiger. Her fingernails clawed his neck and left furrows in his flesh. She slammed her knee in his groin.

Chapo rolled on his back and caught her beneath the arms. With a desperate lunge he threw her forward and out of reach. He scrambled to his feet just in time. Natividad reached into the fireplace and brought out a log that had yet to catch fire. Embers glowed on one end.

She whirled around and charged again. Chapo darted aside and the club splintered the table as she missed her mark. She regained her balance and lifted the log overhead.

Chapo drew his gun. "Enough, little one. Don't make me shoot," he said.

"You won't," Natividad confidently replied, closing the gap between them, step by step. She lunged. Chapo hesitated, then danced out of the way and stuck out a leg to trip her as she stumbled past. Natividad fell face forward onto the floor. "I'll break your skull," she roared.

Chapo holstered his gun and, as the woman tried to rise, toppled her again with a well-placed kick to her derriere. He turned and sat on her thighs, pinning her legs long enough to tie her ankles with his bandanna. He changed positions again and knocked her club away, tossing it back into the fireplace.

"Bastard," she spat, and tried to rise. "May the wolves drink your blood and the vultures tear your flesh."

"Behave, or I'll hog-tie you and put a damn bit in your mouth," Chapo said, dabbing at his shoulder and neck with another kerchief. He stood, and shaking his head in disgust, he crossed the room to pick up the coffeepot he had accidently overturned in the struggle. The brown bitter liquid sunk, steaming, into the packed-earth floor. He lifted the lid and glanced into the pot. With a sigh of disgust, he slapped the coffeepot down on the tabletop and wondered how he would explain the loss of its freshly brewed contents. He dabbed at his superficial wounds and glanced over at the woman who once more sat still and silently staring, firelight reflected in her eyes.

Despite all she had done, no matter how cold-bloodedly she had behaved, he could not help but feel pity for her. Andrés Varela had taken her from a prostitute mother and made her a replica of his own twisted and malevolent self.

Not that this fact excused her actions: it was just that he felt some sympathy for her. Whatever her crimes against John Anthem. Blood dripped from Chapo's nose and stained his shirt. The warning wasn't lost on him—sympathy had almost gotten him killed.

Where were the stars? John wondered, lifting his eyes to the shrouded heavens. They must be somewhere beyond the gloomy residue of winter, he answered himself, and sighed, pressing on through the pass and away from the lights of the cantina. He walked, stiff-legged, into the heart of the night where the moon did not dare to venture, for Cantina Pass, on this eve, was black as a devil's heart. The violence of afternoon had done little to ease John's tension and he rued the many miles that lay between these mountains and Luminaria ... and Rose.

In a few days I might be dead, and then what was the price of my dreams, eh? He shook his head, spat, his mouth felt dry. He resisted self-doubt. He knew he must be alone, must suffer in the night, reach out and take hold, build and achieve and then fight to keep that achievement. Texas was the clay and John Anthem, the potter; Luminaria was the work of his hands. Enemies were a well that never managed to run dry; drive one down and another rose to take his place. After Varela, who would be next—Everett Cotter, that old and bitter man? Well, then, so be it. But first John had to settle with Andrés Varela.

Yet how futile it all seemed here in the heart of the night, following one blind step after the other. For all the labors of his hands, despite the scope of his accomplishments, a bullet from one of Varela's men could end it all.

But, then, I might just step on a rattlesnake out in the dark and die with a leg full of venom. John Anthem reminded himself. So what was the point of speculation? A man lived, a man died, these were the inevitables. How one lived—or died—was within a man's grasp; here one could make a difference. It took courage and a healthy dose of foolish recklessness to walk in the dark, to brace the storms of life, to face down the demons and ghosts of the past, to sleep and then to awaken and begin anew, each day, after day, after day.

John thought of Rose, his Yellow Rose, all golden, her hair a-play in his hands or curled upon his chest as she slept in the crook of his arm after their lovemaking. Rose, whose brown eyes seemed to draw in sunlight and cast it forth as her own sweet magic, in a gaze at once forthright, alluring, and bold.

Images of love faded, unable to compete with the stark reality of ridges looming to either side. In the distance, a horse whinnied as Cole moved among the animals and secured them for the night. Other horses raced through Anthem's memory. Years ago young John Anthem escaped to freedom, with the wind in his face and desperation in his heart. He had ridden through this very pass, Poke Tyler at his side and, hounding them like a pack of mad wolves, Andrés Varela and his militia. John Anthem and Poke Tyler had been free at last, in a desperate bid to save themselves and elude the Varelistas: two fugitives perferring death to slavery and servitude. John Anthem remembered his last glimpse of Varela; it had been at some distance. Anthem had found a spyglass among the provisions on his stolen horse and, pausing on the crest of a hill, had looked back down the valley and seen the general. Varela must have cauterized the stump of his right arm and, nearly mad with pain, led his forces out after the fugitives. John Anthem had turned away and headed north, across the Rio Grande into Texas, and never once had he looked back or hungered 'o ride the barrancas. The memory of his days of imprisonment had become no more bothersome than the scars crisscrossing his back, whitened furrows of flesh whose legacy of pain time had healed.

John dropped his hand to the Dragoon Colt holstered on his right hip, then reached across and patted the belly gun Poke had handed him back at the ranch. Poke wanted revenge. Well, so did John Anthem, for that matter. But not at the risk of Billy's life. Maybe someday, with nothing to lose but his own life, John would have a final reckoning with Andrés Varela.

"Sorry, Poke," he whispered to the dark. "Another chance, another time." And he tried not to dwell on his own deeply felt premonitions of disaster. Blood had been shed. Bustamante and two others had been killed. And so it had begun. John Anthem had returned to the barrancas.

Cole Anthem rearranged the winter hay and apportioned a bait of oats to each mount. They'd take all the horses, come morning, so if Jesse or Manuel wished to warn Andrés Varela in Rosarito, the two men would have to go on foot, a two-day journey on horseback and probably four walking.

The bounty-hunter glanced up as his father left the cantina and started off down the pass. Cole was tempted to follow him but realized how inappropriate it would be. His father could take care of himself. Cole returned his attention to the horses, applied the brush to each of the mounts, and talked softly to the beasts. His voice calmed even the most skittish of the animals. He was Yellowboy, a hunter of men.

Apart and never part of. Even in his father's house, at Luminaria, where he had experienced a special happiness, a restlessness burned in him, always, a need to move on. Perhaps it was a curse that plagued every fiddle-foot, the need to drift, like a leaf in the river. He doubted his mother would ever understand. After all, she longed to have her family whole again.

It took a woman like Glory Doolin to understand how Cole felt. The two of them were cut from the same cloth, with just enough bad in them to be good . . . or as Glory had once put it, "to love livin'."

Ah, Glory. Cole smiled and retrieved the Winchester from where he had leaned it against the wall of the jacal. A wind had sprung up, and it gusted through the gaps in the chinking. Loose branches rattled in the wind and the horses stirred and rolled their eyes, their nervousness permeating the air. One of the mares darted out into the decrepit excuse for a corral and circled the fence line twice before the cold drove her back to protection. The jacal wasn't much, but it was better than nothing at all between flesh and bitter cold.

Cole patted the animal and soothed the mare's rattled spirits, his sure hand gentling the animal. As the bounty-hunter eased himself along the side wall, his black woolen coat caught on a snag. A twig protruding from the mottled wall snapped as Cole pulled free. He cursed, finding the pocket torn. He had held off wearing the riding coat until he was free of the bramble-choked plains just south of the Rio Grande. Cole had to laugh at himself. Here he was in the heart of Varelista country, among enemies who no doubt outnumbered him, Chapo, and Big John. Twenty to one, maybe more. And he was worried about a torn pocket!

Cole pulled the collar of his coat up around his neck and ears and tugged his broad-brimmed hat low on his head. He leaned against the jacal and stared at the amber lantern light seeping through the shuttered windows of Jesse's cantina, and in his mind he silently began the letter he would never send: *Dear Glory*. Cole pictured Glory Doolin stepping into his embrace, the hungry look in her eyes matching his own. Using the still-fresh colors of memory, he painted a backdrop of red satin drapes, a brass bed, feather mattress, and down comforter, and Miss Glory Doolin in all her radiant glory, awaiting him with open arms.

What a way to spend a winter's night, Cole thought with a sigh.

Dear Glory, I wish you were here. Words failed him as he tried to imagine an end to the desperate days ahead. So much for memories. Where was Glory and who was she remembering right this very moment? Maybe Cole. Yes, she had to be. For tonight Cole Tyler Anthem wanted to think he was a part of someone too, on this lonely night in a savage land beneath a starless sky.

23

Cpl. Sancedo had been guarding the road into Rosarito since morning. By afternoon, large fleecy snowflakes began to settle to earth, and through the silent swirling precipitation Sancedo espied approaching riders. He relaxed as he recognized Chapo and Natividad and behind them, sombreros protecting and shielding their faces, two men he took to be Aurelio Bustamante and Esteban. He lowered his breechloader and leaned it against a boulder.

The sentry alerted his companion on watch not to bother stirring from beside a campfire that blazed cheerfully beneath a ledge. Sancedo waved to the riders, who returned his greeting and headed toward the man by the fire. The sound of the approaching horses was muffled by the snow drifting over the barren ground.

"*Buenos días*, Corporal," Chapo called out. "Only two of you watch the road today?" He took the lead, glancing over his shoulder once to make sure John and Cole had their faces hidden.

"*Sí*. The weather is too damn bad, so my men just leave. I ordered them to stay, but they only curse me and go anyway." The corporal held up his hands in despair and he looked over at Natividad. "When your father was well, things were different. Men obeyed—"

Suddenly, Natividad exploded into action. She drove her boot heels into her horse, and at the first touch of her spurs it leapt forward. But Chapo was expecting trouble. Diving from horseback, he wrapped his arms about the desperate woman and dragged her out of the saddle.

"It is Anthem," Natividad shouted, rolling over the hard-packed earth. Chapo tried to clamp a hand over her mouth, but Natividad bit his finger. He yelped in pain.

"What is this?" Sancedo exclaimed, backing away in surprise. "*Señor. ¿Señora?*" He looked up and realized that the other two men were strangers.

Cole stood in his stirrups, his arm crooked back, knife in hand. The arm swept down and the knife cut a path through the falling snow, bounced hilt-first off the corporal's chest, and dropped harmlessly to the earth.

"Shit," Cole said, and reached for his yellowboy.

Sancedo turned and called a warning to the man by the fire. Running to his own breechloader, he took up the weapon. He whirled and looked up in horror at the curved steel blade that swept down through the cold gray of afternoon. Sancedo recognized the ornamental saber of Aurelio Bustamante, but not John Anthem, who loomed over the startled corporal. Anthem raised up in the saddle and slashed out with all his strength.

Corporal Sancedo screamed and tried to block the blade with his breechloader but moved too slowly. The blade bit deep into the side of his neck, severed arteries and carved bone. Sancedo dropped to his knees, rolled over onto his breechloader, and died facedown in the snow.

The man by the fire crawled out of his blankets and,

abandoning his rifle, darted behind a rock. Cole jumped
his horse over the flames and rounded the boulder in
pursuit. John heard a muffled scream and the crack of a
rifle barrel glancing off the man's skull. Cole reappeared
moments later and nodded to the others, signaling that
the second man would not be sounding any alarm. Cole
continued over to where John had dismounted to retrieve
his son's knife.

"I never could throw one of the blasted things." Cole
shrugged, returning the blade to its boot sheath.

"I noticed," John replied, his expression one of exasperation.

"But I can get the job done," the bounty-hunter said,
rising to his own defense.

"Since you both are so damn capable," Chapo blurted
out as he dodged a swipe of the girl's bound fists,
"maybe you could give me a little help, huh?"

Natividad kneed him in the groin, grabbed a rock the
size of a melon, and raised it over his head. Cole rode
up behind her and dragged her away from the segundo.
She dropped the rock and screamed as Cole lifted her
completely off the ground. He trotted back to the campsite and deposited her in a heap on the dead corporal's
bedroll.

Natividad cursed the lot of them. The three men tried
to ignore her and gathered around the warmth of the fire
as the gray light slowly deepened and the ledge above
disappeared beneath a few inches of snow.

"We'll wait until dark," John Anthem remarked, and
turned away from the fire to walk out into the wheel-
rutted road winding down from the hills to Rosarito. The
two day's ride from Cantina Pass had not prepared him
for the emotions he experienced now, standing on the
ridge and looking down at the town and the gray-brown

walls of the fortress and beyond them to the mines of Varela. There John Anthem had slaved for almost an entire year, breaking his back for the general, whipped and beaten and kicked until the day of a cave-in, a day the mountainside took its toll in blood and bone. Men had died beneath tons of ore and rock and timber, died horribly, in the bowels of the mountain. But not John Anthem—he had escaped in the confusion and left the general bleeding in the streets of Rosarito. John remembered and regretted leaving the man alive. Laura's murder, the kidnapping might never have happened . . .

John sighed and turned his thoughts to more pressing matters. He studied the town and the hillside with its mine shafts looming like puckered bullet holes, nasty and black in contrast to the snow-covered slope. It would be a tricky night's work, but he welcomed the task. He had waited long enough. His newly mended leg ached like hell and left him bad-tempered as a grizzly with a sore tooth. Action offered the only release from his misery.

He rubbed his stubbled jaw, massaged the back of his neck, and finally nodded as if coming to terms with what needed to be done. An idea formed, and the rancher smiled, satisfied with the change he had just envisioned in his plan of attack. He no longer needed Natividad; let her stay here bound hand and foot. Let Chapo free Billy. Cole would provide cover fire if needed. John Anthem intended to provide a necessary diversion.

"Look out, you bastards," John muttered, "hell is coming to dinner." He vowed to make it an evening the town of Rosarito would never forget.

Smoke rose from chimneys. Lanterns flickered behind crudely shuttered windows. Dogs barked and romped in the snowfall. Men on horseback reached their destinations, dismounted, and hurried inside jacals and cantinas.

Two weeks before Christmas and it was a night like any other in Rosarito . . . but for the last time.

24

As Hector Varela trudged along the walk, the sentries stationed at various intervals along the wall snapped to attention. He moved his great bulk along the narrow walkway with surefooted ease despite the treacherous surface. His boots crunched in the snow and left a hard-packed trail of icy footprints in his wake.

He had traversed the length of the west wall, found nothing suspect over the south gate, and had started toward the east wall only to find Andrés himself wrapped in a heavy coat and scarf keeping vigil in the snowy dark. The general gazed off to the lights of Rosarito shimmering in the silent storm. A cigarillo, its tip aglow, jutted from between his clenched teeth. The general blew a cloud of smoke and then, cigar in hand, gestured in the direction of the mountain ridge, invisible in the distance.

"We are much alike, John Anthem and I," Varela said. His father's voice seemed stronger than Hector could remember, and he began to take heart. Perhaps the general's health was improving as it did occasionally; the hemp Varela had taken to smoking also helped.

"You still think Señor Anthem will come?" Hector asked.

"*Si,*" Andrés replied. "He will come. He has to, if not for his son, for himself." Andrés exhaled another bluish cloud of smoke that melted snowflakes in its billowing path.

Hector wore a bearskin coat that only magnified his girth. Ice flecked his beard and settled on his broad shoulders and shaggy head. He did not question his father any further but shrugged and leaned against the wall, bracing himself with his beefy hands.

"We are lords of the *monte,*" Andrés mused. "Creatures of pride and honor. We are not moved by expedience but by the will of God. We go where we must and do what must be done. He cut off my hand, I cut off his son."

Andrés fit the cigar between two of the carved fingers on his wooden right hand. "It must be settled between us. He knows as well as I, there can be only one lord of these mountains. And only one prince, too, eh?" He clapped Hector on the shoulder.

"One day you shall lead these men." Andrés leaned into Hector. "Just don't get too anxious." He tilted his head back and laughed aloud. "Men fear you. That is good. But you must never trust anyone."

"Not even my brother and sister," Hector gruffly retorted.

"Especially not your brother and sister," Varela replied. He tossed the cigarillo over the wall, then reached inside his coat and brought out a shiny silver flask. He drank deeply and then passed the brandy to his son. Andrés coughed and spat a mouthful of phlegm, coughed again, and shook his head. His eyes narrowed, his expression turned grim in the night. "These men are rabble.

Not like when we chased the French from the mountains. I can count on my fingers the number of men I would make a stand with. The rest, oh, the rest. Soft, no loyalty, we must find more *men*."

Andrés stared off toward Rosarito, then turned and looked toward the slope rising behind the hacienda. Something moved—there against the white. A shadow?—A coyote? He squinted and studied the terrain. But the curtain of snow was deceptive. He could not be certain. The feeble glow of a winter's moon was a mere suggestion in the sky. Andrés scowled, accused his mind of playing tricks on him. He cursed and faced the valley once more.

Anthem will come, he silently repeated. Tonight, tomorrow, one day. And I will be ready. The general saw the orange-red glow of a fire as flames spread across the roof of the town's only three-story structure, a hotel and cantina owned by Varela himself. He pointed in the direction of the blaze as a second structure, this a barn and storage shed, all but exploded into flame.

Hector stared at the town and his jaw went slack. "What in the name of the saints?" he muttered, and blessed himself. The fire had already begun to spread. Another structure fell prey. Rosarito was burning. He clambered down the steps to alert the men in the barracks. All of Varela's manpower would be needed if the town were to be saved.

Soldiers and Varelistas emerged from their quarters to stumble into the snow-covered courtyard at Hector's behest. Andrés watched in admiration and pride as his son issued orders to the men who continued to stream out into the snow. Some were only half-dressed but quickly donned their coats and sombreros.

A fire in town was enough to alert even the laziest of

souls. Each brothel or cantina burned to the ground meant one less place for a man to find respite from the tedium of his life.

"Get your horses," Hector shouted. "We'll need fire brigades. Hurry!" He started toward the corral and the men in the courtyard ran after him.

Varela glanced around and located the sentries closest to him. A nagging suspicion gnawed at the back of his mind.

"You men," the general snapped, and two sentries, wrapped in serapes and carrying percussion rifles, trotted toward him along the walk. "I want you up at the mine where the gringo is kept. And be quick about it."

The two men managed an informal salute, hid their displeasure, and left at a run toward the footpath winding out from the rear of the buildings and up the mountainside.

Varela dismissed the men from his thoughts and returned his attention to the disturbance in town. Every nerve was tingling. He reached under his coat and felt for the revolver riding high on his left hip.

Fires raged through Rosarito. Inhabitants staggered outside, shouted to one another, and tried to dodge the runaway horses that raced the length of the street, making the avenue a nightmare of thundering hooves and careening wagons.

The violence unleashed on the town seemed almost supernatural in origin, this notion only served to fuel the panic. Flames leapt from thatch roofs to shingles, tongues of fire lapped from windows and open doorways. And everywhere the night rocked with cries and clamor and groans of incomprehension.

When John Anthem set out to create a diversion, he

did it with conviction, excusing thievery as a necessary part of Billy's rescue. Hell, what was stealing compared to the destruction he had already left in his wake? Finding a store had been easy, breaking in and helping himself to an assortment of lanterns and even a saddlebag full of dynamite had been easier still.

Flames leapt up the side of the hotel, flames devoured the stored grain in the stable. John had turned loose all the animals within and the terrified horses bolted toward the center of the town, adding to the madness. He reined the sorrel up alongside a jacal and emptied a tine of lamp oil over the walls. A prostitute poked her head out the doorway as John touched a match to the wall. Flames spread upward to the roof. The whore muttered a startled curse and dashed out with her skirts held high. Her customer, a Varelista, leapt out and bounded down the alley. The jacal was wholly consumed in a matter of minutes. Flames continued to spread to the other cribs lining the back of the alley, turning the snowflakes from pristine white to garish orange.

John sat astride the big sorrel and calmly lit the last of the four lanterns dangling from his saddle horn. Voices carried to him: an angry crowd of prostitutes and soldiers stumbling out of the cribs. John dragged his Henry repeater from the saddle scabbard and waited, bathed in the glare of the lanterns. Here, between the buildings at the far end of the alley, the snow had been trampled to mud underfoot. The storm itself seemed to be abating at last. John shouldered the rifle as the soldiers, in various stages of undress, advanced from out of the gloom. He snapped off five quick shots into the ground, stopping the irate Varelistas, armed with clubs and rocks, in their tracks.

John Anthem endured a shower of stones. A bullet

whirred past his ear and embedded itself in a fence behind him. He fished in his saddlebag and brought out a
stick of dynamite. He stuck the end of the fuse into one
of the lanterns and, when it began to trail smoke, tossed
the dynamite up the alley. A fiery blast illuminated the
mob and sent them packing. Debris shattered windows
and riddled the walls as men and women beat a hasty
retreat.

John holstered the Henry and urged the sorrel into a
trot and then a gallop as he emerged onto Main Street.
He continued across the street until he reached the safety
of a line of shops and cantinas and whorehouses that had
yet to feel his wrath. Anthem nudged the sorrel with his
spurs, took up a lantern, and swung it in an arc, hurling
it up to the top of the nearest building.

The flue shattered and fiery oil spread over the shingle
roof. Someone shouted, a window crashed, and the barrel of a breechloader poked out and wasted a shot. John
winced and hurled a stick of dynamite through the window. The wall blew outward in a cloud of black smoke
and splinters. And the remains of a breechloader.

More and more people were fleeing to the compara-
tive safety of the street, only to find that they risked
being run down. The inhabitants streamed onward to the
outlying houses. No one understood exactly what was
happening, only that somehow Rosarito was being sys-
tematically destroyed. Soldiers and Varelistas and
townspeople alike stumbled awestruck and dazed, past
the burning buildings lining one side of Main Street.

It took Hector Varela to alert the panic-stricken crowd
to the danger threatening the other side of the town.
Leading his Varelistas, Hector dismounted and shouted
orders for his men to fight the smaller, controllable fires.
He shouted and cursed until some of the fleeing soldiers

and citizens in the street finally came to assist the men he had brought from the garrison.

Shopkeepers, farmers, militia, and prostitutes labored side by side, carrying buckets of water, shoveling mud and snow, smothering flames with coarsely woven blankets, striving with all their weary strength to save their town.

John Anthem wasn't about to let them succeed. He came riding at a dead gallop down the center of Main Street. Half a dozen or more sticks of dynamite spewed sparks and gray smoke from his saddlebags. His wild rebel yell rose above the din. After all the weeks of waiting, of doing nothing, of harnessing his rage and keeping it pent up inside, it was time to strike back. The first to suffer his vengeance was the town that had basked so profitably in the shadow of Andrés Varela.

The townspeople scrambled out of his path, dropping buckets and shovels and blankets along the way. The denizens of the cantinas and bordellos, the drifters, gamblers, hide-hunters, fled as the first series of explosions erupted in Anthem's wake. Fist after fist full of dynamite went spinning off to either side. *Whooosh*, and the fountain in the center of town exploded. *Boom*, and the local magistrate's office lost its windows and porch.

Hector saw the man on the sorrel and his intuition told him this wild and terrible figure could only be John Anthem. The son of Varela called to the men around him, but they hesitated, uncertain whether to continue battling the blaze or take on the crazy gringo bearing down on them. Suddenly a stick of dynamite flipped end over end through the cold night air and plopped at the feet of the Varelistas. A couple of the men started for their guns, then thought better of it and scattered like

spooked quail. Hector, on foot now, dropped his shovel
and reached for his revolver.

John Anthem ignored him and galloped past, a
blurred, frightening apparition outlined against a lurid
backdrop of destruction.

Hector turned, swung his gun to center on Anthem's
broad back, and thumbed the hammer. A blast, a world
turned upside down, then Hector landed on his stomach
in the middle of the wheel-rutted street. He couldn't hear
and his serape was on fire. He rolled over onto his back
and let the snow and mud douse the burning fabric and
soothe his burned flesh. His sombrero was gone, his gun
was gone. Hector staggered to his feet and watched a
series of explosions blast to smithereens the facades of
a laundry, two cantinas, and a boardinghouse. The few
remaining horses headed for the hills; dogs ran howling
into the night. Men hurried after them while other inhabitants hid as best they could. In a matter of seconds,
the ravaged center of the town was devoid of life.

Hector wiped a forearm across his bearded, soot-
streaked features and watched in helpless fury as Anthem vanished among the shadows. Varela's son
stumbled forward, still dazed from the effects of the
blast. He started down the center of Main Street, managing one shaky step at a time and weaving like a common drunk through the heart of the conflagration.

A building collapsed in on itself, sending a column
of embers mushrooming into the snow-cleansed air.
Flames reached a supply of black powder stored in a
shed at the south end of town. The explosion flattened
two adobe houses and collapsed the wall of a third.

Hector Varela continued on doggedly relying on his
instincts. Blood streamed from his nostrils and oozed
from a nasty gash on the back of his head. He ignored

the pain, resisted the urge to collapse. Hector fixed his gaze on the fortress and the slope above the hacienda.

Kill him, Hector mentally ordered, fixing the sentry by the mine shaft in his thoughts. The man had his orders—in case of attack, he was to shoot Billy Anthem dead.

"Now," Hector shouted, unable to hear his own voice. "Kill him now!"

Billy Anthem piled the coals around the mesquite wood already ablaze in the center of his prison cell in the mines of Varela. Smoke drifted up to the ceiling where it slipped soundlessly through a fissure in the stone roof and was lost to the night air. Billy gazed with wistful appreciation at the trailing smoke and imagined himself somehow climbing the ropelike vapors and worming his way to freedom through the crack in the earth.

He scratched at his scraggly blond beard and decided a bath might be just the thing.

"Better ring for the servant," he muttered, chuckling aloud as he shoved the flattened board he used for a shovel under the coals. He had arranged his bedding— blankets, skins, and a bear-skin coat—over a depression in the stone floor. Each night he filled the depression with warm coals, covered them with the heavy skins and then one of the blankets. Tonight, as every night, he would sleep toasty warm. And hungry, he mused, wondering what was keeping Hector, Rafael, or Natividad. One of them usually brought up a plate of beans and coffee from the house, sometimes even a chunk of stringy beef on the side. Varela intended him to die, all right, but not by starving him to death. Billy imagined the general had ordered him kept alive and reasonably healthy—no doubt it pleased him to know the son of

John Anthem would enjoy many long months of captivity before being put to death.

Billy had refused to eat during those first desconsolate days after being brought to Rosarito. Thankfully, common sense and a burning need for vengeance had changed his mind. However hopeless the situation, there was always the slimmest chance for escape. Hope had rekindled at the sight of Chapo that afternoon many weeks ago. He knew Chapo would act when the right time presented itself, and Billy intended to be ready for anything. He paced his cell like a caged animal in a circus, but not without reason. Each day he walked the perimeters of his cell, around and around, until he completed a rough mile, in an attempt to keep his muscles limber. Counting off mile after mile, Billy had noted with a grin that he had just about walked all the way to the Rio Grande. Hell, after another few weeks in this cell he wouldn't need Chapo, he'd be home already.

He held his hands out to the fire and frowned, hearing explosions. Though muted by distance and the walls of the mine, the noise was unmistakably the sign of conflict or one hell of a celebration. He shrugged, took up his wooden shovel, and worked it beneath the ashes and embers. What was the point of conjecture? Staying warm demanded his immediate attention.

The clatter of boot heels echoed down the passage leading to the world outside. Billy glanced up from the fire and waited. His hopes rose and were as quickly dashed when a man his own age, clad in serape and nankeen trousers, his features hidden beneath the brim of his sombrero, hurried into the chamber. The Varelista, a clean-shaven and congenial-looking young man, cradled a Sharps buffalo gun in his arms. A cartridge belt had been slung over his left shoulder and a wide leather gun belt circling his waist became visible as he brushed his serape aside and stepped up to the iron bars of the cell jutting out of the walls of the mine shaft. The Varelista wiped a forearm over his mouth, licked his lips, glanced back the way he had come, then stared at Billy, who continued to squat by the fire some ten yards away.

Billy sensed the young man's nervousness, not liking the way the guard pointed the barrel of that Sharps in at him.

"There is trouble in town, *señor*. I don't know what. But *el jefe* has given me my orders of what I am to do." The Varelista thrust the rifle barrel through the bars. His hands trembled with uncertainty. If he needlessly took the gringo's life, Andrés Varela would have the guard flayed alive. But Rosarito appeared to be engulfed in flames. And the explosions, like the roar of cannons . . .

"Stand up, *señor*," the guard ordered, reaching his decision. He cocked the big-bore rifle.

Billy stiffened, knowing his hour had come. He looked down the business end of that heavy octagonal barrel, black and menacing. Well, what the hell, it beat waiting.

"Stand up," the guard repeated.

"Sure," Billy said. His fingers curled around the flattened board he used for a shovel. He bolted upright, scooping a mound of coals and ash in the process. A crimson cloud of fiery ash filled the air as Billy hurled the dregs of his campfire into the unsuspecting guard's face. The Varelista dropped his rifle and raised his hands too late in an attempt to protect himself. He screamed in pain and stumbled back from the cell, falling over on his backside. He clawed at his face and cursed the gringo in the cell.

Billy hurried forward and caught the Sharps by the

muzzle and dragged the heavy weapon through the bars.
The Varelista, still on the ground and in agony, drew a
Colt cap-and-ball revolver and fired blindly. A slug
glanced off the iron bars, another struck sparks a few
feet over Billy's head and ricocheted off into the chamber. The buffalo gun only held one shot, but the .50-
caliber slug fired by a 140-grain load of black powder
carried enough wallop to knock a buffalo off its legs.
Billy aimed at the lock and squeezed the trigger. The
recoil almost knocked him over, the blast deafened him,
but the door to the cell blew open with a loud clang.

The Varelista crawled to his knees and squinted in
the direction of the cell, trying desperately to focus his
vision. He thought he saw movement, more like a flitting
shadow, and aimed. He hesitated and never saw the rifle
butt that clipped the side of his skull and dropped him
over on his side.

Billy raised the rifle butt again to crush the unconscious man's skull, then paused, the rifle poised. He
slowly lowered the Sharps, unable to kill the helpless
guard. He knelt by the Varelista and stripped him of his
coat, serape, and cartridge belts. Billy had just buckled
the gun belt around his own waist when the scrape of
boot leather in the passageway alerted him to the arrival
of a second visitor. Billy scrambled across the chamber
to the side of the entranceway and waited.

The drumming of boot heels on hard rock grew
louder. A second Varelista emerged from the tunnel.
Billy reached out, caught the bandit by the shoulder, and
shoved the barrel of the cap-and-ball revolver against the
startled man's throat.

"Not a sound, you bastard," Billy hissed murderously.
He spun the bandit around but kept his gun trained on

the Varelista, who tilted back his own sombrero and grinned.

"Kill me and you'll have one hell of a lot of explaining to do to your sister."

Billy's eyes widened in amazement. "Chapo!" He lowered the gun and clapped the segundo's shoulders. "Christ, Almighty, I almost killed you."

Chapo took in the chamber, the cell door blasted open on its hinges, the guard crumpled and bleeding on the floor of the prison chamber. "Sorry I'm late," he muttered.

"Yeah, I kind of got tired of waiting," Billy replied. He dressed hurriedly, pulling on the Varelista's coat and serape. The guard's sombrero was a tight fit, so Billy tossed it aside.

"C'mon," Chapo said, and started back up the tunnel to the opening of the mine. "Can you walk?" he asked.

"I can fly if I have to," Billy said with a grin, and started after the segundo. They hurried through the mine shaft and left the confines of Varela's prison behind. In a matter of minutes, Billy stood alongside Chapo. John Anthem's son gulped in the freezing air, dotted occasionally now by an errant snowflake. Billy staggered and leaned against the segundo, bracing himself against a sudden wave of dizziness.

"You all right?" Chapo asked, steadying the younger man. "You haven't been taking care of yourself."

Billy chuckled. "I know," he said in a weak voice. He breathed in deeply, slowly exhaled. "Thanks," he added, and then, "I'm sorry."

"For what?"

"The fight in the barn."

"Wasn't much of a fight, as I recall," Chapo laconically remarked. He good-naturedly tousled Billy's hair.

Billy looked off toward the town of Rosarito ablaze in the distance. An orange glare flickered over the town and lit the surrounding snow-carpeted countryside.

"What's happening?"

"Appears Big John has come calling," Chapo explained.

"My pa . . . here?" Billy asked.

"If you're surprised, then you don't know John Anthem at all," Chapo replied. "C'mon, we better not keep him waiting. Those soldier boys won't stay confused forever." Chapo started down the slope and angled off the path, looked over his shoulder, and saw Billy heading toward the hacienda. Chapo caught up to him. "This way. We got horses outside the walls."

"I have business to attend to," Billy said, pulling free of the segundo's grasp.

"We don't have time!"

"I do!" Billy loaded the Sharps and tossed the spent cartridge aside. "They killed Laura. That son of a bitch Andrés believes in vengeance—well, I'll teach him the meaning of the word." Billy's eyes narrowed, losing the reflection of his mother's gentler nature. He was weak, damn near delirious, but nothing mattered, save the hatred eating at him, a thirst for revenge he needed to quench. "It's what Big John would do."

"The hell he would. Your father wanted nothing better than to get his hands around Varela's neck. But your safety came first. So he's down there somewhere buying you time, maybe with his life." Chapo's anger had reached the boiling point. There was no time to argue; Billy had to be made to see the light and understand. He moved to block the trail leading down to the rear of the hacienda. "Now look, Billy—"

Gunfire blossomed in the dark, reaching out from the

shadows near the foot of the trail. The men who had been left behind to protect Varela, already skittish because of the commotion in town, had emerged from the rear of the house, crossed a covered courtyard, and started up the trail when they espied the men on the hillside above and opened fire.

Chapo grunted, fell against Billy, and slid to the ground, twisting himself around in the process. Chapo thrust his scattergun out from beneath his serape and blasted away with both barrels. The Sharps boomed in his ears in unison with the .12 gauge. Billy lowered the buffalo gun, drew his percussion revolver, and fired another three rounds in the direction of the gunbursts. He heard a muffled cry and then nothing. No answering fire. Only darkness again.

"You nominated?" he asked, kneeling beside Chapo.

The segundo touched his thigh and lifted blood-soaked fingers. "Nominated be damn, I got elected president," he groaned.

Billy helped him stand. Young Anthem discarded the Sharps and the cartridge belt and lifted Chapo onto his shoulders. The slope looked treacherous enough without having to manage it with a bum leg.

"What are you doing?" Chapo gasped as Anthem began to carry him on piggyback.

"Growing up before I get us both killed," Billy replied in self-disgust.

"I won't be carried like a babe in arms," Chapo protested.

"Then you'll die like a man right here," Billy countered. He sucked in his breath and wondered if he had the strength to traverse the slope. There was only one way to find out. Chapo had left a fine set of tracks in the snow and Billy followed them down, leaving the hacienda and his obsession for revenge behind.

On this cold and bitter night, wayward snowflakes drifted in the dark, lost themselves like spent souls discovering a hell not made of fire and brimstone but an awful solitude, a terrible aloneness lasting till the end of time.

Across the face of the mountain, two ungainly silhouettes managed their way, one man clinging to another and both men struggling to stay alive and reach the horses ground-tethered a hundred yards below.

Billy slid, lost his footing, and rammed his leg up against an ice-covered ocotillo. The plant's spiny limbs ripped his trouser leg and lacerated his calf. He grimaced and sucked in his breath, readjusted the weight riding on his shoulders.

"Better set me down. I'll crawl the rest of the way," Chapo said.

"The devil you will," Billy growled in return. "This'd be a whole sight easier if you hadn't been eatin' so good off of Varela's table while I've been living on the slop sent up the hill."

Chapo laughed and clung to the younger man as Billy resumed his descent, his breath billowing in the bracing cold, lungs aching from exertion; muscles trembled and threatened to give out. Despite Billy's efforts to stay fit, imprisonment had taken its toll on his wiry strength and stamina.

Snow obscured the treacherous rift in solid stone and what appeared to be a level outthrust ledge was but a layer of frozen precipitation as brittle as glass. The walls of the fortress loomed to their right, where sentries alerted by the gunfire searched the stark whiteness of the slope and found the struggling figures.

"I see them," a voice called from the hall.

"It's them," another voice replied. A third summoned soldiers from the courtyard below as those few who had remained behind with the general raced to their positions.

General Andrés Varela strode the walkway in a rage. He had only just learned of Billy Anthem's escape. Now his suspicions were confirmed. John Anthem had come to the barrancas. But where was he? On the mountain nearby, or in the town whose very center was awash with flame? Varela hurried to the sentry who had first called out. He was a slight man with dark features. The Varelista checked the cartridge tube on his Spencer repeater and, noticing Varela, snapped to attention.

"What is it? Show me! What do you see?" Varela roared.

The Varelista, a young man known only as García, gulped uncertainly, then pointed off toward the slope.

Varela followed the man's indication and searched the snow-covered slope. "I see . . . wait. Yes!" Varela glanced aside, then squinted, his hawklike features intense. "It's them!" Andrés turned to García and the other four men hurrying to station themselves along the wall. Varela knew none of their names, yet the force of his personality held sway over them. His features turned livid.

Varela, wild-eyed in the fullness of his fury, reached inside his coat and drew his Confederate-issue revolver, a nine-shot Le Mat.

"Anthem!" the general shouted. "Aaannnthemmm!" He opened fire on the figures in the landscape. The soldiers to either side followed the general's example and loosed a fusillade of shots from breechloaders and Spencer carbines. Thunder rattled over the boulder-strewn slope, blossoms of orange flame spurted from gun barrels, bullets ricocheted and careened wildly through the dark.

On the slope, Billy Anthem threw caution to the wind and broke into a muscle-wrenching run over ice-covered slabs of stone and pockets of treacherously loose shale. The nasty whine of bullets filled the air, lead slugs plowed furrows in the frozen ground at his feet.

A hundred yards, a hundred feet, then fifty . . . almost there, but damn, where were the horses? Billy glanced up, searching the darkness. The incline had leveled out now, but the hard rock surface wore an icy sheen that slowed his pace while a veneer of powdery snow provided a bright backdrop for the half-dozen Varelistas lining the wall.

"Hold on," Billy gasped, sliding, then running down the incline. Chapo's weight bowed the younger man forward and forced him off balance. Billy lenghtened his strides to keep himself from losing his balance. Gunfire rattled to his right, to be answered at last by a rapid-firing carbine to his left. He looked up in time to see a tall rangy figure on horseback, leading a pair of geldings out of the rocks. Billy headed for the stranger. He failed to recognize his own brother until he reached the horses and espied Cole's features in the flash of the yellowboy carbine.

Cole had placed the sentries by the muzzle flash of their weapons. He levered six quick shots in return. He raised up in his stirrups and roared a challenge to the soldiers above.

"C'mon, you black snakes, show your heads and I'll pop them off." He fed cartridges into the carbine while

his horse danced in a tight circle below the adobe wall.
Cole loosed another couple of shots.

Chunks of stone spattered Andrés Varela and streaked
his features with blood. The general dropped to his knees
on the walkway and cursed aloud in pain. Following his
lead, his men ducked down out of sight, one of them
cradling a shattered forearm. Varela reached out to the
man nearest him, the one called García, who was
crouched beneath the lips of the parapet.

"I'm all right," Varela shouted. "Don't let them get
away, you fools. Kill them." He grabbed García by the
shoulder and tried to lift him erect. The man slumped
forward, blood streaming from a throat wound. García's
deadweight was more than Andrés could support. The
dead man toppled forward off the walk and landed on
the roof of the barracks, rolled another couple of yards,
and disappeared over the edge of the tile roof. Varela
glanced up and saw the rest of his men were none too
anxious to poke their heads up.

"Bastards! Cowards!" Varela clamped the revolver
between his knees and proceeded to cram shells into the
cylinder. The son of a bitch with the carbine had *ojos
de gato*, cat's eyes, but Andrés would kill him.

Down below the wall, Cole continued to challenge
the men on the wall. Then he lowered his voice and
called to his brother. "Hurry up, Billy boy, those bastards
want your ears for a trophy."

"My God, is it you, Cole?" Billy rasped as he helped
Chapo up into the nearest saddle, but his voice was
drowned out by the crack of the yellowboy and the startled cry of a wounded man who had chanced a shot.

Cole noticed that Chapo had had to be carried.

"What the hell are you doing, Joaquín?" Cole asked,
leaning forward to inspect the segundo's leg.

"Rescuing your brother," Almendáriz growled in disgust and twisted the bandanna he used for a tourniquet above the ragged edges of his flesh wound.

"Could've fooled me." Cole chuckled. He emptied his carbine at the wall of the fortress, covering Billy as he mounted the horse that had formerly belonged to Aurelio Bustamante.

A smattering of gunshots searched the night once again, but the three didn't wait to reply. Now they wheeled their horses and galloped away out of sight.

Hoofbeats drummed a fierce cadence on the frozen ground, as cries lingered on in the night. It was the sound of the Anthems riding to freedom. Voices rang forth in the cold clear dark, reverberated across the mountain slope, and like freedom itself, refused to die.

Rafael Varela fired twice into the latch. The revolver bucked in his fist and thunder filled the confines of the hall. Wood splinters stung his knuckles and the acrid stench of gunsmoke burned his lungs as he shoved aside the wreckage of the door.

The commotion in the courtyard that had roused him from sleep and sent him reeling to the windows had tapered off. No doubt the gunfire would start again. Rafael had discovered a Varelista lying mortally wounded in the kitchen. As Constancia worked to save the man's life, the soldier had recounted the startling news of Billy Anthem's escape. That was all Rafael needed to know—he could conjure the rest. John Anthem had come with a veritable army of gringos and was ravaging the entire valley.

Fires lit the sky in the direction of Rosarito and the night echoed to a succession of explosions. It was only a matter of minutes before Anthem and his men would

breach the walls of the fortress itself. Well, Rafael Varela did not intend to be here when Anthem came. He
concealed his finely tailored attire beneath a ragged serape, then quickly and quietly proceeded to his father's
bedroom.

He took in Andrés' chamber at a glance; then, satisfied the room was empty, Rafael crossed to the chest at
the foot of the bed. Another well-placed shot blew the
padlock away. Rafael dropped to one knee, opened the
chest, and proceeded to stuff a saddlebag dangling over
his shoulder with the contents of the chest, buckskin
pouches jingling with silver coins. He didn't bother to
count them but noticed there were less than he had
hoped for. Still Rafael wasn't about to turn his back on
the treasure. He filled one side of the saddlebag and
started on the other. When the last drawstring pouch was
gone. Rafael tied down the flaps on the saddlebags and
draped them over his shoulder.

He stood and hurried out of the room, then paused in
the hallway to formulate a plan of escape. He considered
sneaking out of the back door, but all the horses were
in the corrals by the barracks. And he had to have a
horse. A man on foot in the barrancas wouldn't live long.
He glanced back at the room, stared at the open chest,
then stepped inside again and walked to an oil lamp on
the table. He lit the lamp and raised enough wick to
make a two-inch flame trail soot above the glass well.

"Won't do to have brother and sister find this chest
empty until I'm well away from here," Rafael said aloud.
The canopy bed would make a nice fire. He tossed the
oil lamp onto the bed and followed it with another pair
of lamps from the mantel. The blankets and bedding
exploded into flame, tongues of fire greedily devoured
the canopy and spread across the ceiling.

Rafael beat a hasty retreat from the blaze and started down the hall. He reached the top of the stairs leading down to the broad foyer and looked over his shoulder to see tendrils of fire curl through the doorway and spread outward across the wooden floor.

Damn. It was spreading faster than he had anticipated and was sure to attract attention before long. He had better hurry.

Rafael started down the stairs, taking the first two in a single stride before coming to an abrupt halt. Andrés Varela stood at the foot of the landing. His cheeks were bleeding, his hawklike features wore a wild and desperate expression. A sombrero dangled between his shoulders and his sparse growth of silver hair was matted to his skull.

"Father," Rafael gasped, "you startled me." The younger man developed a nervous twitch at the corner of his mouth. The tiny blue veins criss-crossing his prominent cheekbones stood out in stark relief beneath his thin skin.

"I can tell," Andrés said. He noticed the haze drifting out from the hall, heard the unmistakable crackling of flames. Rafael's saddlebags appeared quite heavy, and sweat suddenly beaded his forehead and glistened along his carefully trimmed mustache.

"Billy Anthem's loose," Rafael blurted out. "I, uh, I was just coming to help."

"Yes, I see," Andrés said in a cold voice. He raised his eyes to the smoke and started up the stairs.

"There's a fire. I tried to, uh, find someone to help," Rafael explained and retreated to the hall as Andrés bounded up the stairs, reached the top step, and almost lost his balance at the sight of the rapidly spreading inferno.

"What have you done?" he asked incredulously. "You miserable coward, what have you done?" He turned toward Rafael, who panicked and swung the saddlebags off his shoulder and in a vicious arc that slammed into Andrés and knocked him up against the wall. Rafael bounded past the nearly unconscious figure of his father and ran for the stairs. Andrés lunged and caught an ankle. Rafael cried out in surprise and tumbled head over heels down the stairs.

Andrés crawled to the landing, drew his gun, and tried to sight on the crumpled form lying at the foot of the stairs.

Rafael raised up on his elbows as blood seeped from a nasty bruise on his forehead. He groaned aloud and felt for broken bones. "You bastard," he said through puffed and bleeding lips. He spat a mixture of blood, phlegm, and a couple of teeth. Then, reaching for the banister, Rafael Varela pulled himself erect and drew his own revolver. He fired a shot at the man at the top of the stairs. Andrés ducked, then returned the fire, and Rafael darted out of harm's way and headed for the front door. He threw it open and whirled about in the doorway.

"I have your treasure, you old bastard. Every penny," he roared in triumph, and slapped the saddlebags. "And no one's going to stop me. You hear? No one."

Suddenly the darkness behind Rafael was lit by a brilliant orange flash of light and the resounding crack of a Navy Colt fired at close range. Rafael raised up on the balls of his feet, arched his spine, and staggered back into the hacienda. He stumbled toward the stairway. The saddlebags slid from his shoulder, the revolver from his grasp. He twisted around. The back of his serape was singed and powder burned and stained with his life's blood. Rafael stared at the doorway and watched in horror as Hector Varela filled the passage with his great girth and raised the revolver gripped in his hairy fist.

"Wait," Rafael pleaded. "I can explain . . . please."

"I don't have the time," Hector said matter-of-factly, and shot his brother right between the eyes. The heavyset man strode quickly to Rafael's lifeless form splayed upon the stairway. He retrieved the silver-laden saddlebags and then gazed upward at his father, who now stood, outlined in the glare of the flames that speedily consumed not only his house but his entire kingdom as well.

"We have work to do," Andrés said.

Hector nodded. The vendetta had passed to him. "I'll gather the men," he said.

Four riders reached the entrance to the valley and there they paused with the town of Rosarito and the fortress of Varela outlined in flames. They paused to water their horses and gather the other mounts left along with the bound forms of Natividad and the *soldado* Cole had bludgeoned. Cole and Chapo busied themselves with the hasty preparations for the ride north.

John and Billy were left alone in a moment of privacy. John studied his proud but haggard son. Billy waited, ashamed that he had ever doubted the love this man had for him. Action broke their uneasy silence. Father and son moved as one, closed with each other in an embrace that spoke more eloquently than any fumbled words of regret. Then Big John clapped his son on the back and drew away looking toward Cole as the bounty-hunter led the extra mounts out from concealment.

"I hate to break up the reunion, but we better put some distance between us and those folks below. Or we just might wind up neighbors in a cell," Cole said. He leapt astride his horse and shouted back toward the concealed ledge where they had left Natividad.

"Light a shuck, Chapo," the bounty-hunter shouted.

"Your brother's right," John said, handing Billy a pair of reins. The snow had stopped and moon-light streamed through a break in the clouds, transforming the albescent landscape into a sparkling fairyland of silver-dappled shapes and pristine snowdrifts flecked with jewels. But the aura of innocence was illusion. This was killing ground, as was all the run to the Rio Grande. There was a race with death to be won.

Big John Anthem swung into the saddle. He grinned at Billy. "Your ma has set a place for you for Christmas dinner. We got eleven days not to disappoint her." He tossed Billy an extra gun belt and a Colt .44 to replace the cap-and-ball the young man had confiscated.

"I'd purely hate to do that," Billy replied, and saddled up.

John saw to it that each of his sons led an extra horse. Then he looked off toward the brush-choked hiding place where Andrés Varela had posted his sentries. He gazed worriedly back the way they had ridden. As yet, there was no pursuit. But he could make out a swarm of activity and an occasional gunshot was heard as the soldiers, in their confusion, fired at shadows and even some of the townspeople.

"Hurry, my friend," John said beneath his breath, returning his attention to the ledge. "Hurry."

Chapo Almendáriz untied the bandanna from around Natividad's mouth. She tried to bite him, but he expected trouble and was quick enough to keep from losing a finger.

"Son of a bitch," she snapped, and gave a toss of her head that flicked aside her long black hair. She kicked at the segundo as he stood and backed away from her.

"Listen, little wildcat. Your father will no doubt be riding by, sooner or later. If you make plenty of noise, he'll hear you."

Chapo undid the gag from the securely bound sentry as well. Here beneath the ledge, the walls reflected the warmth of the campfire that Chapo hastily built.

"No doubt you might even free yourselves if you don't mind a few burns," he added. "But either way, wildcat, don't come after us." His eyes narrowed and his voice took on the cutting edge of finely honed steel. "In a way, I am sorry for you, little one. With a father like Andrés Varela, you could be nothing else but what you are. Don't make me kill you."

He limped into the underbrush and left Natividad, for a moment rendered silent by his parting sentiment. Then her fury at his betrayal returned anew and she hurled curses into the night.

Chapo continued on, at a run now, to where the others waited. A few moments later he mounted alongside John Anthem, grimacing at the pain that seared his thigh.

"You hurt bad?" John asked, concerned.

"Nothing that home won't cure, Big John," Chapo replied.

John nodded and looked over at his sons, his fine sons, together at last. All of them—Chapo, too—at long last a family again.

"Let's go to Texas," John Anthem said.

And led the way.

25

The woman by the oven did not care who made camp at the spring seeping up out of the ground twenty feet from her door. Any man, woman, or child could eat her tortillas and *frijoles* and peppery chili con carne, everyone was welcome at her table so long as they paid.

Her name was Cecilia, but the farmers down in the valley knew her only as the Widow Flores. Tonight she cooked enough for four men. But only three had ridden up to her door at midday. They claimed a fourth would be arriving later on, and as four shiny new dollars jangled in the pocket of her apron, the good widow wasn't about to argue.

Chapo brushed past the buxom *señora* and lifted the coffeepot from the fire. He hurried to the table before the hot metal handle burned through the cotton towels to his unprotected palm. Flores turned to watch as he filled a coffeecup for himself and resumed eating. He sensed her scrutiny and looked up, wiping his mouth on the back of his hand. She looked from Big John to Billy Anthem and then back to Almendáriz.

"*¿Por qué vas con los norteamericanos?*" Flores asked, her eyes darting once more toward the Anthems.

She remembered John Anthem and another gringo had ridden through about a week ago, following a southern trail into the mountains. And Chapo, too, had stopped to rest his horse and eat her food, but that had been more than two months past.

"He is my segundo," John Anthem politely interjected, catching the widow off guard. "And he is my good friend," John added.

"I did not mean, uh, to be so inquisitive. You do not take offense?" Flores said anxiously. John's command of Spanish had taken her off guard. She wanted no trouble. People came and went—traveling north or south, east or west—she rarely asked questions. She had learned from the example of her husband, who had asked one question too many and had been killed for his trouble. She backed toward the hearth, the hem of her ankle-length skirt brushing dangerously close to the fire.

"No offense," John answered. "Please, *señora*. It would be a terrible loss if one so beautiful caught herself on fire."

The widow Flores quickly stepped forward and checked her gaily patterned dress for any glowing sparks. Her breasts strained against the cotton blouse as she twisted to check the back of her skirt. When she looked back, her expression had warmed. A comely woman in the autumn of her years, her pinned hair flecked with silver and her smooth brown skin free of blemish, she appreciated a man's interest and his compliments, whatever his ulterior motives.

"I hope I am not being forward, Señora Flores," John added, his creased features split by a smile, "but fine food and great beauty have loosened my tongue."

Billy stared at his father in amazement—he had never

seen John Anthem quite so gallant. Chapo struggled to hide his own amazement.

"You are most gallant, Señor Norteamericano," Cecilia said. "Such company as yours I find most welcome." With a swirl of her skirt that showed her ankles, the Widow Flores left the kitchen. She paused in the living room to gather a couple of extra blankets from a cabinet, then continued on to her bedroom, her pace jaunty as she hummed a merry tune of love and spring and a young man's fancy.

John noticed his son's awestruck look and drew himself up, mustering every ounce of dignity. "Well, I wasn't always a thickheaded old man," John growled.

"Yeah, he used to be a thickheaded *young* man," Chapo merrily added.

Billy laughed aloud.

"If you ask me, Joaquín, I didn't beat you enough when I had the chance," John grumbled. He wrapped a tortilla around a spoonful of beans and dipped one end into his bowl of chili before devouring it in a couple of bites.

"I know we'll sleep in the barn, but how about you, Pa?" Billy asked. "You want me to come inside and wake you when Cole shows up?" The young man peeked through the doorway at the good widow busily making up her bed in the next room.

"Look, damm it," John said, flustered now. "At least she isn't afraid of us. And maybe she won't tell Varela when we came by." He held up his hands, palms opened. "Seems to me that's worth the price of a little sweet talk."

"I hope Ma sees it that way," Billy warned.

"I'll be in the barn with you two," John pointedly explained. He slapped his empty coffeecup down on the

tabletop in disgust and shoved away from what was left
of his plate of food. "Hell, I better git before she comes
back."

"What do I tell her?" Chapo called after him. Then
the reason for John Anthem's sudden retreat reappeared.
The Widow Flores stood in the doorway, her fists on her
ample hips, a perturbed frown darkening her expression.
She smelled of rose water and vanilla. A spot of rouge
highlighted her round cheeks.

"He's gone to check the horses, *señora*," Chapo explained.

"Send him to me when he returns," the widow said.
"I have something to show him." She crossed to a cupboard whose wooden paneled doors wore a fresh coat of
white paint. She brought out a clay bottle of *pulque* and
two cups. She turned, caught the two men staring at her,
and misread their curiosity.

"There is another bottle," the widow said. "But it will
cost another dollar."

Chapo searched the pocket of his buckskin jacket and
produced the appropriate number of coins.

"Tell me, *señora*, is it *pulque* or gold?" the segundo
asked. The price of liquor was damn high in this house.

"Gold," the widow answered, and scooped up the
money, opened her blouse, and dropped the coins into a
pouch dangling between her breasts. The widow
hummed a tune as she left the kitchen.

Billy cleared his throat, rose, and stepped back from
the table. "You reckon Pa will be safe with us in the
barn? She might come out after him," he said. He pulled
on his serape and rubbed a hand across his scraggly
blond beard.

"I got a razor in my gear," Chapo said. He had limped
over to the cupboard and found the *pulque* and was bus-

ily helping himself to a cup of the potent drink.

Billy nodded and left by the back door.

Chapo watched him leave and then took another pull from the bottle. In a couple of days they'd be across the Rio Grande and maybe he wouldn't have to meet Natividad ever again. Because he did not know if he could kill her. One thing was for certain though: Natividad would sure as hell kill him if she ever got the chance.

He downed the contents of his cup, felt the *pulque* course through his veins, helping to warm everything but his heart.

From the Flores corral Billy could gaze down across a series of low rolling hills to the village of El Dorado, an assemblage of adobe houses clustered about a central plaza dominated by the whitewashed walls of the village church. It was a sleepy-looking town here at midday. But the appearance of inactivity was only illusion, for El Dorado's inhabitants were busy in the fields, clearing the planting ground of rocks, fetching cut grass for the cows and goats in the meadow. The women prepared the noon meal under a central roof, an open-sided building lined with rows of benches and long tables.

The land around the village was a tableau of low hills checkered with the quickly melting vestiges of a previous snowfall. The fallow fields waiting for the coming of spring—the well-worked ground pregnant with possibilities.

"Hard-won land," John remarked, walking up behind his son.

Billy glanced at his father's reflection in the small round mirror he had hung from a nail in the post. They had spoken of Laura, here in the sunlight to hold the gloom at bay. And Billy felt better knowing she had been given a proper burial and the words read over her. She slept in peace.

Billy returned his attention to the task at hand. He wiped the soap from his face and studied his own features in the mirror. Gone was the young man of summer who had ridden with his love among blue Texas skies. His eyes were deeper set, his cheeks gaunt, and his expression far more guarded; he had hidden his own torment for so many weeks of captivity. Perhaps his buoyant nature would return, but for now, tragedy had leached much of his enthusiasm. He did not know what lay ahead for him. The future was like a book, its contents to be discovered and hopefully—one day—savored again.

Maybe sooner than he expected.

For the air was clean and cold and sweet to the breath with the temperature warming into the fifties. And the sun felt good, touching his back in the absence of a north wind.

"Hard won, like Luminaria," Billy replied.

"I got no complaints," John said.

"Neither do I, Pa," Billy added.

John studied his son, trying to figure the lad. But the change left him puzzled. Billy noticed his father's continued interest and the older man's hesitant desire to carry on some sort of dialogue with his son. Billy finally rescued the man from his diffidence.

"They kept me pretty solitary back in the mine. I guess the more thinking I did, the more it seemed a better way to live. Just watching and thinking and less gab," Billy said.

John softly laughed; he felt much the same way himself. "I guess I expected you to be burned up with hate for what's been done."

"I was for a while," Billy said. "And started to be again until I almost got Chapo killed." He folded the razor into its handle and slid it back inside Chapo's saddlebag along with the mirror. He turned and faced his father in the noonday sun. "If I get the chance, I'll see justice done. But I don't aim to twist my soul up with hate and a thirst for revenge . . . No, sir . . . not for Andrés Varela and his whole dark brood."

Billy buckled his gun belt around his narrow waist. A head smaller than Big John, young Billy Anthem now seemed carved of the same stuff as his father—Texas pride and courage and honest resiliency, the kind of toughness bred in men who have to stand alone.

"I love you, son," John said. The words shocked even the speaker, for Big John could not remember when he had last spoken them. Too long ago, that was for certain.

"I love you, too, Pa," Billy replied.

There was nothing else to say.

A horseman rescued them from silence. It was Cole, riding at a full gallop down from the cholladotted hillside, cutting across narrow gulleys where the snow lay trapped in shadow and paved the yellow slope with streaks of brilliant white.

Cole noticed the men at the corral and headed straight for them, reining his winded gelding to a sudden, savage halt near the post oak fencing. The brown gelding dug its hooves into the hardpacked sod to keep from crashing into timber.

"You're either hungry or Varela and his wolves are a lot closer than we expected," Big John called out as he walked along the side of the corral and up to the bounty-hunter.

"Both," Cole said, and hurriedly unfastened his saddle, slid it off the gelding's back, and slung blanket and leather over the railing.

"Nearest I could count," Cole said, "there's ten of them. And each man is leading a couple of extra horses." Cole pointed toward the stark outline of the ridge a dozen miles to the south. "I used the glass and saw them from up yonder. Varela ought to be sitting down to the widow's chili and beans, come nightfall."

"Damn," John blurted out, and slapped his fist in his palm. He turned and counted the horses in the corral, knowing full well that half of the number were already spent. He had counted on a night's rest. Well, so be it.

"Can you ride?" he asked, peering at his son.

Cole shrugged. "Hell, my butt's already numb. It won't know the difference."

"Go on and get some grub and send Chapo out. I'll saddle your dun," John said. Cole nodded and walked off, clapping Billy on the shoulder and continuing to Cecilia's house, his loose limbed, long strides covering the distance in a matter of seconds.

John ran a hand over his jaw and scratched at his chin. Ten men . . . ten men . . . Why, that would make the fight interesting, no? What on earth? The very idea was madness. He had promised Rose he would bring her sons home and they had better not be shot to doll rags or she might just perforate his vest.

He turned and stared at the ridge down which Cole had ridden, down which Varela would come.

"Shall I saddle up?" Billy asked. "Pa?" He reached out and touched his father's forearm. "Are we leaving?"

"Uh-yeah," John absently answered. His eyes never left the ice-streaked purple ridge framed against a cloudless sky. And his wind-chapped, leathery features took on a hardness that matched the distant cliffs. He was remembering another time, when as a young man Gen. Varela had chased him out of Mexico. John didn't like running then. He liked it even less today.

He was remembering.

And it hurt.

And it made John Anthem angry. Angry as hell.

26

Andrés Varela considered the village of El Dorado to be merely an extension of his realm, an outlying part of his kingdom whose crops were to be freely exploited whenever necessary. His men had ridden up at sunset to the house of the Widow Flores and loosed their horses in her corral.

Varela dispatched Hector and the soldiers to the village and informed the widow that she would be sleeping in the stable. Cecilia might have found the courage to protest had the general not found a silver coin in his saddlebags to appease her. The widow dutifully prepared a meal and left her home and hearth to Andrés and his daughter. She left as unobtrusively as possible after answering all she knew about the gringos who had ridden through. The one called John Anthem had been very handsome; ordinarily she might have lied to protect him, but not to a man like Varela. His vengeance was quick and merciless, and she wanted no part of the trouble he could bring.

Andrés Varela took his cup of coffee out beneath the thatch shelter that shaded the front of the adobe cabin. He studied the cold blue sky. Behind him, Natividad,

whom the general had rescued from the pass above Rosarito, stood in the doorway of the cabin and watched
her father's thin figure. He sipped his coffee and massaged his lower abdomen. He hadn't spoken of his pain,
but she knew it persisted. Sweat clung to his brow on
this cold December night. How much longer would his
pain-racked frame continue to function?

She watched as he set his coffee down on the ground
and rolled a sprinkle of crushed hemp leaves into a cigarette, struck a match, and lit it. He inhaled, then
breathed out a billowing gray cloud. The tension seemed
to leave his body, and he visibly relaxed, leaning against
one of the posts supporting the reed-woven overhang.

"We'll catch them," Andrés remarked, catching Natividad off guard. He hadn't turned around to see her,
yet he sensed her presence. And here, out in the clear
night he had recognized her musky smell. It might have
aroused him in a merrier time. He had no use for pleasure now, wanting only the death of John Anthem, only
the settling of an old score. "Our horses are not as tired,
and we can change mounts more often. In a day or two,
we shall have them."

"But what if they cross the border?" Natividad asked.

"I spit on the border," Varela growled. "What is the
Rio Bravo? What is it but a river flowing between that
which is ours and that which the *norteamericanos* stole
from us years ago. I look across it and what do I see,
more of Mexico."

He raised his wooden right hand and placed the cigarette between two carved unmoving fingers. He picked
up his coffeepot and cursed as he managed to spill a few
drops on the military coat he wore. It was cut of heavy
woolen cloth, dyed blue with scarlet trim, and hung almost to his knees. The coat had belonged to a French

legionnaire slain during the Juárez rebellion. Andrés had found it among the dead man's belongings. It did not matter to Varela that the uniform coat looked odd with the general's purple-stitched sombrero and gialy embroidered vaquero trousers.

Natividad was dressed much the same as any of the Varelistas. A waist-length coat concealed her bosom and a sombrero her long black hair and comely features. She hooked a thumb in the gun belt at her waist, her fingers tap-tapping on the bullets in her belt. Her face, in repose, assumed a hard-edged steeliness that made her seem years older than her actual age.

Natividad stared out at the night, feeling her own sense of anger and betrayal cast a warmth more consuming than any fire. She too knew hatred. Whenever it dulled, she only had to think of Chapo's arms around her, his caressing her, taking her, and all the while playing her for a fool.

"Tell me, daughter," Varela said, his voice cutting through the night stillness. "Who killed Aurelio Bustamante, my old and dear friend?"

"Señor John Anthem," Natividad replied. "Why?"

"Oh, when I kill John Anthem, I want to know all the crimes he answers for," Andrés said. He tried to think beyond this pursuit. Hector had only been able to round up ten men; the rest, the black-hearted cowards, had been too busy looting Rosarito to obey orders. Only Hector's personal guard, men more loyal to the son than the father. The very notion galled Andrés and he intended to correct the situation one way or another.

"Daughter . . ."

"Yes, Father."

"We will have to put Hector in his place, once the Anthems are dead. Put him in his place and . . . start over." Varela sighed, took one last drag on his cigarette, and dropped the remains in the dirt. "You and I must work together . . . closely together."

"*Sí, padre,*" Natividad answered. She smiled and thought of Hector's saddlebags lying on the table in the kitchen. They had a pleasant, comfortable weight and contained just enough silver coins for a father and daughter . . . or maybe just a daughter. "Sí, we must work very closely," Natividad added. She crossed to him and stood at his side, so he could feel the heat of her body close to his, the very image of a loving daughter.

27

Four men came riding a week before Christmas, down through the broken hills of Chihuahua to the land of the Big Bend where the Rio Grande carved its sluggish course through the dry dusty peaks, cutting cliffs of limestone into sharp relief. On the rim, desert shrubs grew blossom to barb, wild rose, and ocotillo, and sotol with its broad, sharp-pointed leaves flourished in arid harmony alongside silver leaf and clumps of creosote bush. Down in the more hospitable heart of Gato Canyon, ash and walnut and stands of buckeye and lip fern struggled to survive and provided shade for jackrabbits and whip-tailed lizards, cougars and coyotes.

The Rio Grande flowed sluggishly southward through the center of the canyon, the river's shallows providing easy crossing. It was a broad canyon, better than two hundred yards across from ridge to ridge, with about seventy yards of river stealing silt from the riverbanks and eating away at the roots of cottonwoods during flood stage.

Linking two countries, Gato Canyon was indeed a sweet Eden offering respite from the harsh terrain stretching out from the rims.

John Anthem climbed down from his horse and let the animal drink at the river. Billy and Chapo followed suit and knelt upstream of their mounts. The two men still had to use their bandannas to strain the grit out of the icy waters.

Cole seemed reluctant to dismount and kept looking back down the valley as if expecting the Varelistas to come riding out of the grove of cottonwoods through which the Anthems had just ridden. He stared at his family in disbelief.

"The water will taste even better across the Rio Grande," Cole admonished. He noticed Big John wasn't drinking and took heart. At least his father was showing some sense. "You tell them, Pa."

"Relax, *mi amigo*," Chapo replied, running a hand through his matted black hair. "We still have a couple of hours lead. And even Varela isn't crazy enough to cross the border."

"He did once, or have you forgotten Billy here?" Cole returned.

"That's what I mean," Chapo said. He stood and donned his sombrero again. "I've ridden with those bandits. They're worried about angering the Mexican government. I don't think they want another border incident."

"Varela won't stop at a river," John said, patting the dust from his coat and batwing chaps. He looked up at the sky, a cold clear ceiling overhead completely devoid of clouds. Nothing but stark space and a molten gold sun to temper the winter wind. It burned high above the canyon, reaching toward noon on its timeless track. "Varela won't stop. Nor would I. Not that it matters, 'cause I'm staying here."

His pronouncement struck like a cannon shell in their

midst. Billy straightened, water spilling from his cupped hands. Chapo had started to light the last of his cigars in celebration of their escape. The match burned down to his fingertips and he dropped it with a start. Cole looked on, dumbfounded. He closed his eyes, shook his head, and muttered, "Oh, shit."

"It's been gnawing at my gut for days now, and getting worse since we left the widow's," John said, turning at last from the distant stand of cottonwoods a quarter of a mile up the riverbank to the artery borderline on his right. He looked out upon the Rio Grande and envisioned another time and a younger, leaner version of himself riding for his life with Varela and his militia in desperate pursuit. "I've been chased across this river once by Andrés Varela. I'll be damned if I'm going to let it happen again." John faced the men around him. "I'll not be hounded again by that bastard. It ends . . . here . . . today." John drew his Colt Dragoon and checked the shells in the cylinder.

"You can't be serious," Cole lamely replied. He reined his horse away from the river. The dun sidestepped and swung about. "Aren't you forgetting your promise to Rose? You said you'd bring Billy home."

"Take him with you," Chapo spoke up. He broke open his shotgun and removed the shells, gave each a shake, and listened to the pellets rattle, then he slid the shells into the barrels. He met John's gaze and nodded. "I'll stay too."

"Oh, Christ," Cole snapped. He wasn't afraid, but there was no point to it. Texas waited across the river and in a couple of days' hard riding they'd all be home. Why get themselves killed? For what? Pride?

"This is my fight," John Anthem said as Chapo limped over to stand alongside the rancher.

"The hell it is," Billy spoke up. He stepped around his horse. The youngest Anthem took the Henry rifle out of Chapo's saddle scabbard and stepped back from the river's edge. A breeze tugged at the hem of his serape and brushed the coarsely woven cloth away from the Navy Colt holstered at his side. It was Poke Tyler's gun, but the smooth worn grip seemed made for Billy's hand.

"I don't need to be taken anywhere," Billy added. "I'm big enough to get there on my own. Maybe you've forgotten, Big John, but I too had a taste of Andrés Varela's hospitality." He balanced the long barrel of the Henry on his shoulder. His soft brown eyes seemed to darken. "And I don't think I thanked him properly."

John looked at his son, saw the image of Rose Anthem, that bold and bald-faced stubbornness that John Anthem knew was futile to argue against. He shifted his gaze to Chapo, hoping to talk some sense into him.

"I ride for the brand. It is my right to stay." Chapo grinned.

"Well, I'm not going to stay," Cole said. "I've seen enough men get butchered for the sake of pride. During the war the streams ran red with blood. No more." His eyes were ice-blue chips, his tone that of a man who had lived by his wits and daring, a man with a healthy respect for profit. The bounty-hunter had the feeling he might just as well save his breath.

"No one's asked you to stay, Cole," said John Anthem. "So, who are you arguing with? Me? Or yourself?"

The tall, lanky gunfighter eased back in the saddle, ran a hand across his blunt, square-jawed features. He slapped the dust from his denim jacket and sighed. "I guess this is where I cross the river," he said.

"Maybe you crossed the river a long time ago," John

said. He moved toward the bounty-hunter. "At least I've one son who shows some sense." He glowered for a moment at Billy, who would not back down for all his father's forceful presence. John lifted a hand and clasped Cole's. "Tell your mother I'll be along."

Cole pulled free and with a tug on the reins headed the dun stallion down the riverbank and into the water. The water was cold and Cole sucked in his breath as the stallion's driving legs splashed water and soaked him to the skin. The bounty-hunter gritted his teeth and endured the discomfort, thankful that the river was low here and only came up to the stallion's belly. Even so, he reached the opposite bank wet and miserable. The stallion emerged from the shallows, trampling a mat of water clover whose tiny stalks dotted the river's edge on the Texas bank.

Cole Tyler Anthem . . . Anthem . . . but that didn't mean he had to be massacred with the rest of his family. He studied the ridges and espied the well-worn trail that led up from the river through a break in the post oaks and to the land beyond the canyon with its broken hills and sagebrush-choked arroyos, to stark mountains and hidden Edens like the canyon surrounding him here in the bend of the river.

He glanced over his shoulder and saw that Billy was tending to the horses while Chapo had built a small fire and begun to boil coffee. Big John was cleaning his rifle. The tranquil scene gave no hint of the violence the afternoon would bring.

Cole checked the grove of post oaks upriver. In a couple of hours Varela and his men would come drifting through the timber. Then Eden would have its own bitter taste of hell.

"Right now I should be holed up at Blind Pete's with

Glory Doolin in my arms," Cole said aloud, and sighed. He glanced again at the trail leading out of the canyon and knew in his jaded heart he could not ride that trail alone. He swung the dun back toward the river. The stallion balked at first, but Cole prodded with his dulled spurs and at the first touch of metal the dun headed down the bank and into the Rio Grande.

Five minutes later Cole rode the animal onto dry ground. He dismounted, ground-tethered the stallion, and sauntered over to the campfire. Chapo, Billy, and John watched him approach. Cole nodded his thanks and took the cup Chapo offered him.

The bounty-hunter looked up at John. "I guess I was arguing with myself."

"What happened?" John asked.

"I lost." Cole shrugged.

John Anthem smiled then. He breathed deeply and never felt more alive.

Let it end here, then, he prayed. It must end here.

28

Eden was silent.

And the men there passed the easy hours, enjoying the rest and the freedom and the taste of strong coffee. The sun overhead warmed the meadow's carpet of dry winter grass. A cooling breeze sent the rushes fluttering there by the muddy bank and stirred the river's placid surface into shimmering patterns of sunlight. Peace reigned here beneath the walls of the canyon, a tranquil tableau of sunlight, gentle winter sky, and sage-freshened air.

An hour passed, and four men waited. A second hour began, and time passed as inexorably as the river's flow, constant and irrevocable. Time to be cherished, to be lived to the fullest. A second hour passed, and four men waited, each alone with his thoughts.

He was called Yellowboy, a hunter of men. And that is who I must be today, Cole Tyler Anthem told himself. He could not afford to think of family, of belonging again. He must be a man alone, with only as much conscience as was absolutely necessary. It was a trick he had never truly mastered. But he liked to pretend that he had. He wiped the stock of his Winchester, balanced the carbine once more in the crook of his arm, and joined Chapo on a log that a flash flood had deposited on the riverbank.

The segundo was busy examining the flesh wound that had already scabbed over on his thigh. But he was far less troubled by his leg than by the role he had played for the past several weeks. It was good to be Joaquín Almendáriz, a segundo, again. It was good to be in the company of people he cared about. And if he was not the same man who had ridden out of Luminaria back in autumn, then so be it; he sighed.

Billy Anthem looked down at the gun in his hand. Firing at dimly revealed silhouettes in the dark was one thing. But today, in sunlight—that was something else. He had never killed a man, unless he had hit someone by accident during his escape from the mines. Today he would have to stand face to face, he would have to kill, and the young man wondered whether or not he could. Billy closed his eyes and pictured Laura, dying in the rain. It was not a pretty memory. But his own expression became more resolute the longer he dwelled on the tragic image. He thumbed the hammer on the Navy Colt, raised it, and sighted on the grove of trees at the upper end of the canyon. Now if those were Varelistas . . .

John Anthem thought of nothing at all. He was stretched out on dry ground with his head propped against a rock and a twig of dry straw clamped between his teeth. Like an Apache, he had freed his thoughts and allowed his senses to mesh with the world around him. He had become part of the turning earth, the breeze, the chattering squirrels in the cottonwoods, and the post oaks upriver, one with the course of the sun and the silence and the sounds of the canyon that suddenly changed.

Flocks of warblers and wild thrushes rose from the tops of the trees. The squirrels ceased their chatter. A fawn bolted from the shadow of the oaks and darted toward the four men. The startled animal hugged the base of the cliff as it raced past, brown eyes wide with terror.

Big John stood and without a word to his sons or segundo headed straight for his horse. With a jangle of spurs and the creak of stirrup leather the four Texans mounted and walked their horses clear of the muddy bank. They reined them to a halt and waited motionlessly, each man's gaze rooted on the stand of timber. They did not have long to wait. A few moments later a line of Varelistas emerging from the trees brought up sharply at the sight of the four men arrayed at the other end of the river bend.

Andrés Varela glanced aside at his son and daughter. "I knew it. I knew he would wait." He allowed his mount to carry him a couple of steps forward. The general winced, sucked in his breath. The grueling ride had nearly finished him. The pain in his bowels was almost unbearable. But now the chase was at an end. Varela wrapped the reins around his wooden right hand. His left reached for his revolver. "Anthem! I know you!"

Hector checked the surrounding terrain, suspicious of a trap, and noticed in the process the worried expressions of those men to either side, hard-faced men used to having their way, accustomed to bullying poor peons, men used to having people run from them. The four statuelike figures downriver were something else again. They weren't running. And this was not a good omen.

"Relax, *compadres*," Hector called out in a soothing voice. "We outnumber them. We are many and they are few."

"*Sí*, like at Rosarito," one of the men muttered in apprehension, the debacle still fresh in his mind. He spoke for all the men.

Hector glared at the bandit but could think of nothing to say in reply. He looked over at his sister.

Natividad tucked her hair up into her sombrero and tied the drawstring beneath her chin. She licked moisture from her upper lip and drew her gun, any gentleness in her gone now, replaced by something as harsh and unforgiving as the desert.

John Anthem recognized Varela in the lead. That was all he needed to see. He slipped the Colt Dragoon from its holster and looked across at Billy.

"Are you Texas-born?" he asked.

"Yes sir," Billy answered.

John Anthem glanced up at Chapo and Cole Tyler, grinned, and shouted, to Billy and the other two, "Come on, then!" He spurred his horse and the animal leapt forward, danced a step, then broke into a gallop. Chapo, Billy, and Cole Tyler started as one, riding side by side in the sunlight.

John Anthem had no use for talking. His Colt Dragoon would speak for him. He waved his sons on and loosed a wild rebel yell. He'd had his fill of the general. It was time the world was rid of Andrés Varela.

"Anthem! You hear me?" Varela shouted. His eyes widened. What were these crazy Texans doing? He had wanted to relish this moment. He wanted to talk . . . to talk . . . He cursed and whipped his own mount. The horse neighed and sped away at a dead run across the meadow toward the charging Texans.

Hector wasn't about to let his father steal the glory

and shouted for the Varelistas to follow him. His stallion lumbered forward beneath the big man's immense weight. The valiant steed finally managed an ungainly gallop. The *soldados* easily drew abreast of Hector but made no effort to take the lead as they spread out in a ragged line of attack. Rifles and carbines and handguns slid from holsters. Several of the men fired wildly at the approaching Texans. Hector shouted for his men to be more careful and make their shots count.

The approaching lines grew closer, the Varelistas wavering before the determined charge of John Anthem and his sons. A hundred yards separated them, became eighty, then fifty. Gunsmoke continued to blossom in the sun-drenched air. The thunder of the Varelistas' gunfire reverberated throughout the canyon. Fifty yards became forty, thirty, twenty—and men began to die . . .

Cole fired, levered a fresh shell, fired again. It was nearly impossible to hit anything from horseback. He rode close to the riverbank where it rose a good ten feet up from the river. The bounty-hunter hauled back on the reins of his dun, slid out of the saddle, and dropped behind the edge of the bank. As the stallion raced clear, Cole climbed up through the mud and raised up on one knee and opened fire with his yellowboy at the *soldados* bearing down on him. A piratical-looking brigand with a patch covering one eye dropped his Spencer repeater and slid from horseback. Cole twisted aside, fired, shifted his aim, and let off a couple of shots. A Varelista wrapped in a black-and-scarlet serape fired, missed, and took a bullet in the shoulder. His second shot spattered Cole with mud. Cole dusted the front of the man's serape, chest high, and the bandit toppled out of the saddle and rolled on the muddy bank to land facedown in the shallows. Cole spaced his shots with murderous effect.

It was what he did best. Men turned and fled from his
deadly gun.

With a sickening thud of horseflesh and the crack of
bones, two horses swerved into each other and went
down, sending their riders sprawling. John Anthem staggered to his knees and watched his own horse stagger
off. "Christ, that was dumb," John muttered. He looked
for his old enemy and saw Varela lying motionless on
the ground. Bullets sliced the air and John swung about
to bring his Dragoon Colt to bear as a slug burned a
furrow across his left forearm. He groaned and opened
up with the Colt. The .44 boomed and a Varelista doubled over, dropped his gun, and rode to safety. Two of
his *compadres* followed suit.

    Then something slammed into Anthem's side and Big
John went down. Andrés Varela, aiming over his crippled mount, roared in triumph and staggered to his feet.

Chapo dodged as Hector fired at him. The segundo
crouched low in the saddle and loosed both barrels of
the shotgun at Varela's son. The distance was too great
for the cut-down .12-gauge to be completely effective,
and Chapo had fired off balance. The shot peppered Hector's stallion, raked flesh, and ripped open the saddlebags
draped behind the saddle. The stallion, a feisty half-
broken mountain pony, leapt, bowed back, and sent Hector flying.

    Hector landed on his rump, the animal on all fours.
It raced off, kicking and leaping and pawing the air and
strewing a trail of glittering silver coins in the wake of
its flashing hooves.

    Natividad recognized Chapo through the haze of
gunsmoke and would have ridden him down had not

Hector's stallion galloped past, littering its treasure. The silver! A fortune to be had. Natividad holstered her gun and gave chase. After all, revenge was one thing, but a fortune in silver quite another. She tugged savagely on the reins, brought herself out of the fray, and sped back toward the trees. She rode at a breakneck pace, desperate to reach the pain-crazed stallion before it disappeared among the timber and the other saddlebags ripped open.

Chapo was too busy reloading to notice the departing young woman. He slipped two shells into the shotgun and looked up as a couple of *soldados* charged. Black smoke and flame belched from their percussion pistols and a lead ball whined past just inches from the segundo's skull as another plowed a hole through the folds of his serape but managed to miss flesh and bone.

"Madre mía," Chapo exclaimed, and blasted away with both barrels at point-blank range. Black powder smoke stung his eyes and momentarily blinded him. He crouched over the saddle horn, gritted his teeth, and braced himself for the impact of a bullet that never came. Two riderless horses galloped toward the river, abandoning the melee. Two men sprawled in the dirt like broken puppets staring with sightless eyes as the segundo rode past.

Behind the segundo, Hector scrambled to his feet, wiped the dirt out of his eyes, grabbed for a revolver tucked in his belt, then froze. A shadow fell across him. Hector looked up into the barrel of Billy's Navy Colt.

Silver was power. Silver was freedom. Silver was a life of luxurious nobility lived in Mexico City or Vera Cruz. Let Hector or Andrés have their stinking mountains. Natividad no longer needed them. She didn't even care about Chapo. Not now. Not when she could have everything.

Riding at a dead gallop, the woman drew alongside Hector's stallion and, leaning low, snared the reins and brought the frightened animal to a skidding halt.

"Mine," she exclaimed. She never heard the gunshot that killed her. Her horse danced to the side. She pitched from the saddle, a bullet through her skull.

"Ours," a chorus of three voices said behind her. Three young hard cases allowed their horses to gingerly step over her lifeless form. They were three of Hector's trusted men whose loyalty had been tested and found lacking at the sight of so much silver. Two of them were wounded and saw no reason to return to the fight by the river. After all, a man could get killed.

Varelistas no more, the three men holstered their guns and, with the skittish stallion in tow, started back to Rosarito in the mountains, leaving the bend of the river behind.

Andrés Varela stumbled around his crippled horse as the animal flayed at the air. The general stood over the fallen form of John Anthem, the man he had just shot in the back.

"I swore I'd kill you," Varela shouted. "Now the debt is paid." The general reached and grabbed the shoulder of the blood-spattered man lying facedown on the trampled earth. "I want this to be the last thing you see," Varela shouted. He held up his wooden hand with the word *Venganza* branded on the wooden palm. He gave a mighty haul and flipped John Anthem over on his back and saw first to his relief then horror that not only was Big John alive, he still had his Colt .44.

"Varela," John muttered, "go to hell." And sent him

there. The Dragoon spat flame, the wooden hand blew
apart, flattening the lead slug before it tore through Varela's throat. John fired again. Andrés raised up on his
toes, tried to scream, and fell backward, a look of complete disbelief on the blood-masked remains of his face.
He landed with a thud, arms outstretched, legs wide and
trembling, then still. John sat up and shot the crippled
horse. The animal ceased its cries of agony and relaxed,
settling into death.

Hector saw his father die. He glanced about, alerted
by the sudden quiet. Then he saw the bodies of his men
and watched, embittered as Cole, alive, climbed up from
the riverbank, and John Anthem, alive, standing now;
and Chapo Almendáriz, alive, who trotted his horse
through the field of carnage.

Hector turned his attention to the young man holding
a gun on him.

"It is finished," Billy said. The Navy Colt wavered in
his grip and there was a hint of desperation in his voice.
"You're coming with me to stand trial for my kidnapping and the murder of Laura Prescott."

"I can see your gun has not even been fired," Hector
dryly observed. He had to act now, while the gringo with
the brass carbine did not have a clean shot—now, while
he was out of range of the shotgun. "You have never
killed a man. *Bueno*. It is not easy," Hector said, raising
the gun he pulled from his belt. "There is no going back
from a killing. You are never the same."

"Don't make me," Billy said.

"I do not think you can, my friend." Hector's dark
features all but beamed with innocence, his voice soft
and hypnotic as he spoke. Hector turned his back and
started to walk way. "*Adiós, amigo.*" There was a horse
grazing only a few yards away and he headed toward it.

"My father is dead. Everything lost," Hector said over his shoulder. "But there will be another day for the house of Varela." He made a pretense of reaching up for the saddle, then sidestepped and whirled, leveling his revolver.

Billy fired, and fired again. Hector grunted as his thickly padded frame absorbed the bullet's impact. He stumbled into the horse, and the animal bolted off. Hector tried to bring his own gun to bear, but the revolver slipped from his hand. Billy kept shooting until the hammer on his Navy Colt struck an empty chamber, and even then he numbly continued to work the action. Hector sagged to his knees, hugged his belly, and groaned. He looked up at Billy, then curled forward. "Another day . . ." he gasped. His face touched the earth. It felt so cool at first. Then nothingness. Billy Anthem holstered his gun.

And Eden was silent again.

"Son?" Big John called out, and Billy heard and started back toward his father.

Big John watched him come and knew there was nothing to be said to relieve the sickening aftertaste of battle and death. It was a hard land that sometimes required all a man could give.

And in return sometimes it gave a life of richness and a sense of purpose.

John Anthem examined the flesh wound in his side. It hurt like the devil, but it would heal. The pain was part of the price.

Chapo rode up with a horse for the rancher, he led Cole Tyler's dun stallion as well.

The man called Yellowboy nodded his thanks and mounted. The bounty-hunter slid the Winchester carbine into its saddle scabbard. Then he waited. Shadows flitted across the earth. Cole shaded his eyes, looked up, and saw the vultures had already begun to circle.

Chapo looked back toward the trees and wondered if he ought to search the back trails for Natividad. But then, he might find her. The segundo resolved to leave well enough alone.

Big John Anthem thrust his foot in the stirrup and swung up into the saddle.

"You better let me tend to your wounds," said Cole.

"Across the river," John replied. His gaze turned from Cole Tyler to Chapo and at last to Billy. We ought to make Luminaria by Christmas.

"Let's go home," said Big John Anthem.

And they did.

HE LEFT HOME A BOY.
RETURNED A MAN.
AND RODE OUT AGAIN A RENEGADE ...

TEXAS ANTHEM

KERRY NEWCOMB

AT THE BONNET RANCH, they thought Johnny Anthem had died on the Mexican border. But then Anthem came home, escaped from the living hell of a Mexican prison, and returned to find the woman he loved married to the man who betrayed him. For Johnny Anthem, the time had come to face his betrayer, to stand up to the powerful rancher who had raised him as his own son, and to fight for the only love of his life.

"Kerry Newcomb is one of those writers who lets you know from his very first lines that you're in for a ride. And he keeps his promise ... Newcomb knows what he is doing, and does it enviably well."
—Cameron Judd, author of *Confederate Gold*

AVAILABLE WHEREVER BOOKS ARE SOLD FROM
ST. MARTIN'S PAPERBACKS

RED RIPPER

❖ KERRY NEWCOMB ❖

NEW ORLEANS, SEPTEMBER 1829. Brothers William and Samuel Wallace board a ship for Mexico with bold visions of wealth and adventure in a new land. But when a vicious storm lands the two on the shores of Mexico, clinging for dear life, a brutal band of freebooters attack the brothers, murdering Samuel in front of William's very eyes. Now William has sworn to avenge his brother's death. This haunting quest will take Wallace to the mist-laden bayous of Texas, where he will become embroiled in the fight for its independence and earn himself the name that strikes fear in the hearts of his enemies . . . The Red Ripper.

SOME CALLED HIM THEIR CAPTAIN.
SOME CALLED HIM THEIR ENEMY.
SOME CALLED HIM THE DEVIL HIMSELF . . .

MAD MORGAN

KERRY NEWCOMB

He came out of Cuba's bloody sugar cane fields, a young Welshman who had been kidnapped from his home and forced into barbaric slavery in the New World. Then on a black night, Henry Morgan made his escape, and soon was commanding a former prison bark manned by criminals, misfits and adventurers—men who owed Mad Morgan their freedom, their loyalty, and their lives.

"Awash with treachery and romance, this well-spun yarn fairly crackles with danger and suspense . . . Colorful, old-fashioned adventure [and] vigorous historical fiction."
—*Booklist*

MM 12/00

READ THESE MASTERFUL WESTERNS BY MATT BRAUN

"Matt Braun is a master storyteller of frontier history."
—Elmer Kelton

THE KINCAIDS

Golden Spur Award-winner THE KINCAIDS tells the classic saga of America at its most adventurous through the eyes of three generations who made laws, broke laws, and became legends in their time.

GENTLEMAN ROGUE

Hell's Half Acre is Fort Worth's violent ghetto of whorehouses, gaming dives and whisky wells. And for shootist and gambler Luke Short, it's a place to make a stand. But he'll have to stake his claim from behind the barrel of a loaded gun . . .

RIO GRANDE

Tom Stuart, a hard-drinking, fast-talking steamboat captain, has a dream of building a shipping empire that will span the Gulf of Mexico to New Orleans. Now, Stuart is plunged into the fight of a lifetime—and to the winner will go the mighty Rio Grande . . .

THE BRANNOCKS

The three Brannock brothers were reunited in a boomtown called Denver. And on a frontier brimming with opportunity and exploding with danger, vicious enemies would test their courage—and three beautiful women would claim their love . . .

AVAILABLE WHEREVER BOOKS ARE SOLD
FROM ST. MARTIN'S PAPERBACKS